FRACTURED
Souls

JESSA L. JAMES

Cover design by Katelyn Groombridge at Design by Kage

Editor Ashley Oliver

For you.

Become your own mother-fucking warrior princess.

AUTHOR'S NOTE

Please note that this is an extreme slow-burn romance. There is no relationship building in book one. Book one is just the start to Harley's crazy story, but it is well worth the wait. Our girl ends up with three love interests she does not have to pick between. This story will also include m/m in later books. I hope you stick around for the ride because I promise, this is just the beginning.

Please be mindful of the **triggers** as these are only the warnings for book one and things do escalate later on in the series. *Abuse from family members, mentions of suicide with flashbacks of attempts, murder, mention of rape, mentions of sex trafficking, mention of drug use, depression, violence, and foul language.*

I hope you enjoy my debut novel!

Jessa L. James

SONS OF SILENCE MC CHARACTERS

RANKING OFFICERS

Rage (Gabriel) - President

Sugar (Colton) - Vice President

Axe (Jackson) - Road Captain

Stone - Sergeant at Arms

Blade (Noah) - Enforcer

Nerds - Tech Guru

OTHERS AT THE CLUB

Blade has custody of "the boys"

Cayden (Blade's brother), Ryker, and Grayson

Club Sluts - Carly, Maya, Rachel

SPOTIFY PLAYLIST

Man or a Monster by Sam Tinnesz & Zayde Wolf
Panic Room by Au/Ra
Hurts Like Hell by Fleurie, Tommee Profitt
Renegade (Slowed + Reverb) by Aaryan Shah
Pushin On by 2WEI, Marvin Brooks
Feel Something by Jaymes Young
Prisoner by Raphael Lake, Aaron Levy, Daniel Ryan Murphy
Turn Our Eyes Away by Ruby Amanfu, Trent Dabbs
Deep End by Ruelle
Warrior by Demi Lovato
Fractured by J. France
I Can't Carry This Anymore by Anson Seabra
bad decisions by Bad Omens
Hurricane by Tommee Profitt, Fleurie
Monsters by Ruelle
Glass Heart by Tommee PRofitt, Sam Tinnesz
Astronomical by SVRCINA

PROLOGUE

August 18th, 2015

As I push the slider open, clutching onto my daughter's arm, I realize my mistake of not having checked for anyone outside first. A man shoves me back into the house and then punches me so hard I fall to the ground. My jaw starts to ache, and I feel blood dripping from my mouth. I hear my little girl scream as three more men come in with the first one. One of them that I faintly recognize from years ago grabs my girl and holds her away as she cries and tries to fight his hold. His cold, dead eyes look at me, and he smiles. His dirty teeth are on full display. My mind threatens to take me back to a dark place, but I fight it. I have to fight for my girl. The other three that I don't recognize lift me and slam me down on a chair. I kick and hit, but I am no match for three large men, so they easily tie me to the chair.

I look over at my daughter, tears streaming down her face as her eyes are wide with terror. A level of fear I am all too familiar with but never wanted her to experience. But I was stupid. So, so stupid. I let myself get comfortable with our life here. Then the three men start to beat the shit out of me. I try to be strong for my baby, biting my tongue to hold back my screams, but I don't think I can be when I know there is no getting out of this.

The pain of watching my daughter have to see this outweighs any physical pain I feel. Which leads me to say things I shouldn't. "What do you bastards want? The old fucker couldn't come deal with me himself? How did you even find me?" I demand as I glare at them.

Not that they care; they laugh and joke, ignoring me. Until *his* voice rings out in the room, causing the tears I was holding back to leak. This is the end.

"Oh, don't worry, the old fucker is here to deal with you himself," he says as he comes towards me from the front door.

I feel my heartrate pick up. Fuck, we are going to die. Unless I can get my baby girl to remember what I told her repeatedly. *"If anything ever happens, you find an opening and you run. You run, Harley. You leave me and run."* I told her that on a weekly basis, always making sure she repeated it back. Knowing the chances of this happening. I needed to feel like she might survive it. As long as no one finds her if she survives.

I take a deep breath and glance at my girl. My brave, brave girl. She has tears streaming down her beautiful face, her bright hazel eyes dulled to an almost brown color right now. I give her a tiny smile and mouth, *It's going to be okay.* She shakes her head and tries to fight the hold of the man holding her, scratching his arms and kicking her legs, but it's no use. He may be old now, with a

2

large belly, but he still is stronger than she is. But if she can escape his firm grip, she may be able to outrun him.

I shut my eyes and lock my emotions down tight, not wanting my baby to see her mom in pain and begging for her life. I'll stay silent as they torture me. It wouldn't be the first time. I can lock my pain down if it protects her from more trauma.

The older fucker laughs in my face, his wretched hot breath filling my nostrils, and I have to hold back a gag. I hate the smell of cigarettes. He begins beating me over and over again, making me as weak as possible. My ribs crack. My baby screams and sobs. I keep my eyes shut, wishing this was a dream. I bite my tongue hard, trying not to cry out. Blood pools in my mouth, and I have to spit so I don't choke. My head throbs, and I can feel my right eye swelling shut.

He calls for the other guys to help him, as they had stepped back while he beat me. They untie me and lift my limp, aching body and drop it on the kitchen table. I think I try to fight them, but my mind is so fuzzy, and pain radiates through my body. I don't know if I am actually moving anything or not. They tie me down to the table, arms spread above my head and legs spread eagle. I can't see my baby now. She's behind my head. I pray her eyes are closed. I want to yell for her to shut them, but I know from experience the old fucker would force her to keep them open if I said anything.

He takes a knife and runs it down the front of my clothes, slicing them open, not caring that he also slices me. "I've waited thirteen years for this. You didn't make it easy. But yet you slacked off. You thought I'd give up." He cackles as he takes the hilt of his knife and roughly shoves it inside me. This time, there is no stopping the scream. I feel the blood from his rough use dripping down my thighs. The pain never eases, and my legs tremble as I do everything I can to show little to no reaction for my daughter's sake. Another piece of me stolen by *his* hands. I faintly hear my daughter screaming and wailing for me behind me as the older fucker throws the knife to the ground and begins raping me. "Oh perfect, perfect girl. Thirteen years and I still remember the feel of your perfect bloody pussy."

I feel myself falling into a numb state. A state I use to be so familiar with, but I hold on. I force myself to feel the pain so I can find a way for my daughter to survive this.

At least an hour passes, if not more. I try to stay silent besides some whimpers that I can't hold back. I still can't see my daughter, but I can hear her crying. I can feel the blood running down my legs from him forcing himself into me. I feel as if I'm being ripped in half with every thrust. His men stand around me, groping me, jacking off on me, cutting me, degrading me, hitting me. It doesn't stop. Even when I pass out from the pain and my mind shuts down.

I wake up when cold water splashes on my face. A scream works its way out of my throat as I feel all the pain throughout my body at once. At some point, the cocky bastards had untied me, assuming I am still the same girl I was before and wouldn't fight through the pain. The old fucker bends over and whispers his plans for my baby girl. I scream, I fight, I do whatever I can to help her. I finally get off the table and can see her.

The man holding her has a knife to her throat. I freeze, trying to get her to realize what she needs to do, and she does it. My baby is the strongest girl there is. She fights like no other and with one good hit, the man holding her releases her. I scream, "RUN. DON'T STOP. RUN. RUN, HARLEY!" My voice is hoarse from screaming as loud as I can as I watch my little fighter take off and not look back.

I can die knowing she will survive and be okay. She has a chance. I have to believe she will make it. I smile at the fucker, and he looks livid.

"GET HER!" he roars at his men. They take off to look for her and he turns back to me, taking his anger on me with his fists. I endure it all, not having the strength to fight back. When he finally stops, he grips my hair and yanks me up from where I ended up on my ground. "I'm going to find her. I'm going to find her and I'm going to keep her for years locked up as my toy. You no good bitch. You were too rotten for me anyway. Enjoy hell, sweet—"

Before he can say more, his men come running back in. "Boss, we've got to go. Cops are coming, and we can't find the brat."

"FUCK!" he snarls.

He ties me up quickly and then has his men set fire to my home. They funnel out while fire swarms around me. I cough and feel myself getting weaker by the second. I'm going to be burned alive while screaming and praying my baby girl makes it out okay and is never, ever in the same room as that man again.

She's a fighter. I have to believe that.

In the end, I did the best I could. At least, I hope I did. There are some things that don't end in your favor. I didn't believe I'd get to live the rest of my life never having to face my past again. But I also didn't expect it to end up the way it did.

I can only hope my sweet Harley gets to live a life full of love and laughter and that one day, she can forgive me.

CHAPTER ONE

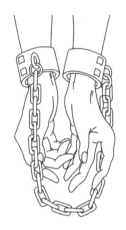

HARLEY

Present Day - October 15th 2018

*A*s I walk on stage, I look out at the audience and a huge
grin comes over my face. There right in the front row is
my mom. Beautiful, elegant, and my biggest fan. I've been playing
piano since I was little. My mom has played for many years as
well. She taught me everything I know and has always shown
up to every event or concert I've had. She signs me up for every
competition there is. Even though money is tight, she always finds
a way for it to happen just so I can do what I love to do. Someday,

I'm going to pay her back for everything she does for me. That'll be the happiest day of my life.

I come out of my daydream when Mother hisses in my ear, "Focus! You need to win this, or you will not like the consequences. Get out there now!"

I sigh. That daydream was just that: a dream. The reality is, I'm walking on stage, back straight, arms at my side, the widest, fakest smile on my face, pretending I'm happy and not in pain. When in reality, my ribs are killing me from Mother kicking the shit out of them yesterday when I told her there was no way I could play in a competition today when I haven't played piano in three years. All because I've been locked away in Mother's basement.

I know this might all seem confusing, but Mother isn't actually my mother. But we'll get back to that later. Anyways, back to what I was saying, she gave me no choice. She told me I'd play, and that's the end of it. She did let me look up the song I knew I could play on the computer and listen to it... once. So, here's to hoping for the best.

I am terrified as I sit down on the bench. Only having listened to the song once, it's just really not enough, but I try to channel my mom and everything she has taught me. I used to play this song with her. I know I can do it. I inhale, then exhale. I let my fingers guide me through the song, muscle memory coming back as I play for the first time in so long. This is a competition between high schools. I still don't know how Mother got me in since I haven't been to school since I was thirteen.

As I play, I can see them watching me out of the corner of my eye. Father looks like he'd rather be anywhere else, and sister glares at me like I've ruined her entire life. Well, according to her, I basically did. Mother is offstage behind me, and I swear I can feel her stare burning a hole into the back of my head.

The warning is clear. If I mess up and don't win, she will follow through on those consequences. I try to push them out of my mind and just find the peace a piano can bring me.

Today is my solo performance where I play to compete for $10,000. However, if I win, I will never see that money. Despite the fancy dress I am wearing, which actually belongs to Mother, I have nothing.

Three years ago, my real mom was murdered. I saw most of it. But I was able to escape, not without scars, both inside and outside of my body, but I walked away with my life and my mom didn't. Just thinking about that time sends a cold chill down my spine. I have so many questions about that day, and no one to give me answers. I can't help but let my mind wander sometimes to the dark places of what if... and who were the people that killed her?

After I lost my mom, I woke up in the hospital two weeks later with a strange woman standing beside my bed. Turns out she is my mom's sister, my Aunt Tammy. After losing my mom, who I thought was the only family I had, I was beyond relieved to see my aunt. To see family, to see someone who I thought would've looked like my mom, someone who could give me a mom hug and tell me it's all going to be okay just like my mom used to do.

Except, I never got that hug. I was never told it would be okay. I never even got to cry as someone held me while I grieved my mom.

That day three years ago when I woke up in the hospital turned out to be my last day of freedom, and the last hug I'd receive was from a nurse who had sat with me every day while I was unconscious.

That day, I learned that people are not always what they seem on the outside. Mother is outwardly perfect. Her mid-length auburn hair is absolutely perfect. Never a hair out of place. She dresses in beautifully tailored clothing. She'd never be seen in wrinkled clothes. But inside, she is the ugliest person there is.

Mother had come down and sent me up to the guest bath early this morning and told me to make myself not look like shit. She had a green floor-length dress and flats, along with hair products, a brush, and stuff in the shower for me to use.

I had gone to shut the door, but Father stopped me and stood at the door watching me do everything... He never says anything. But if I am upstairs, he watches me. Luckily, I was able to step into the shower and pull the curtain closed before taking off my clothes, so he never saw me naked. I had half expected him to rip it open, but he didn't. Even as I took the fastest shower I could, he never looked in. But when I got out, he was still just standing there, his dark brown eyes zoned in on me.

As my solo comes to an end with the last note of Song From A Secret Garden - Piano Solo Version, the audience cheers and claps. I lace my fingers together in front of me to stop the shaking. My head throbs from the noise and having so many people's eyes on me.

Being locked away for so long really changes things when you are out in public again. I walk off the stage, making my way to Mother. She looks beautiful, with a bright smile on her perfectly caked face. A face I wish I could claw to shreds. I see behind that bright smile; I see the demons lurking there. The ones waiting to come out and destroy me for whatever it is she seems to think I have done wrong now.

The concert ends an hour later. I spent the whole time enjoying the sound of a piano again. God, I didn't realize how much I had missed just hearing someone play the piano. It's like finding my way home again, to a time before my life got destroyed and went to hell. When I close my eyes, I'm back home playing piano with my mom while she sings along to whatever we are playing, or she dances around the piano as I play. I feel my lips tilt up at that memory.

Mother nudges me hard. "Whatever you are thinking about doing, don't. You won't get far. I will destroy you."

And there goes that happy thought. I stop smiling and open my eyes but stare straight ahead, not even looking at Mother to acknowledge her, which I'm sure I'll pay for later.

Luckily those who participated in the competition are called back on stage so I can get a tiny reprieve from Mother Dearest. Me and five others head up to the stage. As much as I don't want to win this money, since I know Mother will take it for herself, I know if I don't, the following weeks won't be pretty. On the other hand, my real mom and I shared a bond through playing piano, and she is the one who wanted me to play in every competition there was. I remember my mom signing me up years ago, but she said the waitlist for it is crazy and apparently, I got in now but not as who I was. As Harley Wilson. So many questions.... so many fucking questions I'll never get the answers to.

I'd like to think she would be beyond proud of me for doing this. My fingers itch to touch my scar on my face running from below my right eye across my cheek through my lip and ending on my chin. I don't dare, though, knowing Mother's and Father's eyes are on me. I zone back into the director's speech as it's coming to an end.

"...And we thank each of you for competing, but unfortunately there can only be one winner. The winner of the Allstar Competition of 2018 is... Harley Wilson!"

For a split second, I forget how horrible my life is and just remember the feeling of winning something. Of people clapping and cheering for me. The fact that I won! I haven't even played in so long but yet it all just came back to me. I have to think it's my mom who helped me with today. Watching over me from heaven. That moment is short-lived as we all walk offstage, and Mother is waiting there with a smug grin on her face that I'd love to slap off of her. Maybe one day, I'll get to.

The second we pile into the car, Mother rips the check from my hands and with a snarl says, "At least you did something right for once." Honestly? It's a compliment coming from her.

"Thank you, Mother," I say, trying not to add an eyeroll. The bitch always wants to be thanked as if she did something good by opening her mouth. The woman currently sitting in front of me in the car will never even compare to my mom. But calling her Mother is better than what would happen if I refused. Trust me, I've tried.

3 Years Ago

As we leave the hospital two days after I wake up, I feel uneasy. My aunt has been quiet and seems to just stare at me unless someone else comes into the room; then she smiles and is a bubbly, kind person.

I tried talking to her about my mom, but she shuts me down and just keeps saying, "Now is not the time." I don't understand why now isn't the time. My mom is dead. I feel so lost. But Tammy seems just fine and not bothered. I haven't even seen her shed a single tear. But also, my mom never mentioned any family. This whole thing is so confusing. I just want my mom.

Once we get out to the car, she leads me around to the trunk where we are blocked from anyone seeing us. Then she grabs my hair hard and yanks me back before shoving me against the car.

Completely stunned with tears stinging my eyes, I reach for her arm that is gripping my hair and try to pull it away, but she only further tightens her grasp. I let out a yelp of pain, and she shoves me harder into the car. Then her hauntingly dead voice speaks low in my ear, and I freeze.

"Shut up, you little shit. Let me get a few things straight," she sneers. "Your life before today no longer exists. Don't worry, I have lots of connections to important people who owe me. It will be wiped away. You are Harley Wilson now, and I am your mother. You will not speak of Lilian ever again. She is not your mom anymore. I am. You will address me as Mother at all times. You now have a brother and sister, and you will call them as such. Don't worry, I'll come up with a story about where you have been all this time. Maybe a long stay at the psych ward. I do have lots of connections as I said," she cackles, her fist pulling harder at my hair, making more tears stream down my face.

I don't understand. I'm only thirteen. How could she be saying these things? How am I supposed to just forget my mom? I don't understand. A sob breaks loose from inside me and comes out, and she slaps me hard across the face. Pain blossoms through my cheek.

"SHUT UP!" she yells. "You will do everything I tell you to do, or there will be consequences. Until I decide what I will tell people about where you came from and where you have been, you will not leave the house. So enjoy the ride home." She laughs like a crazy person as she opens the trunk and starts to shove me

inside. I fight as best I can, but I'm still weak and can't do much, so she overpowers me quickly and slams it shut behind me.

That night, I learned what the consequences looked like when I spoke without being spoken to and called her Tammy instead of Mother, even though I had no idea I wasn't allowed to speak. She whipped my back until it was bleeding and left me curled up in the basement, in the dark overnight. Little did I know that would be my new home.

The next day, after that first beating, I woke up crying and in pain. Mother came down and kicked me in the ribs for crying, and I was forced to spend the day cleaning and scrubbing while in excruciating pain, trying to hold back my tears.

I asked why she would change my last name to Wilson, and that got me slapped and screamed at for asking questions she claimed were none of my business. I prayed this wouldn't last. I prayed someone would save me and prayed this was all just a bad dream.

Those prayers didn't do a damn thing. In my world, the devil was very much real, and her name was Tammy Wilson.

Little did I know that to beat the devil, I would have become the devil myself.

Welcome to my hell.

CHAPTER TWO

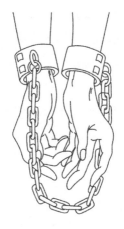

HARLEY

I wake to something hitting my mattress repeatedly, jostling me awake from another night of restless sleep. I try to sit up quickly but groan in pain. My ribs hurt from the beating I got two days ago because Mother felt I needed one. For the most part for the last year or so, I have been left alone in the basement. Unless they might have guests coming, then I get sent upstairs to clean before they arrive, then sent back down before they come in. It's like some twisted, fucked-up Cinderella shit. You know the whole evil stepmother makes her clean and shit? Jokes on me because Cinderella was my all-time favorite Disney movie that my mom and I watched together.

Other than the cleaning, I'm left to my own thoughts in this shitty basement unless Mother gets bored; then she comes down and beats me. Or if she thinks I magically did something wrong while locked up in a basement alone. The beatings used to come almost every day at first, but after about two years I think she got bored because I stopped begging and crying and trying to fight back. I just took it. Hell, I haven't fucking cried in almost two years. I gave up on that shit after one full year here. So I think she just comes when she feels like it or needs a release. Or like yesterday when I had the competition, she beat me in spots no one would see the day prior to keep me too weak to run.

"Rise and shine, bitch! Mommy wants to speak to you," says a shrill, awful, squeaky voice as she continues to kick my mattress. God, I cannot stand my sister's voice.

She is fourteen, two years younger than me, and she does not care how her mother treats me. She thinks she is the shit when she's really just a spoiled brat. I bet if you even poked her, she'd break out into sobs and cry about getting hurt. I laugh internally thinking about just slapping the bitch once and watching her cry. Okay, maybe I'm slightly insane.

Tabby, who is a spitting image of Mother—perfect clothes, auburn hair, and cold, mean eyes—unlocks my chained cuff that's around my ankle and then takes off upstairs. Yep, a chain. It spans the length of the basement from the middle of the floor and just barely reaches the bottom step to the basement. The basement isn't super big. It's the size of a large bedroom, I think. There is a small bathroom in the corner that they took the door off of, and it has a small standing shower, a toilet, and an old sink. I have a twin mattress on the ground with one throw blanket, an old pillow, and my small stack of clothes next to it, and that's it.

I get up as fast as I can and head upstairs. Mother, Father, and Tabby are all sitting around the table eating breakfast. I stand in the corner of the room with my head down waiting for permission to move, speak, or do anything. This is the most I've been up here lately. They haven't had me clean for them in a few months, and yesterday was my first time out of the house in three years. Seriously. I hadn't stepped foot outside until yesterday for the piano competition.

As I stand here waiting, my thoughts go to where they have randomly gone over the years I have been locked away here: my dad.

I have no idea who he is. But I like to daydream about him. He'd be loving and kind. A knight in shining armor I remember thinking as a child. I wish he would swoop in here and save the day. Or I just wish that I knew who he was, so if I somehow magically got out of this hell someday, I could find him and hopefully he'd want me. But unfortunately, I don't. Just another unknown to throw in the mix for me.

I zone back into the room as Mother opens her mouth. "Well, Harley, it would seem my connections came through and you will be starting school tomorrow, with rules that you will be agreeing to and be obeying at all times. Don't worry, if you don't, I will know. I have eyes everywhere."

This is not the first time Mother has mentioned connections. What the fuck does that even mean? Like people she knows or something? Will people be watching me? She is extending a lot of faith that I won't say anything. But maybe she knows I am too scared. Or she really does have these connections. I just wish I knew what or who they were.

"Also, just because I can, and I don't trust you, dear darling daughter, you will drink that." She points to the other end of the table where there is a glass with something in it, but I'm not sure what. I just stand there staring at it. This can't be good.

When I don't move fast enough, Father flies out of his chair, knocking it over and grabbing me by the back of the neck before shoving me towards the table. "When your mother tells you to do something, you do it, you stupid bitch!" Father spits at me.

I tremble but try to cover it the best I can. Even after so many years, they still terrify me, but I try to mask it and pretend like nothing they do bothers me anymore. It's hard, and sometimes I feel those walls cracking. Like I might just break one day.

I grab the cup off the table and take a small sip, instantly gagging. I have no idea what this is, but it *burns*. My throat is instantly on fire.

Mother gets up and slowly walks towards me. She grabs the cup with one hand and grips my hair with the other, then tilts my head back roughly and shoves the glass at my mouth. Father plugs my nose, so I have no choice but to drink in order to breathe.

19

It feels like time stops as I slowly gulp it down. It tastes awful, and the burning sensation in my throat gets worse with each swallow.

Mother steps back. "Speak," she orders, narrowing her eyes.

I try to talk, but it comes out choked and really quiet. It hurts too bad to speak loudly, and what I do get out is raspy. Mother beams triumphantly like she just won some game.

"As I was saying, rules you will be following. You will be mute. I have already informed the school. If I find out you are talking at school or to anyone at all, that,"—she points to the cup—"will happen again. And again. Maybe every day until you really can't speak, so I suggest you keep your mouth shut. You will come and go by bus, and I expect you to be on time every day, not staying late ever. If you are ever late, you will get locked in the doghouse that night."

My mind threatens to drag me under to memories of that doghouse, but I immediately shut them down, blocking it all out.

"You are to brush off bruises as being clumsy. You were in a mental hospital from age ten to sixteen because you struggled with self-harm and anger issues and are ill. If we are not home when you get here, you will walk around back and wait on the back porch until we get home. Harley, you will not like the repercussions if you disobey. I hope the last three years have taught that stupid brain of yours something useful. You are starting as a junior like everyone else your age. I do not care that you are behind. Succeed. We will get you some more clothes later today. You are dismissed. That is all."

With my head spinning with everything she just said and my throat on fire, I nod and turn around to head back towards the basement but before I can get far Father is behind me grabbing my hair and yanking me back, "When your mother is being so generous you could show some gratitude, you stupid, ungrateful bitch!"

Stupid mistake. Always thank Mother. I knew that. *You're a fuckup, Harley. You never learn.*

Father drags me into the kitchen and shoves me down onto my knees as he fills the sink with water. Oh no. This has happened before; it's his favorite thing to do. He always tries to make it last longer and longer. Last time was two minutes.

I can do this. I can do—

He grabs my hair and yanks me up, then immediately shoves my head into the sink full of water. I try to take a deep breath first but don't have time. I try to stay calm and breathe, but it's always terrifying when you can feel your head being held down. I try to find some sense of peace in the water so I don't panic, but I can't when I have no positive experiences with water.

I know passing out isn't an option. Last time I did, I got beat until I couldn't walk. I had to be carried downstairs, and healing took months. I just need to remain calm; panic will not help me... I can... what the fuck! My mouth pops open on a silent water filled scream as I feel the whip hitting my back, my thighs, my ass. I feel the burn as I realize they are hitting hard enough to break skin. Tears leak down my face without my permission.

Don't panic.

Hold your breath.
You can do this.
You've survived worse.
You are strong.
Hold on just a little longer...

It feels like my mind is turning blank. Words don't come. I can't keep myself calm. The pain, the water—it's all too much. Maybe this time, just maybe, this is it. It'll be the end. They'll let me go. Free me from my chains, I'll be free, free to finally die.

Mom... Mommy, I'm coming to you...

Pain. Searing, all-consuming pain. I feel like my chest is caving in on me. That's when it hits again, and I cough and gag as I choke and spit out water all over. My throat hurts and burns, but I can't stop coughing. Each cough sends a stab of pain through my throat. It takes time to get it under control and breathe properly, but when I do, I realize I am not dead.

I sag back onto my back on the floor of the kitchen where I realize that they must have been doing CPR on me. My chest hurts, and it feels like a ton of bricks are sitting on me. I know I'll have a bruise tomorrow from that.

As I regain all my senses, I realize Mother is yelling at me, and I open my eyes to see her standing over me with her arms crossed and a look of disgust on her face.

"AGAIN? Are you insane? Maybe you really should be put in a mental hospital. You did that on purpose, you stupid girl! Get your ass downstairs. I don't want to see or hear you anymore today! GET OUT!"

I scramble up as fast as my aching body can and head to the stairs. Father follows me down and locks my ankle cuff back in place. "She wouldn't be so hard on you if you'd just be good for once. This is your fault, Harley. Try harder, sweet girl." He runs his hand up my leg and squeezes high up on my thigh.

I freeze, unsure how to react. *What is happening?*

Then he leans closer and whispers, "I've been waiting three years. Please stop making me wait. Be good and I'll get to spend some time with you, sweet girl." He releases me and turns to walk back upstairs.

I stare at the spot that he was touching on my thigh. My stomach revolts with the thoughts of his hands on me. *Please don't let more happen.* I think if I had anything in my stomach, I would be hurling right now.

I sag onto my bed, and tears threaten to leak out of my eyes, but I refuse to let them. That... That has never happened before. I don't even know how to process that.

I mean, my mom had the birds and bees talk with me when I was twelve, but that couldn't be what he means, right? He's my uncle! I mean, he's always watching me. If I'm upstairs for any reason, he's just always there watching, but he hasn't touched me before. His words repeat through my head as I try to rest, but soon it's just too much and I jump up to do something, anything, because I can't be left alone with my thoughts right now.

When I thought this might be it, I was happy, and I just feel like I'm not supposed to be happy about that. It's the same as when it happened a year ago. I tried to kill myself, and I was happy when I came up with my plan.

That's not normal, is it? I start pacing the small space, counting my steps as I go, from my bed to the far wall by the stairs, and then I turn around and go back and do it again. My body aches and screams at me with each step, but I let the pain in. Let the pain distract me from my mind. The chain hooked to my ankle cuff drags along the concrete floor as I pace, the sound like nails on a chalkboard.

My hands start to shake, and I feel like I can't drag in a full breath. I think I'm suffocating. I can't focus, and my vision is going blurry. I can't breathe; everything is all too much. After who even knows how long, I collapse onto the concrete floor and start sobbing so hard my body hurts and begins shaking uncontrollably.

Damn it! Get it together, you stupid girl! This is probably all your fault. Maybe you're crazy? Who feels like they are dying just from pacing? Who breaks down like a weak bitch? This is insane! Why won't they just kill me?

I'm not strong enough for this. I can't handle it. I'm weak, I'm alone. I need my mom again.

My breathing is coming out in sharp pants. It hurts so bad to breathe.

I can't handle this anymore.

And just as that thought crosses my mind, everything starts going black, and I can't help but let that darkness take over.

CHAPTER THREE

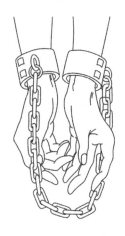

Harley

When I wake up, I'm still in a ball in the middle of the floor. I slowly sit up and try to stretch out, but everything hurts. I must have passed out. God, I really am crazy. I feel like I'm losing it. It's like some days I find a new sense of power somewhere in me to want to fight and survive, but then other days, like today, I feel so beat down that I don't know why I keep trying.

What's the point? Why am I trying to live when I don't even know how to get out of this situation? What's their end goal? I just have so many questions and no answers.

I drag myself up and onto my bed. My body hurts, but at the same time, I feel half numb to the pain. I'm so used to having cuts, bruises, marks, and being forced into water that it doesn't bother me as much as it used to.

Sometimes I just wish I could talk to my mom again and that she could give me some direction. It was just her and I for thirteen years. She was who I spent most of my time with, and I don't know how I am supposed to live without her. It's been three years, but I feel like I haven't had a chance to stop and think about it or talk to anyone about her. Any time I have mentioned her name around here, I've been beaten black and blue for it.

I may have gotten away, but my mom didn't. She died, and I know the men who... I shudder thinking about that day. I know they had to have killed her. But it was brushed off so easily. I want to know what happened. The truth. Which I am not likely to get here.

I wish that I knew who my dad was. Maybe he'd have answers. But since my mom never wanted to talk about my dad for whatever reason, I used to come up with these crazy fairytales when I was little. I remember playing and making the knight save the princess. The knight always ended up being my dad. I had a good childhood. I loved my mom so much, but I wish I had my dad around. Now more than ever do I wish he was around. Although, now that I'm older, I can't help but wonder why mom wouldn't have told me about him.

Is he a bad man? *Don't go there, Harley.* It's so easy to spiral down that path when I ended up with Mother. My mom never told me about her either. Is that because all of these people are bad? I think I'll just let the child in me wish and have hope for her knight in shining armor.

As I lay on my bed trying to get somewhat comfortable so I can try to nap, I prepare myself for the onslaught of bad dreams that always come, only this time, they don't.

It's dark. It feels like a tunnel almost. There is a light breeze blowing my crazy hair in my face. I push it aside to look around. What the fuck? Where am I? Is this real?

"No, my baby, this isn't real. You are dreaming." That voice...

"M-mom?" I sob, feeling my knees give out, but before I can hit the floor, a gust of wind pushes me back to standing. When I open my eyes, I see the most beautiful sight I have ever seen: my mom.

"Oh, my baby girl, your poor face. I am so sorry you got a scar from my lack of preparedness." She has tears in her eyes and reaches forward, but her hand just goes right through me.

I feel tears falling down my cheeks. I want to hug her. This isn't fair. I feel like I'm being taunted.

"Oh, I know it feels awful. But it will be okay. You will survive. You must remember everything I have taught you. You remember all the stories I told you? Be strong, Harley. Don't give up. You are so much stronger than I ever was, and you will get to the other side of this. You will conquer and come out stronger. My beautiful soul, my warrior princess, you are not shattered like me. You, my baby, you are only fractured."

"Mom, I don't think, I just... there are so many things I want to say," I say on a choked sob. I never want this to end.

"I don't want it to end either. Our time is up, though. I love you to the moon, baby girl."

"Wait! You're supposed to say to the moon and back."

She gives me a sad smile, and then everything fades away.

I wake with a jolt, sitting up in bed quickly. Mother is standing by my bed with a stack of clothes. She drops them on me. "Here, you lazy shit, clothes for school. You better be ready for tomorrow," she sneers before walking out.

I slump back down on the bed, rubbing my hand over my chest where an empty ache seems to be. It felt like my dream was so real, but yet it's fading so fast, I can't remember what it was about. I brush off the weird feeling; it was probably another nightmare. I should be happy not to remember it.

I slowly sit back up and look down at the pile of clothes. I'm not ready for that yet, so I get up and slowly make my way to the tiny bathroom to pee and clean up a little.

Maybe this could be a good thing. It might not be so bad. School means leaving the house alone. Maybe I could come up with a plan to get away from here. But I'll have to be smart about it.

I remember mom teaching me about money and saving and bills; she always told me to save as much money as possible, so you're never left in a bad spot. She struggled to pay all our bills, so she worked two jobs and was tired a lot, but she said she'd do anything for me. I want to be like my mom, so that means I need to do anything for me too. She'd hate this. I just know it. Maybe I could find my dad? Maybe there is a way to figure out who he is. Although, I don't even know how I would go about that. I just feel like he can't also be a horrible person. Right? Everything is so confusing, and I feel like I am never going to truly know who I can trust from now on.

I need to find a way to get money first. Maybe I can find a way to get some from Mother or something, but that's doubtful. Ugh, this is going to be impossible.

After I finish in the bathroom, I go to look at the clothes Mother brought down. I've spent the last three years only wearing the same worn-down sweatshirt, two shirts, and one pair of jeans, but now I've been given four sweatshirts, all appearing to have been used by Mother and Tabby, two pairs of Mother's old jeans, a pair of leggings and a pair of old blue Converse shoes. I also now have two oversized plain t-shirts. I'm guessing they belonged to Father. They are way too big, but I think I can work them if I use my one hair tie to tie the end together in the front.

But I only have one, so then I'd have to keep my hair down, which with it having been who knows how many years since getting it cut last, it's now longer than it's ever been, falling to my butt in thick copper waves.

I remember I need to wash my underwear; I only have three pairs, and I'm not given access to the washer and dryer, so I've been hand washing them down here. I get up to wash them so they have time to dry. Once I'm done, I organize all the clothes I now own on the floor at the end of my bed. I don't have any bras because they haven't given me any, which is okay because I have small boobs so it's not like I need any.

Once I get everything set up the best I can since I don't have a closet or dresser, I decide to wash my hair. I only have one bottle of shampoo. It's about half gone and I have no idea when they will give me more, but it's been a while since I washed my hair last, and I want it to look nice for school since this'll be the second time in three years I'm leaving this house! I'm terrified but also a little excited. I used to love school. I hope I still do.

The next morning, I'm up at sunrise. I have no idea what time it is, but I can see the sun rising through the small, barred window down here. I quickly wash myself in the shower and then get dressed for the day the best I can.

With my ankle cuff on, I can't change my pants yet. But when I shower, I pull them down and leave them around the chain so I can shower without getting them wet. I leave clean underwear and a pair of jeans on my bed while I wait for someone to come down and get me. I'm wearing a black plain hoodie today with light blue jeans with holes.

What feels like hours later, the door to the basement opens and Mother comes down the stairs, taking off the cuff and watching me as I change my pants and underwear. Once I'm done, I put on my Converse and look at her.

She smiles, but it's not a warm, welcoming smile. No, it's sinister. "Speak," she says.

I try to speak, but barely anything comes out, and it hurts really bad. I tested my voice early this morning, I can talk, but it burns, and I just end up coughing. I really hope whatever she gave me doesn't do permanent damage.

She nods, pleased. "Good. I shouldn't need to remind you of what can happen if you disobey any rules today."

I nod. Mother turns around and goes back upstairs. I follow slowly behind her.

She tosses an old backpack at me and then takes me outside, handing me a piece of paper with what looks like an address on it. "This is our address. Memorize it. The bus will pick you up at the end of the driveway. Off you go. Remember, come straight back here after. Do not miss the bus."

I nod and take off towards the end of the driveway, which is longer than I remember it being, not that I've been out here much. It doesn't look like any neighbors are close to our house, not that I can see too far since we are surrounded by trees.

By the time I'm at the end, I'm breathing heavily. It's been three years of barely any movement and plenty of beatings. My body is tired. This is going to be harder than I thought it would be, especially if I'm already winded. I don't know where Tabby is or why she isn't with me. Wouldn't she be in school too? I wait by the mailbox that is right by the road for the bus. This road is pretty isolated. No other cars are going by, and it's mostly woods all around. I can see the start of someone else's driveway across the street and to the right a little, but I don't see any other kids out waiting for the bus.

When the bus finally pulls up the driver opens the door, and I take a deep breath. I can do this. I walk up the steps and find a seat. There are only three other students on right now, so I take a seat towards the middle of the bus and slide in to sit by the window. As we keep moving, I can see more clearly that we are farther out from town and the neighbors are all spread out with lots of woods in between and long driveways. You can barely see some of the houses. The driveways are so long.

What feels like maybe five minutes go by before we are around more houses. It looks like a normal neighborhood, kind of like what I was used to living in with mom. The houses are closer together, and there are groups of kids waiting in random spots throughout for the bus.

The bus makes its way through a few neighborhoods and quickly fills up. Luckily, no one sits by me, which helps me breathe easier. I am a little nervous about being around a lot of people now. I am not sure how to act around others anymore. Especially since I haven't been around kids my age in a few years. The bus soon makes its way into a larger part of the town where there are less houses and more businesses and shops.

When we arrive at the high school, I follow everyone else off the bus and realize I am not sure what to do. I look around at the large parking lot, at the end where the main road is. There are large trees that block it off so you can't see much past the road. The school itself is two stories tall, and I am standing in front of large double doors that students are walking into. I follow them in and luckily see signs pointing to restrooms on the left and the office on the right.

I follow the sign around the corner to the office. There are large windows looking in with a glass door in the middle. When I head inside, there are chairs along the walls and a large front desk with a hall on either side of it that looks to lead back towards offices.

There is a very beautiful blonde sitting behind the desk bating her fake lashes at the tall man standing in front of her with his back to me. When she sees me, she looks me over and rolls her eyes, seemingly annoyed I'm distracting her from the guy she was trying to talk to.

Honestly, he doesn't seem that interested. He's pretty tense right now. If I can see that, why can't she? I'm the one who's been locked away for three fucking years.

The lady asks what I need, and I watch as she examines my face. A look of disgust as her eyes land on my scar. I feel my face heat with embarrassment. I already hate my scar as it is. I hate that other people can see it so easily. I open my mouth only to feel that burn at the back of my throat and remember I'm supposed to be mute.

I grab a pen off the counter instead and try to signal with it that I need paper to write. She looks at me like I'm stupid before letting out an exasperated huff, "What do you need? Speak already."

I roll my eyes. If I could, I would, lady. I zip my lips with my fingers then hold up the pen again. The lady sighs, then hands me a sticky note.

I quickly write my name and that I'm new and not sure what I need to do or where I need to go and hand it to her. She takes it then says hang on and walks away.

The guy she was talking to earlier is now standing at the side of the counter with his hard eyes trained on me. I glance up at him and get caught in his stare. His eyes... they are blue, the brightest blue I've ever seen. They have this gold shimmer to them that makes his irises look like blue fire. Then I realize I'm staring too long and quickly look down. The heat of his gaze bores into the side of my face as I try my hardest not to fidget. It feels like butterflies are in my stomach, and I so badly want to look back up at him.

Just as the office lady comes back to the desk with a man behind her, I hear a chuckle to my right where the guy was and when I glance over, he is walking away with a barely concealed smirk on his face.

The other guy who came with the office lady is the counselor. His name is Mr. Wright, an older gentleman with a clean-shaved face and mostly gray hair with square black glasses on his face. He gives me a warm smile. "Welcome to Jackson High. I have your schedule here and your locker number and combo to get into it. Here is a map of the school. I unfortunately don't have anyone who can show you around right now. Our office admin, Mrs. Seagle, is out right now, which is why we have a student helping. But if you have any issues, come back here and I will help you." He hands me the papers and wishes me luck.

Well, I guess I'm on my own. It makes much more sense now why that lady was so okay with being a jerk. She doesn't even work here and is just a student.

I take a deep breath, then turn around to leave the office, only to stumble slightly. The same guy with the gorgeous eyes is leaning against the wall by the door. I inhale sharply, then start walking. As I pass, I can smell him, and holy shit, the man smells heavenly. It's like a mix of musk, leather, and something else I can't quite pinpoint.

I find my locker easily with the help of the map. All juniors have their lockers in the same hall on the first floor. Luckily, I am able to figure out how to get it unlocked fairly fast. That leaves me time to walk and find each of my classes before first period. Once I locate all my classes and make sure to circle them on the map, I head back towards my first class. I'm still early, so I just sit in the hall by the door and study my schedule:

1st: English

2nd: History

3rd: Piano

LUNCH

4th: Study Hall

5th: Math

6th: Gym

I'm nervous since I'm so far behind in everything. My body is also already tired from all the moving I've done so far this morning. I get winded really fast, and there is a slight ache in my ribs when I move too much. It makes me wonder how I am going to do gym and pass it when I barely even get a meal a day; I'll probably end up passing out. I didn't even get a meal yesterday, so I'm extra hungry today.

I make it through first period confused as hell, but the teacher seems nice and gives me some handouts to help me get caught up that I'll study later. As I'm leaving the classroom, a girl steps into my path. She's short. Shorter than me, which is pretty short because I'm only 5'3. She has cropped black pixie hair, bright green eyes, a black ring in her nose and another on her lip, dark skin-tight jeans, and a green cropped sweater with black ankle boots.

She flashes me a bright smile and says, "So you're the new girl, huh? You're the talk of the school today. It's okay, I know you are mute. I figured you could use a friend, and I can talk enough for the both of us."

I'm pretty sure she didn't even breathe while talking. She talked so fast. She looks delighted before quickly grabbing my hand and pulling me along. She doesn't see the way I flinch when she grabs me, but I don't pull my arm away, instead trying to seem normal. I really could use a friend. Well, I'm not sure if having a friend is the best idea, but it would be nice anyways.

"Do you have your schedule?" she asks as she drags me along next to her.

I nod, still in shock and very unsure of what to do or how to feel. She holds her hand out, and I realize she is waiting to see my schedule. I hand it to her, and she scans it over before looking back at me. "Sweet, dude! We have history together for second and study hall after lunch and gym for sixth. Although, I am going to work as a TA during study hall some days, so I might not always see you. But I'm claiming you as my friend. You play piano?"

I nod and trace a heart over my chest. She smiles and says that's awesome. We walk into history, and I realize I don't even know

37

this girl's name. When we take our seats, I get my notebook out and write, *Name?* And show it to her.

Her eyes get wide and then she laughs loudly, "Oh my god! How the fuck did I not tell you my name? I'm Lexington, but I go by Lex. I fucking hate Lexington, and I already know that you are Harley."

I nod and offer her a small grin.

"I really like the name Harley. Does it have a special meaning?"

I write, *I don't know. Mom always said it was from the best memory of her life until I came along. Then I became the best. So she wanted me to have a piece of it, I guess. She wouldn't ever give me any more details than that.*

Lex reads it and nods. "Huh. Mysterious. I like it."

All throughout history, I felt eyes on me. Eyes that felt like they were burning a hole in me, seeing all the things I never want anyone to see. It's the same eyes from the office this morning, I realize. The guy that was in there with the batting lashes girl is sitting in the back right corner staring right at me. I look away quickly and sit still the rest of class, trying hard not to fidget with the weight of his stare on me.

When the bell rings, Lex grabs my arm and pulls me along after her. She walks with me to my piano class and whispers, "It seems you've caught the eye of the resident bad boy." I look at her confused, and she continues, "His name is Cayden, and he doesn't talk to anyone really besides his two best friends. But girls throw themselves at him all the time. Just be careful, okay? I've seen him staring pretty hard, and you've barely been here. Him and his friends aren't the best company to keep."

She says it like it's nothing and then takes off waving and smiling, leaving me standing there wondering what the hell that means and why that dude Cayden was staring at me. She said he is a bad boy and apparently not good company, but why do I get this nagging feeling that is the farthest thing from the truth?

Something about him is telling me that there is nothing actually bad about him. *But who the hell am I to trust my instincts? Just listen to Lex, Harley.*

I'm most excited for piano since I haven't played since my mom died besides at the Allstars Competition last week. When I walk into the class, there are only five other students. Two at each piano besides the third one, which only has one guy sitting at it. There is an older gentleman at the front of the room writing on a whiteboard, and he turns to look at me as I come in.

"Ah, Miss Wilson, I presume?" I nod. "We work in sets of two and have a rotation system for playing since we are all stuck in one room with the three pianos. Luckily, now you will even us out! You will be working with Mr. Anderson. Please take a seat with him, and he will bring you up to speed and explain how class works."

He points to the one guy sitting alone. I nod and walk towards him. He hasn't taken his eyes off me since I came into the classroom.

I take a seat next to him and keep my eyes trained on my lap, scared to look at him being so close to me now. Slowly, I see a ringed finger reaching towards my face, and I flinch before I can stop myself. *God damn it, Harley. Why? You saw it coming towards you!*

His pointer finger touches my chin and tilts my head up to meet his eyes, almost so dark they could be black, but up close I see the brown within them. He has cropped short hair with it shorter on the sides and longer in the middle. It's not styled and looks as if he runs his fingers through it all the time. He's slim, but I'm guessing he is built under the hoodie he is wearing along with dark jeans and black boots. He has a ring on almost every finger.

Through my intense staring I realize he still has his finger under my chin. I try to duck my head, but he won't let me. He studies me intently before asking in a deep baritone voice, "Are you good?" I nod, and he gives me a slight smirk. *Holy butterflies.* Then he nods in return as he removes his finger. "You play before?" I nod again; I'm really getting tired of nodding so much. I feel like a fucking bobble head.

He goes to say more, but then the teacher comes walking by. "Ah yes, Mr. Anderson, it would seem Miss. Wilson is our Allstar Competition winner of the year. Congratulations, my dear." I give a small smile and nod.

I hear a quiet snicker followed by a whisper, "What's wrong with her? Can't she talk?" to which someone else responds, "I heard she went crazy and can't talk now."

I feel myself tense up, which doesn't go unnoticed by the guy sitting next to me.

"Enough," who I know as Mr. Anderson says in a deep, dark voice that makes the hairs on the back of my neck stand and my pulse kick up at the same time. Holy shit, his voice is commanding, and you'd think it would terrify me, but instead I just get this intense tingling feeling working its way through my body.

The teacher chides, "Alright, class, that's not how we treat new students. Back to work. Mr. Anderson, catch up Miss Wilson. She'll be your partner now."

"Got it, Mr. B," says Mr. Anderson. I pull out my notebook and write, *Name?* and show it to him. He gives me another tiny smirk and says, "Ryker." Then he stares at me before letting out a deep chuckle. Holy hell, I feel like I could listen to that chuckle all day long. *What is wrong with me?* Before I can get lost in those thoughts, he says, "You gonna tell me yours?"

Oh shit. Oops. I write down my name and show him.

"Badass name for a badass chick." I scrunch my nose up at that, and all he does is smirk at me before focusing on the piano again. "So, we are just creating our own pieces now since we spent the last month learning to read notes. Can you read and write them?"

I nod and write, *I've been playing since I was four, and I've written my own songs before.* He reads it and runs a hand through his hair, "Right, sorry, dumb question. Since you did Allstar you would've had to show proof you can compose. How did you get on so young anyways? I heard the waitlist is crazy and usually only seniors get in."

I write, *My mom's mentor heard me play when I was twelve, and he put in a recommendation to get me on the list to compete, and since it only happens once a year, I just got accepted this year.* Not adding the parts where my mom is actually dead, and I have no idea how Mother got me in now with a different last name and so young.

Thinking about that brings to surface a memory of when mom told me about it four years or so ago.

"Baby girl!" Mom yells for me.

I was outside talking to a few of the other kids that live close by. I say bye and run back up to the house.

Mom is standing on the back porch holding her phone bouncing on her toes. She has a huge grin on her face, which makes me smile back at her. I love my mom's smile; it's infectious. When she lets out her big one, like right now, she gets this dimple in each cheek, and her eyes spark the brightest hazel color I have ever seen.

"What's up, Mom?" I ask her as I skid to a stop.

"That was Josh I was just on the phone with! He had news he wanted to tell me." Josh is my piano instructor. Even through all of our moves, he still teaches me. Sometimes it just had to be over video chat.

She bounces on her toes again, looking like a rocket ready to take off at any second. "Okay," I draw out with a chuckle. "What is this news?"

"You know the Allstars Competition we had talked about with Josh at your last practice?" I nod. "Well, he said that he talked with

a friend of his that helps run the competition every year, and he might be able to get you on the waitlist to compete."

I scrunch my brows. "But you have to be older. I thought a junior or senior."

"Yes, normally you do. But since you are homeschooled and very smart,"—she bops my nose as I roll my eyes—"you are technically ahead. Plus, you have been working closely with Josh for many years, and he said he would be able to swing it for you. You would be on the waitlist, so it would still be two or three years away, but baby girl, the money you win could help so much for your college fund! Or a 'whatever Harley plans to do in the future' fund."

I chuckle at how she uses air quotes. Mom is a firm believer that I can go do whatever I want after I graduate. She said I have a good head on my shoulders for being so young. She always ends up crying when she says it, though.

"Wow. That would be so cool. But nerve-racking. Mom, I don't know if I am even good enough for that," I say as I wring my fingers together in front of me. I couldn't even imagine trying to play by myself in front of so many people right now. As amazing as it would be, it's scary.

"Oh baby, you would do amazing. And we still have a few years, so don't stress about it right now. Just be excited!" She hugs me tight and squeals as she tells me how proud she is of me.

The memory fades as Ryker nods and says, "Well, I've heard it's a big deal and colleges will be after you next year since you're a bigshot now." He winks. "I'm only taking this because I can play half decent and didn't know what else to take for my arts credit."

I nod, and my lips tilt up a fraction, I write in my notebook asking him if I can warm up before we get started. He nods and makes room for me to play. I take a deep breath, straighten my back, lay my fingers on the keys, and then let the power of the piano take over.

I close my eyes and play, a huge grin forming on my lips as I keep playing, everything just coming back to me, as if it's only been days since I played with my mom and not years. As I finish, I open my eyes and realize the room is silent.

I look around and notice all eyes are on me. I automatically turn my head to search out Ryker next to me, as if I'll find comfort in those dark eyes of his. *Wow, okay, slow your roll, Harley... You don't know this guy.*

His eyes are on me, and he has the biggest smile on his face. It automatically calms me down, and my shoulders sag. I didn't even realize I had gotten so tense. Ryker lets out a low whistle and starts clapping, which seems to pull everyone else out of their intense daze, and they also start clapping.

I feel a blush come over my cheeks as Ryker leans towards me and whispers, "I've never seen someone look so goddamn beautiful and at peace as you just did playing. You enrapture me." His voice and words send a shiver down my spine, bringing tears to my eyes that I quickly blink away.

I should not be feeling so strongly based on a few words from a stranger.

The rest of the period flies by, and I find myself smiling more than I have in three years just from being around a piano again. At least I'm telling myself it's the piano and not the company. I should've known it wouldn't last.

Chapter Four

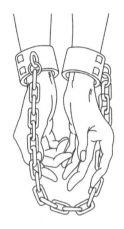

Harley

After class, Ryker winks at me and takes off as I wait for Lex outside the classroom. When Lex and I walk into the cafeteria, a lot of eyes turn to look at us, and I feel the need to turn back and leave, but Lex drags me through to a table in the middle that has two other guys and a girl at it. Lex introduces us and lets them all know I'm mute. I get weird looks, but they soon move on to have conversations between each other.

The cafeteria is a fairly large room with long rectangular tables set up throughout. When we first came in, we walked by the food area, and just smelling all the food makes my stomach grumble. I want to eat, but I don't have money to get anything. So instead, I am sitting here trying to ignore my rumbling stomach.

As I zone out, I feel eyes on me and look around the room, spotting a corner table in the back. Ryker from piano class, the guy from the office who I know is Cayden, and one other guy are sitting there by themselves, and all three of them are staring at me.

When I look at them, the third guy looks away, but Ryker and Cayden keep staring right at me. Ryker winks at me and quirks an amused grin. I look away and with shaky fingers grab a notebook from my bag and write to Lex that I'm going to the bathroom. She nods and returns to her lunch and chatting.

I shakily stand and try to calmly walk out of the cafeteria to find the closest bathroom. I go in to hide in a stall; I know it's pathetic, but I'm not used to this. I've been locked away for three years. It's hard to adjust.

I take some deep breaths and work on calming myself down. I know I just need to adjust to it all. So much noise, the strong smells, eyes on me... Just as I start to calm down, the bathroom door bangs open, causing me to jump, and some other girls come in. I raise my feet up on the seat with me wanting to stay hidden. They talk about makeup and their classes for a while, and then it gets quiet.

"So what do you think of the new girl? Did you see how Lex has been attached? She probably has a crush on her," one girl says.

Then the other one pipes up, "Cayden has been staring at her all day. I saw him doing it in history and at lunch. Ryker and Grayson, too."

Before she can say anymore, someone who I am assuming is Queen B speaks up in her high-pitched, shrill voice. "I'm not worried. She's a freak who can't even talk and dresses like a homeless person. Ry and Cade are mine. I'm still working on getting them away from Grayson, which I need to talk to Lex about anyways. Let's go, girls."

They all leave, and I stay for a few more minutes. Why would she need to talk to Lex? That's odd. But not my business. I try not to take offense to what they said, but it still sucks. I just wish I could talk so I could at least protect myself better.

I hide in the bathroom for a few more minutes before I decide I can't just run and hide from things all the time. I am supposed to make use of this time out of my hell. I leave the bathroom and wander around. I find more of my classes and the library. I round a corner, planning to just head towards my locker since I still have ten minutes before class, but I stop short when I see Ryker, Cayden, and the other guy, Grayson I'm guessing from what that girl said in the bathroom. Fuck.

I turn quickly, trying to get away before they see me, but that plan goes to shit when I plow right into the wall. Ow, fuck. That hurts. I rub my nose and then realize I am supposed to be getting away. Before I can even take a step, a deep chuckle comes from behind me.

I turn slowly and see Ryker standing there. "You okay there?" he says with a look of mirth. I nod and give a thumbs up. He shakes his head and tries to hide a smile. "Come on, come hang out with us before the bell rings."

Before I can try to figure out how to get away, he loops his arm with mine and pulls me towards Cayden and Grayson, who are still standing by the lockers. Cayden looks stone-faced while Grayson's lips are turned in a kind smile.

"Are you okay? That looked like it hurt." I nod again at Grayson's question.

I seriously wonder if Mother would truly know if I talked. Not being able to fucking sucks. But I think this is one of those things that's not worth the risk. My mom used to say to me, 'Pick your battles. Sometimes they aren't worth your energy, and sometimes they are.' I think this one isn't worth it. I don't want to jeopardize Mother pulling me from school. Especially since I don't know why she's sending me here.

A throat clears, pulling my attention from my thoughts. I look at them and all three are staring at me. The differences between these three astonishes me. Cayden is silent and broody. He looks like he's always calculating things with his eyes. Grayson seems gentle, softer. His eyes show his emotions. The complete opposite of the brute next to him. Ryker, though, is hard to understand. Maybe that's just because I'm not used to being around people, but he seems like the funny, loud one. Still, when I look at his eyes, they show a different story. It's confusing to me.

"How's your first day going?"

I realize I can't actually respond. Before I try to pull a notebook out to answer Grayson's question, a rectangle is shoved in front of me. I glance at it and see a white screen and then what looks like a tiny keyboard. I glance up at Cayden, who is holding it out to me.

I must show my confusion because Ryker jumps in, "Harley, do you not know what this is?" I hesitantly shake my head, getting worried about where this conversation is going. Ryker glances at Cayden and Grayson before looking back at me. "It's a phone. Do you not have one?"

Oh, a phone. Wow, I feel like an idiot. My mom had one, so of course I know what it is. I just haven't seen one in three years. And this one looks fancier than what I remember Mom having. I shake my head at Ryker's question. He grabs the phone from Cayden and shows it to me. "Just type on the keyboard part and we can read whatever you put. It'll be easier than always having to pull out a notebook."

I give a tiny smile. Tears burn the back of my eyes, but I blink them away. They are being so nice to me. I don't understand. I take the phone from him when he offers it to me.

"Do you use sign language? I don't know it, but I've always been interested in learning it," Grayson says, his cheeks turning pink when Ryker picks on him for being nerdy.

I shake my head.

"You don't? How do you communicate with your family at home?"

They all stare at me. I squeeze the phone in my hand, feeling myself getting irritated. I can't answer their questions. I wouldn't even know what to say for a believable lie.

This isn't their fault, but part of me feels myself getting angry at them anyways.

"Harley? Did you recently lose your voice? Can you tell us anything?"

Before I can respond to Ryker, Grayson jumps in again. "You don't have to tell us anything. We are just curious. If you ever do want to tell us, you can."

They need to stop. I squeeze the phone harder. My breaths turning into pants. Fuck. Cayden reaches over and pulls the phone from my iron grip. He types on it then hands it back to me. I read it.

I see your rage. They only want to offer help. Sometimes when people hurt us, we turn our own hurt on the wrong people. Don't do that to them. But remember they would drop anything to help you. Even if they don't know you. Trust me. I know. Go calm down. I'll stop Ryker from following you.

I shove the phone back at him harder than I mean to and wince. I haven't felt anger like this before. I'm not even sure who it's aimed at. But I also hate how easily he read me. Can everyone? Does Mother? How will I ever get away if they can read my face so easily?

I turn and take off down the hall at a brisk pace and go back to the bathroom to hide until the bell rings. *Great going, Harley. You didn't even last ten minutes outside the bathroom.*

The rest of the day goes by slowly but not bad. During study hall, we only have to check in with our teacher, and then we can study anywhere unless told otherwise. Math was hard. I'm going to struggle since I can't ask questions and I'm so far behind.

Grayson was in my math class. He's tall, I think slightly taller than Ryker. He has longer brown hair that is more of a messy bedhead look but yet still looks good. He dresses differently than Ryker and Cayden. He has on fitted dark blue jeans and a nice black button-up shirt with the sleeves rolled up to his elbows.

Who knew I'd find myself attracted to arms? Because wow.

He sat by me but didn't talk. When I got stuck on a problem the teacher was having us do, I was just staring at my paper when Grayson reached over and took my notebook and wrote out how to solve it, explaining in detail. When I looked over at him when he was giving the notebook back, he blushed, shrugged, and went back to his work.

I had to fight off tears for the second time today over another guy. *You can withstand beatings without crying but not two insanely attractive guys doing something nice or saying something nice? What's wrong with you?*

Gym was just dodgeball and the coach let me watch since it's my first day. Thank god, too, because my body is exhausted from so much today. But I am really worried about it because my body is really weak, and if I'm already struggling this much, how am I going to make it through gym every day?

Besides all of that, I enjoyed being out of that house. It's a good reminder that there is more out there than what I've been given for three years and someday, hopefully, I can get away or possibly get answers for why all of this has been happening.

When I get back to the house, the door is locked, and no one is home. So I do what they told me and head around back to wait on the back porch. It's October, so it's 50 degrees and I'm wearing ripped jeans and an old hoodie. I'll definitely get cold sitting out here waiting, but there isn't much more I can do. There is an old shed in the corner of the yard that mother calls the doghouse, but it's cold in there too, and there is a big padlock on it; that is the last place I want to be right now.

I once talked back to Mother, testing the waters to see how real her threats were, and she dragged me out to the shed and locked me in it for forty-eight hours. No food, water, toilet, light, nothing. It was miserable, and I never want to experience that again.

I cried and screamed almost the entire time. I felt so hopeless. I really thought she might leave me out there forever.

I shiver at those bad memories, and then I decide fuck them and walk around the house, testing every window, but none of them are unlocked. There might be one open on the second story, but I have no way of getting up there, and even if I did, my body aches right now from moving so much today on top of having bruised ribs and not having done much in three years. I also only get two canned goods a day and yesterday they forgot to give me any, so I'm starving right now. It's not the first time they've forgotten and probably won't be the last. I really need to find a way to get food at school.

I sit on the back patio, the cold cement making me shiver, and pull my knees to my chest. Fighting off the tears that burn the back of my eyes. Fuck crying. I'm sick of feeling like I need to cry. I refuse to, anyways.

I hate this. I know my mom would hate this, too. I have to get out. I have to find a way to escape. I won't survive forever this way. After the first year, I was crying so much and was so incredibly devastated from being beaten all the time and then left alone for hours or days on end. I wanted to die. I could only think there has to be something better than this. I was fourteen at the time and in just one year my life had been flipped upside down and became absolute hell. I didn't understand why they were treating me this way or doing any of this to me. I still don't understand. Only difference now is that I feel a need to do something to live a better life instead of just giving up. I can't let Mother win.

At some point after a year, I stopped asking why, I stopped crying, I stopped begging for mercy. I just laid there and took whatever was dished out. Until one day I thought I couldn't take anymore so I decided that I should end it myself. That memory makes me shiver as goosebumps rise, the thought that I could be dead right now. By my own doing. I never want to think of it again. Obviously, it didn't pan out, and the beating from that day will never leave me. Literally, a lot of my scars are from that day.

I don't know how long I sit out here, but eventually my whole body is shaking from the cold, and I can barely feel my fingers. I get up to start moving around, hoping that helps to warm me up a bit, but from the lack of food, the strain of moving so much today, and the cold, I fall to the ground and everything goes black.

I jolt awake when I feel ice-cold water hit my face. A scream wrenches its way out of my throat, but as soon as I start to scream, it's cut off by my entire body jolting then shaking uncontrollably while it feels like a million bees are crawling and stinging under my skin. It feels like hours before the feeling finally fades and my body slumps back down on the cement.

My body is freezing cold and shivering. I can hear Mother telling me to get up.

I slowly start to, but everything hurts, so it's not going fast enough for them. The blow to my face comes so quick that I don't even see Mother move. She has a wicked arm and can hit hard. I stumble, but before I can hit the ground fully, Mother grabs my hair and yanks me up so I'm standing in front of her. I feel the blood dripping down my chin from what I am guessing is a split lip.

She sneers, "I should only have to call your name once and you respond immediately. You shouldn't be sleeping anyways, you lazy, no-good piece of shit."

I try to say I am sorry, but my throat still burns from what she made me drink yesterday and from trying to scream just now. She pulls on my hair harder. "ARE YOU EVEN LISTENING? Should we get the taser again?"

I try to shake my head, but she has such a strong grip on my hair that I can't move without pain ripping through my head.

I faintly hear Father from somewhere behind her, "Tammy, that's enough."

She shoves me back inside through the open slider and tells me to get out of her sight because I am not worth any more of her time. As I'm stumbling to get to the door for the basement, I see the taser in Father's hand… I can't believe he actually tased me. But I guess I also can. They can be ruthless when it comes to hurting me. Once Mother had Father hold me still as she made cuts up and down my thighs for no other reason than, "She liked the sight of the blood."

I shudder at that thought as I head down the stairs to the basement. On my way down, I overhear part of Mother and Father's conversation.

"You can't keep losing your temper so fast and hitting her where people can see now that she goes out in public."

I internally scoff. For a second there I thought he was going to tell her not to hit me at all. But who am I kidding? He would never. I don't understand their relationship. Mother is so much worse than Father is, but in my mind, he is just as bad because he never stops her. I just wish I understood why. Why is he okay with her hurting me?

Tammy huffs, "Fine. I will call the school in the morning and let them know Harley had an accident."

I don't hear more because I am already at the door to the basement. It takes way longer than it should to get to the bottom of the stairs since my body is throbbing, causing me to wince with every step down.

When I get downstairs, Father comes and joins me a minute later. He cuffs my ankle like usual, then sighs, "You are such a disappointment, Harley. You will never be enough for anyone. Especially if you can't even be good enough to make your mother happy." His eyes scan me from head to toe with a predatory gaze that has me freezing where I stand, not even daring to breathe. He then stares at me in the eyes and licks his lips. "Someday, Harley, someday, and I can't wait for that day."

I curl up on my bed, too exhausted to even shower right now. Tears threaten to leak out, but I remind myself I am not supposed to cry over the things they do to me anymore. That gives them a power I don't want them to have. But yet at the same time, being around people and out of this house is reopening all the doors to my feelings I locked down years ago.

Chapter Five

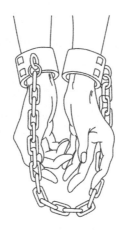

HARLEY

The next morning, I wake from a restless night of sleep. I try to stretch out, but my body feels like it's been hit by a truck, and even little movement sends stabbing pain through my body. I have no idea how I'll make it through today.

I slowly get up and go pee, then stand at the sink. I no longer have a mirror in here, so I have no idea how bad my face must look. Not that it would matter anyways; I have no way to cover it up.

I quickly shower, unsure of what time it is, just that it's well after sunrise. I pull my jeans I still have on from yesterday down around the chain like normal so I can shower and not get them wet. I was so exhausted I passed out right away last night. I get my hoodie on and set clean jeans and underwear to the side so they are ready to be put on when someone lets me out of the cuff. I finger comb my hair the best I can and call it good.

A few minutes later, Mother comes down and unlocks me, not saying a word as I keep my head down and change my pants. I follow her up the stairs after I'm done and as I head towards the front door, I see Mother and Father behind me, so I stop and wait for whatever comes next.

"Go to the guest bath. There is concealer to cover up the bruise on your face. Do a good job. You look disgusting, and no one needs to see that. I already informed the school that you were playing with a soccer ball outside with Tabby and the ball hit your face and you fell on the porch. That is where your bruise and cut came from. Understood?" I nod my head, and Mother walks away.

I go into the guest bath and as usual, Father comes and stands in the doorway to watch me like he does anytime I am upstairs. I cover up the best I can, but I have no idea what I'm doing, and it does nothing to cover my split lip. All it did was dim the coloring on the bruise, which is much worse than I thought it was. My lip is slightly swollen and cut, and the bruise on my face goes from under my eye and covers my entire right cheek. I shrug and call it good enough. Hopefully I won't see Mother again before I leave.

I make it out of the house and as I walk down the driveway to wait for the bus, my stomach grumbles at me. I haven't eaten in over twenty-four hours and with all the strain my body has been through the last two days, I need to eat something. If Father had not been watching so closely and following me around then I would have grabbed something at home, but that wasn't an option.

I'm one of the first stops, so when I get on, there are only four other students. I sit in the same seat as yesterday, directly across from a girl who is leaning over the seat in front of her talking to the girl sitting there. There is another girl up front and then one guy behind me who is sound asleep.

I start to think of what I can do for food when I glance over at the girl across from me and see her wallet sticking out of her purse. I can't be that insane. I'm not that kind of person. I quickly look away.

I've never thought of myself of being the kind of person to steal, but when it comes down to it, I feel I don't have many options left. I look behind me and find the guy is still sound asleep. Then I look at the girl, seeing she is still half bent over the seat in front of her talking to the other girl. I'm not sure why they just don't sit together... *Okay, focus, Harley!*

I take a deep breath and scoot to the end of my seat and look around one more time. When it all seems clear, I reach over and snag her wallet really fast and scoot back in my seat, putting my bag up next to me to block anyone from seeing. With trembling fingers, I snatch out the cash. There is $60, so I take a $20 and a $10 and stash them in my bag. Then I check around me before quickly sliding back to the end of the seat and returning the wallet.

Not even a minute later, she reaches for her bag, and I take a deep, shaky breath. Holy shit, that was too close. I can't ever do that again.

About twenty minutes later, the bus pulls up to the school, and we all start to get off. The guy walking in front of me has cash sticking out of his wallet that is in his back pocket... Okay, that's just too easy. How can I resist?

I snag it really fast and shove it in my jeans pocket. I don't even know how much it is, but I couldn't help myself, and it honestly feels kind of good. I know it shouldn't, but I need to eat and truthfully, I could stash the money to save. I have a while before first period, so I go to the bathroom to count my cash. I have $30 from the girl on the bus and $70 from the guy. Shit! I didn't mean to take that much. As I stare at it trying to decide what to do, another bad thought comes to my mind. I could keep doing this... It's not like I can get a job and I can't snoop Mother's house for cash easily... So I could do this, save, and then run away.

Shit, this is bad. But my life is bad, and in order to survive, I think it's time I sharpen my walls. Do whatever it takes because I can't stay here forever. I know Mother has something planned. She wouldn't have put me in school otherwise.

I have no intention of seeing those plans in action, so staying is not an option. I am hoping I can figure out something else or even try to find my dad. I at least want to know who he is. Him being a good person would be a huge plus, too. Maybe he'd even have answers about my mom and what happened to her and why it happened.

I shove $90 into my bag. I need to find a really good hiding spot for it. I keep $10 out hoping I can use it the rest of the week for food.

Today is Tuesday, so hopefully it'll last all week. Maybe I'll just eat in the mornings and hope Mother or Father give me canned goods like they normally do in the evenings. That should work.

I head towards the cafeteria and see a vending machine, so I stop and get two protein bars for $2 and a water bottle for 50 cents that I can keep and refill here with the water fountains and in my sink at home. I just have to leave the bottle in the bottom of my bag. Hopefully they don't plan on going through it. If they do, I will lie and say it was free or someone gave it to me. I eat one bar now and save the other one for later.

As I wander the halls to kill time before class, I see Ryker, Cayden, and Grayson walking towards me. They see me and stop, and Ryker beams, "Hey, Harley, did you—" He's cut off abruptly by a growl coming from Cayden.

Ryker and Grayson look at him shocked, but he doesn't notice as he's too busy staring at me. Well, my mouth, or more importantly, my cut lip.

I start to panic, so I smile, wave, and start to walk around them, but before I can, Cayden grabs my arm and I flinch.

"Wow, Cade, chill. What's going on?" Ryker asks.

Cayden growls again and points to my lip and glares at Ryker. "Cut," he grunts out.

Ryker turns his attention back to me, and I glance down at my feet. It's quiet for a minute, and I can't run because Cayden is still holding onto my arm. I feel two fingers touch under my chin, and I flinch again and internally cuss at myself for it. *Stop being so weak!*

The fingers raise my face up, and then I'm looking straight into the brightest green eyes I've ever seen. Grayson. He gives me a tiny understanding smile, then looks at my lip, and a look of anger crosses his face.

But before anyone can say anything, someone walks up behind me and throws their arm around my shoulder and tugs me towards them, so Cayden's hand falls away from my arm.

"Hey, Harley! I haven't seen you since yesterday," Lex says. She glances back at the guys. "Sorry, girl talk time." Then she yanks me away from them.

Once we are out of sight, she stops and looks at me. When I see her notice the cut lip, I tense. I'm not sure how to get out of this one.

She looks at it and then back up at my eyes. "Are you okay?"

I nod and try to give an encouraging smile. Luckily, she changes the subject after that.

"I saw the guys stop you and everyone was looking, and it looked mad uncomfortable, so I got you out of there. Also, you should try to avoid those guys like I told you yesterday. They aren't good news and come from a gang on the other side of town and trust me, you don't want to catch their attention. I've heard things about them, and none are good."

I nod, but I'm not sure what I think or how to feel. I point towards my class and then mouth 'thank you' to her. She looks pleased as she takes off for her class. As I'm walking, I start to think about how just two days out of that house are changing me and I know one thing for sure: I am tired of being beaten and used and abused, but I don't want to die anymore.

I want more, I want better. And I get this weird feeling it's out there for me. I just have to find it and stop all this self-pity shit.

One Month Later

It's been a month since I started school, and things are going good. Well, at school anyways.

Lex and I have become good friends. I wait for her every morning at the front of the school, and we hang out until the bell rings. She spends lunch with her friends, but during the classes we have together, we sit together and always work together when we can. She also joins me in the library during study hall when she has nothing to do as a TA. I really enjoy being around her; she has so much energy and is always smiling.

Well, that is until she sees Ryker, Cayden, or Grayson staring at me, which they do a lot. Then she gets a weird look on her face. But she always masks it so fast that I haven't really thought about it too much.

Speaking of the guys, though, things have been weird, but I guess good. They all watch me all the time. Grayson is quiet, but he is sweet with his actions. He always holds doors open for me, and he meets me at my locker all the time and carries my books and bag for me. He also walks me to any class he can. He smiles at me, but we don't really talk, besides in math which he helps me with during class.

Whenever I smile back at him, his cheeks turn bright pink; it's cute. Cayden follows us most days but keeps his distance and never talks. He feels more like a silent protector, or a stalker, but it doesn't bother me. Oddly enough, it's peaceful being around them.

Ryker is much more talkative. Any time I'm around him, he likes to chat and joke around, and I think he flirts with me, but I'm not really sure.

It's all odd to me, and Lex hates them with such a passion that I don't really know what to do. She gets mad if she sees me with them. But they just don't go away. Even with me not being able to talk, they are always around. I also, well, I don't really want them to go away. Lex is my friend, but I just... something is telling me not to listen to her about this.

She won't even tell me why she hates them, so that doesn't help me think they are bad, especially since they are so kind to me.

I find myself keeping to myself as much as possible. The last thing that I want is more people questioning bruises or just anything about my home life. The guys keep a distance too for the most part; they have mostly just watched me over this last month.

Since those first two days when they were asking questions and trying to get close, they have backed off. But yet are still around.

I thought at first I was just too fucked up and they finally caught onto that, but they are still around. Just silent in a way. I feel like I should find it uncomfortable or bad, but I find that I kind of like them always watching me. Well, besides that it makes pickpocketing a little harder because I have to try to make sure their eyes aren't on me.

I've continued to pickpocket and have a total of $389. I've had to use some of it on the days that Mother and Father don't feed me but other than that, I've been stashing it all. I found a small hole in the concrete at the base of the wall right next to the stairs in the basement, and I've been rolling the cash up and sticking it in there. It works for now. Somehow, I haven't gotten caught, and honestly, I think I'm getting pretty good at it. I also enjoy it. It gives me something to do. It's becoming a hobby I guess one would say.

Though, I always worry that Mother will look in my bag after school, or they will beat me before I can get downstairs and the money will fall out of my pocket and they'll see it, so I found the best space to hide it for transport from school to the basement at home. My panties. Yep, just stuff the cash in there and I don't have to worry about it.

My classes are all really hard, but I have so much time to study that I've been able to keep up for the most part. Mother has been careful not to hit my face again since last month when I went to school with the bruises and split lip. I also got that cup of shit that burns my throat again last week because I spoke at home and apparently the mute thing is to be kept at all times, not just at school. Not sure how the fuck I was supposed to know that, but I don't think she cared that I didn't. The rotten bitch just enjoys hurting me.

Father has been coming downstairs more often and just staring at me when he thinks I'm sleeping. I'm not sure what to do with that, so I just pretend to sleep, but it's starting to scare me.

My body hasn't gotten any stronger, mostly because I still get beat all the time, so it's kind of hard for my body to heal fully and gain strength. Most days, I'm so exhausted when I get home that I can't do anything to stop the beatings. Mother does something at least once a day, almost like an addict. I seriously think she is addicted to hurting me. I also think she is purposely keeping me weak, so I don't start getting stronger to run or fight back.

I found out Tabby goes to private school and can do whatever she wants, so she is barely ever around. Robert or Rob, my oldest brother, is at college, but I overheard that he comes home for Thanksgiving this month. Hopefully he's not as bad as everyone else. I have yet to meet him. I don't think he knew I was here when he lived here. But he was also rarely ever home that I knew of.

Being able to go back to school this last month has been such a blessing. It's given me a new sense of hope. Reminding me that there is better out there and not just what happens in that basement. I want to be out; I need to get out.

I've been thinking a lot about how I can do that. I know my best bet is to run away from school, but I have to be careful and do it right or else I could make things worse. I've been trying to think of people my mom might have known that I could go to. But I can't really think of anyone yet. I know that if I run away, I'll probably go back to where I was raised in Auburn, Massachusetts. It just seems like it would be the best option. But until I can actually get out and even think of a plan to get away, I just need to keep getting money and saving as much of it as I can.

Mother has been better at bringing me cans of food again, so I only get protein bars from the vending machine sometimes. I know I don't eat enough, but it's the best I can do right now. My body is weak unfortunately, but I just have to make do until I come up with a plan.

I come out of my thoughts as Mother comes down to uncuff me so I can go to school. I get my pants on, then head up after putting my shoes on and take off. We don't talk in the mornings which is a rule she set because apparently, it's just too tempting to hit me if she's around me for too long, and she saves those blows for after school. I head to school and instead of waiting for Lex today, I head towards the courtyard.

Before I can get there, however, the school's mean girls, or as I like to call them, the Barbie Bitch Squad, step in front of me. There are three of them.

Steph, who is the queen barbie, wears so much makeup she seriously looks like a barbie. She has always given me nasty looks, but this is the first time she's directly come up to me.

Her minions cross their arms. I don't even know their names, but they are basically bitch one's—sorry, Steph's—minions. You never see her without them, and they dress like her. They wear just as much makeup, too.

"Stay away from the guys. Ry and Cade are mine. They always have been and will always be. You have no shot with them, so back the fuck off." She smirks at me.

I have to bite my tongue to keep from saying something since I'm not supposed to talk, but it's fucking hard. Something about her calling them by nicknames and excluding Grayson really grates on my nerves. I'd like to punch her in the face, but I know I'm weak. I'd be no match if she threw a punch back at me. So instead, I clench my fists and raise a brow.

"Oh dear, I forgot you can't speak. Whoops. Well then just listen to my pretty voice. Stay away, mutt, or else I'll make your life hell. Once I have the guys, no one will dare to even look at me wrong." She smirks again. "Come on, girls." She walks away, not even looking back at the girls to make sure they are following.

I roll my eyes as they follow like pathetic little ducks. Sorry, that's disrespectful to ducks. They follow her like the pathetic barbie bitches they are. I sigh and keep heading towards the courtyard, wishing I could've said something to her.

It's been a few days since I pickpocketed someone, and I feel an urge to do it again. It makes me feel better the more money I can stash. So, I walk around until I pick my victim and then get to work with a giddy feeling and my veins pumping with adrenaline.

Honestly, I love doing it and it's time I start thinking about myself.

Got to become the devil, right? Step one: pickpocket.

Chapter Six

Ryker

I'm standing in the courtyard with my brothers, Cade and Gray. We watch as the cute little redhead comes walking into the courtyard prowling around looking for a victim. She picks out a nerdy dude who is standing with one other guy with cash literally just sticking out of his back pocket. *Idiot.*

Harley walks by and bumps into the nerd's friend and gives a shy grin, then ducks her head. As she rounds them, she snags the cash.

It's fucking smooth, if I'm being honest. She's gotten better at it over the last month.

Yep, we've been watching her. We first saw her pickpocket the lunch lady three weeks ago. The fucking lunch lady. We all got

71

a good laugh out of that and ever since then, she's gotten better and better. The little shit stole from our piano teacher, too.

No one has seen anything. We notice, but we keep our distance and make sure no one else does. Hate to have to kill them. But so far, our little redhead has been very good at not getting caught or being seen by anyone.

I couldn't be more proud. *What? I'm not fucking normal.*

Over the last month, we've kept an eye on her and have slowly started talking to her, but we don't want to overwhelm her. It's not hard to tell she is skittish. So, we keep contact to a minimum for now. Hopefully that'll change soon. I don't have much patience. But until then, we watch her.

Okay, well, I watch her a lot. I've skipped a lot of classes just so I could keep an eye on her. I want to follow her home, but I haven't found a way onto her bus yet.

Plus, Gray keeps telling me I'm taking it too far.

Maybe he's not taking it far enough.

Cade growls, his normal communication, which he seems to do way more of lately, especially when it comes to a cute little redhead.

I look at him and follow his eyes to see Harley walking away but keeping an arm around her ribs. It's not something most people would notice, but because all three of us have seen and had injuries on our ribs, we notice. She definitely has some broken ribs with the way she's been holding them all week.

It makes my skin boil, and I want to kill whoever is hurting her. No one should lay a fucking hand on her. Ever. The day that

Cade pointed out the mark on her face, I was pissed. I wanted to do something right then and there but couldn't, so I settled for sparring with Cade at home, and he and Gray talked me down.

"Give her space," they say. Well, I fucking hate space. If I want something, I go for it. I also don't like sitting back and watching. A month. Four fucking weeks is too long.

So, we don't say anything because we have a feeling she would shut down or run, and we don't want that.

Since the day that we talked to her in the hall, we have backed off. We still try to be friendly and be around her, but we mostly just watch her from a distance. Cade never told us what he wrote on his phone and showed her before she took off like her ass was on fire. But he keeps telling me we need to just back off some. That overwhelming her will only make things worse and with how she responded to a few simple questions we asked, we don't want to push it more.

But It's driving me insane that Cade won't say what he said to her, but he's a stubborn ass, and I won't get the answer out of him. *Doesn't mean I won't fucking try.*

Something about her calls to us. She's special and not like other girls. I think she'd actually understand us. But we need her to trust us before we can try to help. Us being crazy cavemen wouldn't help her right now. That doesn't mean it doesn't piss me the fuck off to sit back and watch.

"I'm really getting sick of this shit. We need to do something. I can't stand to watch it. It's been a month, a fucking month! I'm done sitting back and watching," I spit at my brothers, not intending for my anger to be directed at them, but they know that.

"I know, brother," Gray says in his usual calm, soothing tone, always the voice of reason. "But we have to play it safe. We don't know what's going on, and we need to form a plan. Maybe it's time we take this to Noah? He could give us some ideas and maybe get Nerds to look into her."

Cade growls, which means he agrees. Trust me, I understand growling now like it's his own language since the fucker barely ever talks. I nod at Gray and take a deep breath while looking into his calming eyes. He gives me a small smile, then goes back to watching Harley.

Harley starts heading back into the building, so we all follow her. I normally don't tag along for their little quiet walk to class; I don't get how they can just walk quietly next to each other and having caveman Cade at their backs following silently. Fucking awkward.

You know, I kind of like caveman Cade. Maybe it's time for a name change in my phone. Before I get a chance to do that, we catch up to Harley when she gets to her locker. She looks back at us, and shy, cute-as-fuck smile comes over her face before she quickly looks away.

She loads up the books she needs into her backpack, and Gray takes it from her. Usually from what Gray says, she doesn't try to write anything, but apparently today, that isn't the case, as she grabs a notebook and pen from her locker before she shuts it and writes, *You know you don't have to do that. I can carry my own bag.*

Before Gray can do anything, Cade leans over and reads it. He growls, "No."

Harley flinches at his tone and then drops her gaze to the ground.

I slap Cade on the back of the head. "Knock it off, caveman." Then I step towards Harley. "It's okay. Gray likes to carry things; it makes him feel more manly."

Gray gasps and Harley's head shoots up to look at me before she glances at Gray. When she looks at him, he blushes, and I chuckle. *It's so easy to make him blush.*

Thank you, Grayson, Harley writes and passes it to him before dropping her eyes to the ground again.

Everything seems to just stop. We all don't know what to say to make her open up to us, and she seems terrified to try to be open, or maybe she just wants to run away. *Not that it would work anyways. I'd chase her. Huh, now I kind of want to try that.*

Cade is just staring straight into Harley's soul. I just wish she knew he wasn't angry. He's staring so hard because he cares and he's trying to memorize every part of her, but the poor thing won't make eye contact with him. Gray just gets shy and doesn't know what to say. I think Harley is the first girl to ever really grab his attention. So that leaves me.

"Well..." Before I can get anything else out, Lex shows up. "Girl, where were you? You weren't waiting for me." She glances at us and quickly discards us.

Harley looks at her, her eyes wide for a second. Then she grabs the notebook back from Gray when he hands it to her, but she stares at it. I'm assuming she's not sure what to say, not wanting to lie to her friend, even if said friend is sketchy.

"She was with me. Sorry to hold up your girl time, Lexington. Had to chat with my girl."

Harley makes a startled noise and looks at me with wide eyes. I just wink at her.

But Lex turns a nasty glare on me. "She isn't *your* girl," she sneers. "So why don't you run along and leave her the hell alone?" She makes a shooing motion with her hands.

Before I can open my big mouth to probably make things worse for Harley, Gray puts a hand on my shoulder and opens his mouth, but to everyone's surprise, it's Harley who grunts and writes fast, making her pretty handwriting look sloppy, then she shoves the notebook at Lex. I step towards Lex so I can read what it says.

Lex, please don't be mean. They haven't done anything. They just walk me to class and carry my bag.

Lex turns her glare towards Harley, and Harley drops her eyes to the ground and lets her shoulder slump as if she thinks she disappointed her friend.

Alright that's enough of that. "Lexington, knock it off." Harley's eyes shoot up to mine, wide and fearful. "Harley can talk or walk with whoever the hell she wants. Stop trying to shove whatever problems you have with us onto her. Got a problem? Take it up with me." I take a step towards her, and she backs away, eyes wide. "And one more thing, don't you ever, and I mean ever, turn a glare on Harley when she was nothing but polite. Now, fuck off. We are taking Harley to class."

Lex shoots Harley a look, almost like a, you can't seriously be siding with them look, but Harley doesn't say anything. Instead, she's staring right at me, almost as if she's trying to read me. The fear I saw earlier is gone, and I'm not sure why she's not showing fear now.

Lex storms off, and I nod my head to the guys. We all start walking with Harley to her class. She wraps an arm around her ribs, trying to keep from wincing with every step, but I see it. We really need to get home and talk to Noah.

Noah is Cade's brother, but Noah has kept all of us out of trouble for as long as I've known him. He's all our brother, and we'd be fucked without him. He's the enforcer at The Sons of Silence MC, where he goes by Blade. We all have had shitty childhoods, and now we all live at the clubhouse with Noah, and he has guardianship over us. It only worked out that way because Nerds, the MC's tech guy, hacked the system and made it happen. No way would a judge actually grant a twenty-two-year-old custody of three teens and have them living in a motorcycle clubhouse.

Gray and I are sixteen and have been with Noah and Cade for two years now. But we've been best friends with Cade since we were eight. Cade is seventeen already, having had his birthday at the beginning of the school year, and Noah has had custody of him since he turned eighteen.

I grew up watching my dad hit my mom, and when I tried to stand up for her, he turned his fist to me and from then on beat both of us. Seeing Harley hurt brings something out of me. I'm not that kid anymore; I can protect her. I need to. I feel this pull to her that I've never felt, and I just know I need to help her and be in her life in some way. I shake off those thoughts of my childhood as we watch Harley head into her class. I know Lex is up to something; I'm just not sure what yet, but we've had a tail on her for a while. Even before Harley came around, we've been watching her. But now with Harley in the picture, I'm worried. Lex has never picked up new friends. She hates just about everyone, so whatever this is, I have a feeling it's not good.

During piano, I get to see Harley look delighted with a sparkle in her eyes as she loses herself to the music. She did admit once that she has no way to play outside of class, so I make sure to practice any other time I can so she can play a lot during class. I want to give this girl the world so that peaceful look she gets when playing stays on her face forever.

When she's done warming up, she glances at me and gives me a small smile, then she grabs a notebook and starts writing before handing it to me. *Thank you for this morning. I'm sorry about Lex. I'm not sure why she doesn't like you guys. But thank you for standing up for me.*

I look over at her, and she blushes and bites her bottom lip but doesn't duck her head like she usually does. That sends a warm feeling through me I want more of.

"It's okay, Harley, no worries. Lex has her own shit, but she doesn't get to take any of it out on you. You deserve better."

Her eyes go wide, and her cheeks turn bright red. I see a sheen of tears in her eyes, but she quickly blinks them away and turns back to the piano. She starts playing again, working on the piece we were assigned to learn. I watch her, completely entranced by her. When she's done, she peeks over at me, then drops her eyes, her cheeks instantly flushing again.

I chuckle and lean in close to her, making sure to move slowly so she sees me and can move away if she wants to, but she stays still.

"I think you will be my little flame. Beautiful red hair." I run my finger through a few strands of her hair as I say it. "And your cheeks turn the brightest shade of red sometimes." I slowly run my finger lightly over her cheek. "And, well, little because you're tiny, but I think there is an unlit flame somewhere inside you, and you just need someone to light it for you."

She turns her head towards me, my finger still resting by her cheek, now lightly touching her lip. Her eyes are wide at how close our faces are. I can feel her breath on my face. I give her my most genuine smile, and she very slowly reaches up and runs her finger over my dimple on my left cheek before dropping her hand. She sighs heavily and opens her mouth but immediately shuts it.

I scan her face but don't understand what changed. I decide to let it go for now, figuring that I've probably pushed her too far already.

"Alright, my little flame. Let's practice this shit." She grins and nods at me.

After school, we head back to the clubhouse. It's about a fifteen-minute ride from the school. We all take Noah's truck together since Noah mostly just rides his bike. As we get closer to the club, the houses lessen. We are farther out away from town. You turn down a side road that leads to a farmer's land on the left, and on the right is the compound. It is all fenced in, and we pull up to the gate where a prospect is in the gate house. He opens the gate for us, and we head through down the road. It's all trees on either side until you reach the main building. Then it's an old-style warehouse that was renovated long before I was around. It's three stories with the first floor being half a huge garage and then the main room, kitchen, and offices. There is a basement with a gym and the second and third floor is where members live.

As we pull up, all you can see is the huge warehouse with the garage and main parking lot to the left, and to the right the road continues around the warehouse. Cade parks the truck in our normal parking spot, and we all head inside to talk with Noah about Harley.

The two new prospects that came on over the summer are at the bar drinking beer. Pretty sure they are supposed to be doing prospect duties but when prez isn't around, they fuck off and do whatever they want. They aren't good guys, and I still don't get how they even were able to make it on as prospects. But I think we see a different side to them than the prez does.

Daniel smirks at us as we walk past. I don't know why he acts all tough; I have kicked his ass before, and I sure as hell can do it again.

We find Noah in one of the offices on the phone, talking about a new security business he is getting up and running. He plans to let us work part-time at it once it's going until we turn eighteen and can prospect for the club. We take a seat on the couch and wait for him to be done.

Prez set up a bunch of offices off one hall from the main room about two years ago for anyone to use. Noah has never told us, but we know that the club used to be dirty when Rage's dad was around and now Rage is turning it around and trying to make things more clean. One of his new things is if you want to run a business or start something up, the club will back you. So he created the offices for all members to be able to use. They are bare bones. Just some shelves on one wall with a desk in the middle and a few chairs on the opposite side, along with a couch on the back wall. Basically, all the other open offices look the same, as well.

Noah finishes up and looks up at us. "What's up, boys?"

We all glance at each other, realizing we never did decide how to bring this up.

Noah looks between us, then sighs and leans back in his chair. "Spit it out," he commands, bringing out the enforcer in him.

I speak up first, being the most sane to hold a conversation. *Ha. If only you knew what a joke that is. I'm the craziest out of my brothers.*

"Alright, so, last month, this new girl started at the school, Harley. We knew something was up day one but couldn't tell what then. On her second day, she came in with a split lip, and I'm pretty sure her face was bruised too—"

"Pretty sure?" Blade cuts in. "Brother, we don't do pretty sure. You either know or you don't."

I nod. "Well, I know then because she has a scar on her face going from below her eye to her chin, and it was half covered like she had some kind of makeup shit on. So, I'm going with my gut here. She was bruised. Anyways, after that, we've kept our distance just watching her and have noticed that she started pickpocketing people. She still is, and she's gotten damn fucking good at it.

"Now, the thing is, we've been watching closely. We see the limps, the stomach holding, the careful movements, the getting out of a desk slowly. Also, the girl only owns two pairs of jeans and four hoodies. At least, that's all she ever wears. I don't know, man, we decided to come to you because something is off. This is our town and yeah, it's just not right."

Before Noah can respond, Cade grunts, "Talk."

Noah has a moment of shock before he quickly masks it. *Yeah, I get it, dude. He talked last month in front of her. I about shit my pants; it's been so long, and he sounds scary as shit. If I didn't know my brother, I'd run from the fucker.*

I cough. "Yeah, that's the other thing: She's mute. Can't talk, but we're not sure why. We had Gray get on the school network, but all it says is mute and no other details. Kind of weird."

Noah opens his mouth to say something but yet again before he can, Cade grumbles, "Gotta do fucking everything," so quietly I don't even know if Noah heard him across the desk but Gray and I sure did. "I don't think she's actually mute," he grunts out, his voice raspy and deep from barely any use.

Of course, as soon as the words are coming out is when prez, the club's president, walks in and stops dead in his tracks. I don't think I've ever seen the man shocked before. He's been in our lives since we were younger and is always the badass prez, not this shocked to his core pussy he is right now. *Oops... probably shouldn't call the prez a pussy.*

I guess I can't blame him, though, because Cade doesn't talk. He's always been on the quiet end, but when he was younger, his dad wanted him to be like him. Since Noah wasn't going to be, for his own reasons. So, he tried to force Cade to be like him. He'd beat him to make him talk and force him to say horrible things to his mother and beat on and yell at other kids or anyone his father wanted.

We don't know everything he went through, but I do know from a drunken night about a year ago that Cade doesn't like to talk now because he has the choice. He said maybe someday that'll change again, but he was forced so much as a child that he needs to feel like he's in control now and has power.

I don't think he even remembers telling Gray and I that since that night he was so drunk, but I'm glad he did. It gave us a better understanding. I hope someday he tells us everything so we can seek out some revenge on his behalf.

Prez clears his throat, wipes the shock off his face, then comes in and shuts the door before leaning against it and looking towards Noah. "Blade, what's going on?" Blade is Noah's road name; he nods his head to me, and I repeat everything back to prez that was just said.

Prez, or better known by his road name, Rage, nods. "Alright. What's her last name?"

Grayson pipes in and says Wilson. Rage gets a look on his face that I can't quite read. "Wilson? You sure the kid's name is Harley? The Wilsons only have two kids. Tabby and Rob."

"Yeah, we're sure. Gray got into the school system and checked her out. Nothing is on there. Just her name, no middle name, her home address, and that she's mute. Oh, and her emergency contact is Tammy Wilson."

Rage looks at Noah, his brows scrunching up in confusion and says, "I want them on her."

Noah nods. "Of course, prez. I think this is different because these fools seem to have come to a liking of the girl, so I'll allow it. I'm assuming there's more to this?"

Rage grunts and turns around, opening the door. "Finish this, then my office, Blade." With that, he storms out, slamming the door behind him.

The only reason Rage put it to Blade is because none of us are old enough to be prospects yet. You have to be eighteen, so technically we aren't a part of the club. But we are family, so it's different. But everything goes through Noah since he's our guardian. Although I doubt he'd ever tell his prez no. *Pussy.*

"Alright, boys, make friends with her. Be fucking nice." He glares at Cade, who simply grunts. "Try not to overwhelm her. The main goal right now is being her friend, and then we'll want to try and get her here at some point because prez will want to see her and talk to her. Also, if possible, I want pictures of bruises. I don't know how to get them, but you fuckers are smart, so figure something out. Gray, I'm going to put Nerds on her as well. I'd like you to sit in with him.

"And one more thing: Cade, if you think she can talk, get her talking. I don't care how. I want answers. Get them. I gotta go see what's up my president's ass now. Later, boys." He gets up and walks out, leaving us alone to think about how we are going to figure out Harley.

Part of me gets a bad feeling about all of this, but the pull to that girl is so strong that there is no turning it off. *Ready or not, here we come, little flame. Time to light that fire.*

BLADE (NOAH)

I leave my brothers and head towards Rage's office. I haven't heard my brother Cade speak a word in over a year. To say I was shocked is goddamn understatement. What is it about this girl that brings him out of his own head enough that he speaks willingly? He mostly definitely didn't have to say anything out loud. Usually, he just texts us what he wants to say. I know one thing for sure: I will do what I can to help them figure out this girl. If her pure presence alone can drag my little brother from the depths of his own hell, I will owe her my life.

Rage has been like a father to me since I was little, so I know I can get away with a little more than others normally would. I barge into his office, making sure the door hits the wall. "So, prez, what the fuck was that shit?" *What? I got a flair for the dramatics.* Prez glares at me like he knows I did that shit on purpose. I shrug at him, slam the door, and sit down across the desk from him. "Well?" I draw out.

He rolls his eyes at me and sighs, "You know, if you were anyone else, you wouldn't get away with that shit."

"You know, prez, you tell me that all the time. But I really don't care. Your fault for making me your enforcer, so you're stuck with me all the time."

He rolls his eyes and grumbles, "If you weren't so goddamn batshit crazy, I wouldn't have needed you as my enforcer."

"Alright, alright, I get it, I'm fucking special as shit. Want to tell me what's up with the Wilsons now? Or more specifically Tammy?"

He sighs and runs a hand through his beard. "Tammy and I dated many, many years ago. For a long time, I thought she was the love of my life, but I was in high school and so stupid. She was also dating two other guys, at least that I know of. Her main goal was to make sure she was with someone who was going to prospect for the club when my dad was still prez so she had a chance at being someone's old lady. My dad caught her fucking another guy behind my back; it was someone in the club who knew I was seeing her. Dad had him brought down to the cells and let me decide what to do with him. Well, I was so head over heels in love with this bitch that I went into a blind rage and killed him. Dad said he was proud of me. Fucking fucked up he didn't stop me. I'd never let one of the boys go through that shit so goddamn young.

"Afterwards, I broke it off with Tammy, and she was asking for the club member I killed, and I said he was gone and it was her fault I was so angry. She turned around and went to the cops and got us raided. She was kicked out and never allowed on any club property again. Her current husband, Richard, was one of my close friends back then, and she spun the story to fit her best, and he took her side. Refused to even hear me out. Not that long after that, I found out she was pregnant, but she lost the baby. No one knows whose it was, but she lost it early on.

"My dad always thought it was intentional. Anyways, none of it makes sense now because Tammy has two kids. I've kept track of her over the years to make sure she didn't try any other shit with the club. She stuck around for some reason but hasn't been on any club property in many years, and neither has Richard," he sighs and sits back in his chair, closing his eyes and taking a deep breath.

I know this isn't the time for joking, so I give him a minute. Prez being the president of the club means he doesn't get to be vulnerable very often, if at all.

First kills are always the worst, and they never leave you. It's like marking your soul and turning you into something else; you will never be the same.

I should know. My first was at fourteen. Why do you think they call me Blade?

CHAPTER SEVEN

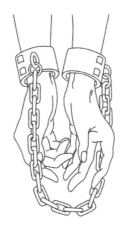

HARLEY

I t's about a week before Thanksgiving, which means I'll be doing a lot of cleaning around the house soon. Which also means being upstairs, so it's time to start thinking ahead about where to look for money, information, anything at all honestly.

I am on the bus on my way home. I don't think anyone will be home when I get there today, which means waiting outside, and it's freezing out. I stuffed an extra hoodie in my backpack when I left this morning, and I have a t-shirt on under the hoodie I'm wearing now.

After the bus drops me off, I decide to check the windows again to pass the time. As usual, they are locked, but I can see inside a few. One is Tabby's room. It looks like she keeps cash on her desk in a change jar, so that's good to know. The next window I can see in is an office. I can't see too much, but it looks like there's a safe in the corner which I wouldn't be able to get into myself. But if I ever got the chance, I could go through the papers stacked on the desk.

The only other place I can see in is the slider, but it's a small gap the curtain doesn't cover, and there isn't too much to see. Ugh, this feels so useless, but I need to do something. I'm tired of not being able to do anything to change my situation.

When the beatings first started when I got put with Mother, I sobbed every day begging for it to stop. Then after a year or so, I gave up on that and shut down. I felt like the only way to survive then was to completely shut down and pretend I had no feelings at all. But now, I feel all those feelings bubbling up like I can't keep them shoved down anymore.

But I refuse to let the full weight of my reality hit. I will not give Mother and Father that kind of power over me. So, I have to try to do something to get away.

I sit on the cement on the back patio and after about ten minutes I decide fuck it. I haven't been beaten in a few days. My body is healing up, so even if I do get caught, I should be fine. The worst that'll happen is they won't leave me alone outside anymore which is fine by me because it keeps getting colder. But I need to start testing boundaries and figuring out what I am going to do to get the fuck out of here.

I stand up and head towards the woods at the back of the yard. I try to make sure I keep in a straight line, so I don't get lost. After about what I think is thirty minutes, I finally reach a road. It goes left and right, but I know that right is going back into town. So that's a good start, but if it did take thirty minutes like I think it did, I need to head back now before I get caught. Next time, I'll run and start from the bus, so I have some more time.

I begin to make my way back and once I'm in sight of the house again, I hear a car door. My eyes widen, and I freeze for a second before getting my ass into gear and bolting towards the back patio. As I get closer, I see lights inside the house turn on, so I push with all I can and get up onto the patio, diving onto the cement, pretending I'm shivering so it makes sense for my heavy breathing.

Just as I land, the curtain flings open, and Mother opens the door and steps out. "You better not be passed out again!"

I raise my head and look at her. She motions for me to stand, so I do. She stands, blocking the slider so I can't walk inside and eyes me like she knows what I've been up to.

My heart beats faster, and it takes everything in me to stay calm and not give myself away. She reaches forwards and grabs a leaf off my hoodie and looks at it and then looks at me and raises a brow. I shrug and act like I'm not sure where it came from.

She glares at me. "I don't know what it is you're up to, but I will find out. You can't get away with anything, you stupid girl. I will always know. Get downstairs."

She steps aside so I can pass, and I go inside and head downstairs. As soon as I reach the basement, I take my shoes and pants off before anyone comes down to put my cuff on. I take off my hoodie and that just leaves me in my panties and shirt, which goes down to right above my knees, so I grab my leggings and put them on too. Sometimes it gets cold down here at night.

A few minutes later, Father comes downstairs with two cans of food and sets them down, then locks my cuff on my ankle. He stares at me before clenching his fists and taking off upstairs. I have no idea what that was about. I've barely seen him these last two weeks. He hasn't even been home much that I know of.

I get as comfortable as I can and grab a can. It's always the pull tab cans, so today it's Chef Boyardee and peaches. I eat one now and save the other for later.

I soon get lost in my thoughts of what I'm going to do. I've got a total of $514 from pickpocketing, but it's not enough to last me very long. Still, I might soon run out of options and just need to go anyway. I might start keeping it in my bag, which is a risk, but if I ever need to run, it would be from school, and I wouldn't be able to come back and get the money.

Ryker, Cayden, and Grayson have started talking to me way more over the last two weeks. Well, Cade just growls and grunts mostly, but they seem to have decided to be my friends, which is odd, but I don't really mind. It'll just be sad when I have to run and leave them and Lex behind.

Speaking of Lex, she hates that I'm friends with the guys. She has gotten mad at me a few times but yet still comes around and is my friend, so I'm not sure what to do about that. I haven't really had friends. Mom homeschooled me, and she was my best friend, so I'm not too sure what I'm supposed to do or what's normal.

Ry asked me the other day about my voice and when I lost it and if I can speak at all, and I panicked. I had no idea what to do. I panicked so bad I almost passed out, but luckily Grayson helped me. He said I had a panic attack. I didn't know what that was, but I'm pretty sure I deal with them almost every day.

Which reminds me of the conversation Gray and I had today in math class.

It was after the panic attack that Gray told me a little bit about himself, "I grew up in a bad home. My oldest brother was killed when I was pretty young, and my parents blamed me for it, even though I now know it was not my fault at all. It brought on a lot of panic attacks. They would get pretty severe, and I had no one to help me through them. But I learned something through that time. When you find people who can help you, you should let them. Even if it's terrifying. You let them because there is nothing worse than fighting off hidden demons alone. Especially when those demons live in your head; they have a way of twisting everything around you, and you need someone else to untwist it for you.

"I tried to hide mine away and keep to myself. But it only made it worse. Harley, I'm telling you this because you have people too. You just have to choose to see them through the darkness and allow yourself to let your walls down."

I had stared at him; it was the most he had ever said to me. I wrote, *What if... those people you think can help you actually turn into even bigger monsters than the ones before or the ones in your head?*

He sighed, "I can't answer that for you, but I can tell you that I know a couple of people who would ask how high if you asked them to jump."

So I wrote the one question burning in my brain. It's been there since the minute these guys looked at me and didn't immediately run from my scars. Then still didn't run from my brokenness. *Why?*

"I wish I could answer why, but I can't. I also can't make you trust us, but I can promise you that you won't ever have to fight alone again if you let us in. We see the scars, and I don't mean the one on your face. I mean the ones in your eyes."

Before anything else could be said, the teacher had gotten everyone's attention.

I had looked down at my notebook, feeling tears in my eyes, but I blinked them away. I wrote down, *What if I don't want to fight off my hidden demons? What if I want them to consume me?* I stared at it, then I had ripped it out of my notebook and folded it up, promising myself that if he ever found it, it would be a sign I can let them in, trust them, even though I don't know them. Then I reached over and dropped the paper into one of his backpack pockets when he wasn't looking.

The rest of the day went by like normal, and I'm not sure whether to hope he finds the note or never finds it.

I get pulled from my thoughts as I hear shouting in the house. I've heard fights before, but nothing like this. Mother and Father are screaming at each other. But it's too far away for me to hear what it's about. Next thing I know, Mother is storming downstairs and pulling me by my hair off the bed.

"What have you done?" she screams at me. "I SAID, WHAT have you done?" She shakes me so hard my vision goes blurry for a second. My throat is still raw even though it's been a while since she made me drink that awful drink.

I whisper in panic, "I don't know."

She screams as she starts raining down blows on me all over from my head to my ribs. She gets tired of hitting and starts kicking me instead. When I don't respond, she rips me off the floor, grabs part of the chain that keeps me trapped down here, and wraps it around my neck, squeezing it. I start to struggle as I'm losing air and can't breathe.

She keeps going as she's screaming at me, but I can't make out what she's saying. I'm kicking my legs and trying to scratch at her wherever I can, but I can feel myself getting light-headed.

The next thing I know, I drop to the floor and Father has Mother pushed back. "We can't kill her. Calm down, Tam. There is more at play here. We will keep her home until after Thanksgiving and find out what she did and what she knows during the week. Go upstairs, take a break."

Mother stomps up the stairs, muttering to herself.

Father turns around and glares down at me. "One chance, Harley, one. Tell me what you did, and this next week will be easier on you, otherwise I will put you through hell until you tell me everything."

I shake my head and rasp out, "I don't know what you're talking about."

He shakes his head and sighs. "You are such a disappointment, Harley. A waste of space. If you weren't needed for a bigger purpose, I'd have killed you years ago or sold you. Of course, after I had my way with you first." He walks back upstairs, slamming the door behind him.

What the hell is happening?

CHAPTER EIGHT

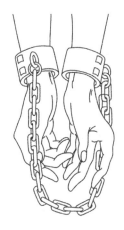

HARLEY

E verything hurts, and I feel like I'm going to be sick. I haven't felt this much pain in a while. I can't even drag in a full breath. I think some ribs are broken, and my neck is so sore it's raw and hurts to the touch. My throat is on fire. I think I have a concussion from being shaken so hard, and my vision keeps going blurry. I can't even process what just happened.

I haven't spoken to anyone! This makes no sense. I wish I knew why she did this shit or where any of this is even coming from, but I'm clueless.

I want answers for once. I am so sick and tired of never understanding or having any answers. I didn't do anything! My mom died. Mine. I did nothing wrong. I have to hold that in my head, otherwise all the shit they tell me will break through and I'll believe that whatever it is they think I did is my fault.

Leave. Run. Something else has to be better than this. It almost feels like my mom's voice is in my head sometimes whispering for me to run. That I am strong. That I can survive. Whether it's real or not, I want to listen to it because I'd do anything to be out of here and be able to talk about my mom freely. She was a beautiful person, light-hearted and fun. God, I miss her so much; it feels like my heart is cracking into pieces when I think of her. Fracturing even more knowing I have no one to tell about her, because I never want her to truly die. It's unfair. *Run, Harley.*

I have to try. $514. That's going to have to work. It will work, right? It has to. $514. I can do this. I can make that money my bitch.

I crawl slowly back over to my bed and lay down on my side, already breathing hard just from that little movement. There is no way I can run right now. Not that it matters; I don't even know how to get this stupid ankle cuff off.

Maybe I can run from school tomorrow. Yeah, that could work.

Wait, shit. I heard him say I won't be going back until after Thanksgiving. Fuck! I don't know what to do. I lay here fighting off tears that threaten to spill over, not wanting them to come down and see me cry.

At some point, I fall asleep and wake up to the door opening and more than one set of feet coming down. Mother and Father stop in front of me, and then Father lifts me up as Mother cuffs my hands and then raises them above my head to hook them on a hook in the ceiling.

I'm so tired and in so much pain that I can't even try to fight them off. I've never been strung up like this before. The hook is up high, so I'm stuck on my tippy toes, and the cuffs are cutting into my wrists.

Mother walks in front of me and holds up a cane. She swings it once. Twice. Three times. Hitting me across the front of my thighs.

I refuse to make any noise, so I bite the inside of my cheeks until they bleed. Fuck! That hurts. It's agony, and I know it'll only get worse, so I do the best I can to shut down and lock up any feelings.

I can survive this. I have to. I need to find answers someday as to why this shit happens to me.

"What did you say, Harley? Who did you talk to?" Mother asks in a scarily calm voice that I've never heard before.

"No one."

"DO NOT LIE TO ME"

SMACK.

SMACK.

SMACK.

SMACK.

Holy fuck, that hurts so bad. She hit the same spot on my thighs over and over. I can feel blood in my mouth from biting the inside of my cheeks so hard. *Lock it down, Harley.*

Mother backs off, and Father comes to stand in front of me. He has a knife in his hand and slowly brings it towards me and slices the front of my shirt open. I squeeze my eyes shut, terrified of what might come next. Father stares at my chest before running his knife across the top of each breast, pushing just enough to leave two small cuts. One above each breast. I bite my tongue to hold back a whimper.

Mother comes towards me with a belt and loops it around my neck, pulling it tight. "Tell me who you talked to, Harley."

I shake my head and open my mouth to say no one, but before I can, she pulls on the belt and starts choking me. She keeps doing it over and over again, only letting up when my vision goes blurry. I know the skin on my neck has to be raw by now.

"Who? Give me a name, goddamn it!" She slaps me hard across the face, making my already bruised face ache even more.

I'm trying to hold it together and hope they get tired of it and stop, but I don't know how much longer I can. Everything aches, and my wrists are taking more and more of my weight. I know they are bleeding from the cuffs. I can feel the blood running down my arms.

Father stares at me for what feels like hours before he finally sighs, "Let's leave her. She obviously needs time to think. The worthless bitch needs to remember her place here."

Mother nods and walks up to me, whispering in my ear, "I do this because I loved your mother, and she'd be so disappointed in you. You spoke to someone. You betrayed your family. I can only imagine how disgusted she'd be with you." She follows Father out, shutting off the light as she goes. Leaving me in the dark.

I can feel my walls crack. The longer her words repeat in my head, the more the walls break until... *shatter.* I can't hold it any longer, and a sob breaks out of me. I feel tears running down my face as I let out a hoarse scream that makes my already aching throat burn even more.

"*Why?*"

GRAYSON

We haven't seen Harley since Thursday. It's now Tuesday and today was the last day of school before we are off for Thanksgiving, and we don't come back until next Tuesday.

I've been working closely with Nerds, the club's tech guru. He got his name from his love for tech and Nerds candy. The guy always has a bowl of Nerds in the tech room with him. He's a great guy in his late twenties who's been around here since before Rage's dad died. He's like a big brother to me and has been teaching me all things tech for a while. I'm definitely not as into as he is or as good as him, but I like to know how to do most everything, so he helps me out.

I sigh and run a hand down my face. Our president has been talking with Richard some just to feel him out, but Richard thinks something else is up. We have been watching his phone, and he has been texting his wife saying he thinks something is going on.

I've been trying to find more about Harley Wilson but keep coming up with nothing. There is nothing before the age of ten, and from ages ten to sixteen, it looks like she stayed at the mental hospital one town over, but whoever the idiot was that put this on here did a horrible job making it look real. We knew it was fake almost immediately. For one, there is no information from her stay at all. How would every other patient have a huge file and she has nothing? And secondly, they didn't give her a room, and she's not documented on anything in their system.

So that means we don't know where Harley was from ages zero to sixteen. She just randomly pops up. Nerds has been getting pissed he can't find anything on her and is staying up all hours trying to find something. Cade has been asking for jobs to stay busy so he doesn't go storm over there and get Harley like he wants to.

Technically, we can't work for the club yet, but since we are closer to some of the ranking officers, we are allowed to go along with a patched member for any legal jobs. So that means working at any of the legit businesses or helping with odd jobs that may come up.

Ryker is doing what he does best, being a psycho and constantly making jokes to mask his fear and anger. But I can see through it. He's my best friend. I can read him like no one else can. Ry is the funny, down to earth guy on the surface, but inside, he has a vicious streak and can be absolutely terrifying, but he doesn't let it out because he isn't good at controlling himself. So he puts on a front of being a jokester and the club psycho so no one sees that he feels everything and is scared.

But I see him. I always have, and I always will.

I'm sitting in the tech room with Cade's dog, Bear. He's a huge black great Dane with large, tall pointed ears. The dog is huge. He comes up to above my waist and I am 6'2. He doesn't really like people, and for the most part he keeps to himself if he isn't with Cade, but today he has decided to hang out with me.

The tech room is about the size of an average bedroom; it's bigger than the other offices mostly because of how much stuff is in here. When you first come in, you see a large desk with four monitors on it. That is Nerds's main desk, and he is the only one who really uses it. On the wall with the door are three TV screens that are hooked up to the security cameras around the property. Then in the center are two desks pushed together, and I am currently sitting at one of them. They each have two monitors on them. There is also a closet on the farthest wall, but Nerds is the only one who goes in it. He keeps all his tech gear in there and has it all organized the way he wants it, so we all stay out of it. The room is fairly dark; the most lighting coming from the LEDs along the baseboards and then the tiny bit of light shining from the blackout curtains over the window by Nerds's desk. Sometimes I think we should call this room the Nerds Cave.

Nerds went to go shower and sleep since he's been in here since last night, and I took over as soon as we got back from school. I'm taking a break, sitting back and trying to think of what else we could do to get information on Harley when the screen in front of me dings with a notification. I click on it, seeing Tammy Wilson is getting a call from an unknown number. Nerds was able to clone her phone and make it so we can listen in and see everything on it. I hit the button to listen in and make sure my screen is recording so I can show the others if it's important.

Just as she answers, Ry comes in. I wave him over, and he comes to listen in with me.

"I told you I need more time, Tammy."

"And I told you that you don't get anymore. Get it done. I am tired of waiting, and I know the bitch spilled something to someone, but she won't admit it. I'm still working her, but I can't kill her. We need her alive for now, so it's going slow. The bitch is weak and keeps passing out on me."

"Tammy, she's only sixteen. What good is she going to be? Just sell her already. I have a lineup of girls ready to go. I know we don't usually take minors, but I can fake her age to my boss."

"No! We have other plans for her. Right now, I just need to make sure that he gets taken out. You hear me? Get the job done. Three days. That's all you get."

The call cuts off after that. Ry and I stare at each other before he pulls out his phone and starts texting. A few minutes later, the door bursts open, and Noah, Rage, and Cade all come barreling into the room.

"What's going on?" Rage demands.

I wave them over and play the phone call for them.

Cade growls as Rage looks, well, like his name. Full of rage.

"We can't let this slide, prez. If they are selling girls in our town, we need to stop it. Who knows what kind of shit they've gotten into and who is involved? We need to shut them down and find out," Noah says. He has a switchblade in his hand and is spinning it around, a sign that he is on the verge of losing his shit.

Rage must notice this as he looks at Noah's hand and then sighs. "I know you're right, but we have to be smart about how we approach this. I've been talking with Richard throughout the week as you know, and he isn't giving me much. Keeps saying they mind their own business and stay away, and we need to do the same. But they've only been allowed to stay in town because of me, so I want to check in.

"Blade, you and Sugar will go with me Friday after Thanksgiving. We'll visit their home and see what we can find out. Blade, you will go without your cut and be Noah for the day and say you are a friend of Harley's so we can try to get you alone with her, and I want you to tell her we can help."

Before prez can say any more, Ry is standing up with a look of murder on his face.

"No! One of us should go with and talk to her. She isn't going to trust Noah when she doesn't even know him. She is barely even trusting one of us, and we've been around her since the start of October. Also, what the fuck are you going to do if you don't get shit from them? Leave Harley there to deal with the fallout? No way. No! We need to get her the fuck out of there and a hell of a lot sooner than Friday."

"Ryker, back the fuck off. That is my president you are speaking to. I respect the hell out of you for wanting to protect your girl, but back the fuck up before it leads to someone getting hurt, boy," Sugar snaps from the doorway.

I didn't even see him show up, but he's pretty good at staying in the shadows. Sugar is Rage's vice president. Don't be deterred by his name. Sugar is one huge, scary dude.

Ryker goes to open his mouth, and before I can jump in to stop him from saying something stupid, Noah speaks, "No, Ryker. Enough. You said your peace. You are getting away with no hit. Take it as a win back the fuck off and let your prez speak."

Ryker glares at Noah for a minute, and I swear he is going to start a fight, so before he can, I get his attention, "Ry, everyone is doing the best they can. Why don't you fill Blade in on everything we know so far? And since you spend the most time with her, think of something he could say to Harley that would get her to realize he knows you and he is safe. You know we can't go with them; we aren't part of the club yet. Take it in stride, Ry."

He stares me down, and I don't back off from it. He eventually nods and sits down.

I look at Rage. "Why wait until Friday?"

Rage glances between Ry and I, then rubs a hand down his face. "We have a run tomorrow, then family day is Thursday, and we need everyone here for it. For family time and for protection since family day makes us more vulnerable. So Friday is the best day."

A while later after plans are finalized, Cade takes off to go for a run with Bear, and Ryker is with Noah doing who knows what. Sometimes those two left alone together isn't the best idea because they both can be a little reckless, but I have some odd feelings, and I need to dig into them.

I left the tech room to shower and eat after Nerds came back earlier. But now I am heading back to the tech room, and Nerds looks up as I come in. "Whatcha doin'? Thought you were done for the night, kid."

I shake my head. "No, I just have a gut feeling about something, and I want to do some digging into Richard and Tammy and the selling of girls."

Nerds nods and says he'll help.

We dive into searching and about three hours later, I come across it. I knew something seemed off. So far, we have only found that Tammy and Richard sell to wealthy people in a few different cities; there are offshore accounts I've found connecting certain people to Tammy and Richard. Honestly, these people aren't very smart if I can find this information. I'm not even half as good as Nerds is. It doesn't look like they are working with any larger gang or Mafia groups, so that's a good sign; it makes them easier to take down. I just want to check as far back as I can find to see when this started.

I go through the offshore accounts and their personal accounts, along with phone records I've pulled, and it's leading back at least twenty years. This is insane. I don't know who would've been running this back then because Tammy would have been in high school then. I keep looking and eventually find that Tammy is getting deposits of large amounts from an account I can't seem to get the information about. I ask Nerds to help me, and he does his thing while I watch.

Once he's done, he has a name. The name on an account that has millions of dollars in it and has been funding a lot of the things they need to pull off taking people and getting them ready before selling. I don't even know what I'm supposed to think right now. How could he do this?

"Nerds, can you print all of this information for me?"

He looks at me like he knows what I'm about to do. "Kid, this isn't a good idea. I know that look. Don't go getting yourself killed over this. We have no idea what this shit means, so let's take it one step at a time."

"No, you don't know. Just print off the papers, Nerds."

He slowly nods and gets to it. I can't believe this. I may be the quiet one, the one who prefers not to get involved in certain things, and I keep what I say out loud to a minimum, but this? This affects my family. The people I care about the most. This changes everything.

Nerds finishes and hands me the papers with a sigh. Good. I'm glad he's not going to try and stop me. I don't think anything or anyone could right now.

I leave the tech room and head towards the offices. If I'm right, he'll still be awake and working in his office. I don't even bother knocking. I slam the door open; my heart is pounding. I don't do confrontations, but I have to protect my family. I'll do whatever it takes.

Rage looks up from his desk when he hears the door slam open, and he looks pissed that I didn't knock. I don't even care right now.

I march in, throw the papers on the desk, and cross my arms, preparing myself for whatever is about to happen. Rage looks down and picks up the papers, slowly beginning to flip through them. The more he reads, the more his brows furrow with confusion.

"Grayson, what—"

I cut him off, "Please don't lie to me, Rage. I am a lot of things, but I am not stupid, and I know what that says, and I fully understand it. We have a problem."

Rage nods, letting out a deep breath. "We do."

CHAPTER NINE

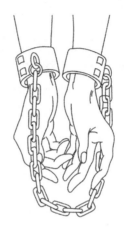

HARLEY

"*I do this because I loved your mother, and she'd be so disappointed in you. You spoke to someone. You betrayed your family. I can only imagine how disgusted she'd be with you.*" The words replay in my head over and over again as I lay here.

It's been a few days. I can't even tell you what day of the week it is. I've been stuck in the basement. The beatings are bad. My whole body is aching all over. I know I have some broken ribs and I'm covered in bruises and welts.

I feel numb. I don't know what I'm supposed to do now. They think I told someone something but they won't tell me what it is I apparently said or to whom. I wish someone would take me from here. Tabby came down here last night. I thought she was coming to help me, like an idiot. But she just said I was trash and belittled me and then laughed and left.

I slowly get off my bed and limp towards the bathroom, but before I get there, I stop and my whole body freezes up as memories from the last few days hit me all at once.

...Father fills the sink with water and dunks me in it over and over again, barely letting me breathe, screaming at me while Mother stands to the side yelling about how I'm failing and disappointing my mom...

...Mother rips me up off the floor, throws me into the shower, turns it on cold, cuffs my hands to the handle on the wall of the shower and locks me in. They left me for well over an hour. With freezing cold water raining down all over me and no escape from it with the shower being so small. When she got me out, she used a violet wand on me over and over again until I passed out...

...I'm left hooked to the ceiling again. Father comes down and says Mother had to go run an errand, so it's just him. He stares at my breasts and tells me it's a shame he can't sample me. He grabs my breasts in a bruising grip then looks amused as he pinches my nipples as hard as he can before laughing at the whimper I let out before he leaves...

...Mother comes down later on. "Whoring yourself out to your father? You disgust me." She stares at the big handprint bruises forming on both of my breasts and then sneers, "I was going to let you down, but I think you need to stay longer, you whore."

111

I scream, my voice hoarse, "No, please! Please don't leave me up here. I need to pee. Please, Mother, please."

She laughs, "Whores don't get a say." She slaps me across the face...

I come out of my memories of the last few days to realize I fell to the floor and I'm sobbing hard. I try to pull it together, but it takes a while, and I end up in more pain from sobbing so hard. I can't do this anymore. The first chance I have, I am gone. I will never ever come back here again.

At least a day later, Mother comes down and takes off my ankle cuff. "Tomorrow is Thanksgiving, so you need to clean the house today. Do not try anything, Harley. You are no match for me."

I follow her upstairs and get to cleaning. It takes almost all day because of how slow I am moving. They always keep an eye on me, which I can't even fault them for because if I had a chance and knew I could make it, I'd have left right away.

I feel so broken down and devastated. There are so many questions swirling around in my mind, and I have no answers. I can't ask for any either, my body is already struggling, and I can only imagine what else she would do to me if I asked questions. I've done everything that they have asked. I don't even try to talk to anyone at school. I play the mute girl, not that I could talk much anyways with whatever it is they make me drink.

But still, I don't even try. Why not? Obviously, whether I listen and obey or not doesn't matter. They still assume I did something wrong, and I don't think that'll ever change.

I think I hold onto this false hope that there is no way Mother can always be this bad. Maybe it is just me and I need to find a way to be better and then maybe she'll change. I mean, how can my mom and Mother be sisters when they are so completely different? *Simple, one's a devil and one's an angel.*

I need to let go of that hope that I know will never become a reality and just plan to get the hell out of here.

Sometimes I feel myself slipping into believing what they say to me.

"You are worthless."

"You disappoint Lilian."

"You will never be good enough."

"What the hell is wrong with you? You're so stupid."

"Being a slut again?"

"Acting like a whore?"

"No one will ever love you. How could they?"

"You make us do this to you."

"You leave us no choice. We don't want to do this to you."

I shake off the thoughts that bombard my mind. I can't let it get to me. I can't. I need to just remember what my mom would say, if only I could remember everything... Sometimes I think things are fading, and I hate that. I constantly have dreams I can't remember, and I almost feel like they are my mom talking to me. So why can't I remember them?

Mom, I need you to tell me what to do.

Mother comes storming into the bathroom I was working on cleaning. "What the hell is taking so long? Hurry the hell up, you lazy bitch."

I stand to tell her I am done but before I can, she yanks me towards her by my neck, making my eyes water involuntarily from her squeezing and it being so sensitive from the chain and the belt. She pulls me close, choking me as hard as she can, cutting off my air. I try to fight her off, but I don't have much strength, so it's futile to even try.

Mother licks her lips tauntingly. "If I could kill you, I would, but I can't. Yet."

She cackles, and for the first time in a long time, true fear runs through my veins. Not just hopelessness and giving in to whatever she says. What she is saying, she means it. I have to get out of here. It's my last thought before my vision starts going blurry, then Mother releases me, and I crumble to the floor.

"Pathetic. Hurry up and finish! I am tired of seeing your nasty face up here."

I get up, fighting off the tears that threaten to come, not wanting Mother to see me cry any more than she already has. *Mom, I need you. Help me.*

BLADE (NOAH)

Thanksgiving was tense. No one knows what happened, but according to Nerds, who isn't even saying much, Grayson stormed into Rage's office Tuesday night and shortly after, the door slammed shut, and there was some muffled yelling for about ten minutes before Gray came storming out. Gray isn't even telling Ry and Cade what happened, which is causing some issues because the boys don't keep things from each other. Whatever happened has Gray on edge like I've never seen him before, and I can tell he isn't sleeping, but there isn't much I can do to help until someone spills.

I tried hounding Rage, but he said he's not spilling yet. He needs to figure out something first and wants to see how today goes with our drop in at Wilson home. Which is what we are up to now.

Rage, Sugar, and I are heading out to go over there. I'm leaving my cut behind so I can play the part of a high school kid who's friends with Harley. The boys are all tense and still not happy they can't go. It's not helping that Gray usually keeps Ry in check, but since Ry is annoyed at Gray and Gray is being standoffish, he is kind off his hinges right now.

Actually, everyone in the club is kind of off their hinges right now, especially with the news spreading that right here in our own town, for the last who knows how many years, women have been stolen and sold to be used by horrible people. That's not easy to hear, especially when we have worked hard to turn the club around, but apparently this is all connected to our club from when Rage's dad was alive and running things. This news has the potential to take the club down even though it has nothing to do with us, who we are, and what we stand for now.

We try to protect our town as much as we can. We keep drugs off the streets and have turned around a lot of the bad businesses. There is no more money laundering, no gun selling, no drug dealing, but this? This is huge and just fucking awful.

I really hope that when we take them down, I get to play with some of these bastards.

We soon reach the Wilson family's house, which is a nice two-story home with a small front porch on the other side of town and away from prying eyes of neighbors. After knocking on the door, we can hear whispered yells but can't quite make out what they say. Then a door slams shut. A few seconds later, the front door opens to whom I believe is Tammy Wilson.

"Rage? What are you doing here? And with... others." She looks Sugar and I up and down like we are dirt on the bottom of her shoe.

"Tammy, we are here for a little chat. Mind letting us in?"

Tammy looks behind her, then steps back and opens the door wide, holding a hand out to welcome us in. We head in and see Richard, her husband, and who I am assuming is their daughter—Tabby I think her name is? I wink at her when she stares at me, and her cheeks turn pink.

Tammy clears her throat. "So, what can I do for you?"

"Well, darlin', we heard your other daughter came back from, what was it? A stay at the mental hospital? We just thought we'd check in since this is our town and we like to keep an eye on everyone. Noah here is friends with what's the kids name? Harley?" I nod. "Yeah, and he wanted to check on her since I guess she wasn't at school the last three days before break," Sugar says in that southern drawl that usually melts women.

Tammy blinks at him, then seems to shake herself from his charm. "Oh, well, Harley is out right now visiting some friends. So, unfortunately, you missed her."

Rage looks ready to say something that can't be good, so before he can, I cut in, "Oh, darn! Well, can I leave her a note with some schoolwork she missed? I can just leave it in her room if you point me in the direction?" I ask with my sweetest smile.

"You can leave it on the kitchen table for her," Tammy says, starting to look agitated but trying to hide it.

Before Sugar or I can stop him, Rage steps up to Tammy. "What are you hiding? Don't play games with me, Tam. This is my fucking town, and if you are up to something, I will find out."

"I have no idea what you think I am up to, Rage, but you should be careful with what you say. Wouldn't want another accident like your father to happen, would you?"

"Tammy! That's enough out of you. Go upstairs!" Richard snaps.

We all watch as Tammy storms up the stairs. Once we hear a door slam, we look back at Richard. I personally think he's pussy whipped, but I will say he looks a little tough right now considering he's facing off three deadly bikers. "So, what is it? What are you after? Spit it out and let's deal with it so we can all go back to our separate corners and leave shit alone."

Before Rage can say anything, Sugar speaks up, "Well, Richard, as we said, Noah is friends with Harley. We didn't know you had a third kid and just wanted to check in and make sure everything is okay. We don't want to cause problems, and we ain't lookin' to get into shit that don't involve us."

Richard nods and looks to be deep in thought before he turns and looks at me. "Friends, huh? What has Harley been saying to you?"

I tilt my head and look at him with a confused expression. "Saying? You do know your daughter is mute, right?"

Richard blanches before pulling it together quickly. "Of course, I just meant writing or some shit, I don't know, however she likes to communicate. Anyways, she is fine. She'll be back at school Monday, so no need to worry about her. Now, I have lots to get done today, so it's best we be done now."

He walks back to the door and opens it wide. I guess that's our cue to leave. I glance at Rage and Sugar and see barely contained anger, so it's probably best we go. I gesture for them to walk ahead of me, and I make sure Richard can't fully see me behind them as I pull the mic out of my pocket and stick it under the table along the wall heading towards the front door. It's not much and will only hear conversations in the entryway and part of the kitchen and maybe the start of the hall, but that's better than nothing.

We head out to the truck we brought instead of our bikes and hop in. As soon as we drive off, Rage lets loose lots of curses. I don't even know if those are all in English.

"What the hell? I feel like there is more going on here than we even know. Why are they hiding Harley? Something is off with this situation with the girl, I just know it. I need to find a way to get her over to the club so I can meet her and feel things out," Rage grumbles.

"Rage, I respect the hell out of you as my president, but kindly as your VP, what the actual fuckin' hell was that shit back there? Since when does our prez not keep his shit together? If the boys are right and they are hurtin' that girl, then you might have just gotten her another beatin'. So whatever the hell is wrong with you, figure it the fuck out and real fast."

I nod my head even though neither of them are looking in the back at me. As much as I want to say something, I'll keep my mouth shut. For now. I may be the club's enforcer, but I know I can be kind of a pain in the ass, and now isn't the time to piss off my prez even more.

"I know. I didn't mean to go off, and usually I don't do that kind of shit, but Tammy just brings up a lot of old memories, you know? Between her being my first love, to the woman who broke my heart and made it so I trust no other women, to then my first kill being around that time and all the awful memories it brought to surface, I just felt like exploding or even strangling her."

I can only imagine how hard it is to keep your composure when some of the worst things in your past come back up. I know I

119

wouldn't hold it together as well as he does. Adding on to it, his own father was sex trafficking women. That would be a hard pill to swallow.

We soon get back to the club house and as we walk in, we hear yelling and things breaking. When we come into the main room, Cade has Ry pinned to the ground holding him down while two prospects are on the ground bleeding and groaning. I glance around the room to see most of my brothers looking at Ry with a wariness I haven't seen before. Gray is standing off to the side, his face deathly pale.

"What the fuck is going on in here?" Prez commands. Everyone stops and looks at Rage. "If you were not involved, get the fuck out!"

Most of the brothers rush to leave the room. A few brothers, Gray, Cade—who is still holding Ry down, and three prospects stay.

"Someone start talkin' now!" Sugar orders.

Gray steps forward, staring right at Rage. "This is on you."

I swear the room fucking freezes. Grayson Tanner is not one to talk first. He's not one to show anger or hatred towards someone; he's always calm, cool, and collected. It's partially from his childhood trauma, but I think it's mostly just what keeps him centered. Being in the background but still being there and being a voice of reason and calm when needed. But right now, he is looking at my president like he could kill him on the spot.

His voice is dripping with venom as he continues, "Ryker, Cade, and I don't keep secrets. I kept yours because I thought I was doing the right thing. But it's not. I'll take whatever punishment is going to come my way for this, but tell them now or I will."

"Kid, I don't know where you get off thinkin' you can speak that way to Rage but—"

Before he can say more, Gray shocks us all again and turns his death glare to Sugar and cuts him off. *Jeez I kinda want to see more of this Grayson... Wait, I'm not supposed to think that.* "I get OFF, Sugar, by saying that because the last few days have been hell and now I've just watched my best friend drink and cause fights because I can't tell him what I know, out of respect," he spits the word like it tastes bad coming out of his mouth, "for YOUR president. Do I need to remind you why Ryker would react that way when one of his closest friends is keeping something from him?"

Sugar looks a little guilty and shakes his head, sighing.

At this point, everyone looks stunned by all the shit happening, and Ryker is now standing staring at Gray. I decide it's time for me to open my mouth. *What? Sometimes I can be helpful.* "Alright, folks, that was a great show and all." Everyone turns and glares at me. *Oops? Wrong thing to say?* "But," I drag out the word, "maybe we should all take a beat, okay? Things are stressful right now, but this isn't helping. Ryker, sober up. Gray, go with him. Cade, feel up to coming with me for a job?"

I grin, knowing he'll want to, and it'll piss off Ryker because he can't go drunk. Ryker goes to interject but I cut him off with a glare.

"No. You got drunk in the middle of the day and got into two fights. You're done for the day. Test me and you'll fight me. Sober." I glance at Rage and Sugar. "Prez, take the day off and figure your shit out. Sorry, but whatever this is, you need to clue in the people it affects or who can help. Sugar, be the VP and take care of prez. PROSPECTS, get the fuck outta here. You're on cleaning duty the rest of the day. You dumbasses know better than to get into fights. We all will meet bright and early tomorrow and discuss everything from today and anything else we need to talk about.

"Prez you can dish out my punishment for telling you what to do then. Let's go, Cade." I turn and walk out, making sure to slam the door. A grin comes over my face. *See? I totally got this down. Fuck you, Dad.*

CHAPTER TEN

RYKER

Fuck, fuck, fuck, fucking, fuck shit. I really screwed up.

I follow Gray as he leads me upstairs to our area where Noah, Cade, Gray and I all have rooms next to each other. We go inside my room, and Gray rounds on me as soon as I shut the door.

"What the fuck was that? Look, I get it, after all the shit with your dad and then your aunt right after, you have trust issues. But you can't do shit like that. Right now, Ryker, we are here strictly because of Noah. Yeah, Rage cares and sees us as his boys, but the club comes first. You think he won't boot you when you're eighteen for doing that? He will!" He flings his arms out wide and then turns away from me.

Shit, Gray never curses; he's pissed at me. And he called me Ryker not Ry. I can't even remember a time he's been this upset with me.

Panic takes over; I feel like the walls are caving in, and all I can hear is my dad in my head.

"You no good piece of shit."

"You'll never amount to anything, you stupid boy."

"You ruin everything and everyone around you."

"Your mother is sick because of you."

"No one likes you, boy. They all report back to me with everything you fail at."

"You disappoint your friends by being this weak bitch."

"You hurt me when I have to hurt you."

I feel myself hit the floor as my hands shake and my breathing is coming in uneven pants. Bright green eyes get level with my brown ones. I can see his lips moving, but I can't hear him. He grabs my arms and pulls me towards him and wraps his arms around me, holding me. It centers me. It brings me back down from the panic. Quiets my dad's voice. Brings me back to reality. I can hear him now.

"Breathe, Ry, breathe. It's okay, I'm here. You are everything. You are amazing. Just breathe, fight through it. I got you."

His words bring me so much peace, I take a deep breath, then scoot away from him until my back hits the door. Gray scoots back until his back is against the wall to my right. We just sit there in silence until he breaks it with the question I knew was coming.

"You need to talk it through, Ry. Everything. Why you really pulled that crap today and this panic attack. Eventually, Ry, if they get worse, we have to tell Noah, and he'll have to tell Rage. I know you don't want that, but if we don't get a handle on it, you'll have no choice."

I sigh and run a hand through my hair. I get what he's saying. It's dangerous in this world to have these kinds of episodes and have no one know about them. Especially when my triggers are all over the place. Gray may have pulled me out fast, but when he isn't around, they can last hours.

I'm frustrated but know I need to talk it out, and Gray will listen without judgment.

"Harley."

Gray looks over at me, waiting for me to continue. The fucker won't crack. He has the patience of a nun.

I let out a grunt and sigh again. "Fine. It's Harley. I just... we know what we are seeing. We know shit is happening, Gray. We saw it with each other. I don't know why, but I can't sit back and watch that continue for her. She's so goddamn beautiful and sweet. It's like a magnet, and hers is so strong that it's just pulling me right along. Then there's Cade, who is our brother and doesn't even talk to us but yet Harley unknowingly has pulled more words from him in the last two months than any of us have in years. I know you feel a pull too. I've seen you watch her, and you never show any signs of liking a girl, so don't deny it."

I take a deep breath, preparing myself to just get it all out now.

"Today... today I was pissed. You wouldn't tell me what the fuck happened with Rage last week, and I hate being in the dark, especially about people I feel it's my job to protect, and it really hit a nerve. Particularly because, well, you know my aunt and dad. We also haven't seen Harley since last Thursday. That alone sends chills down my spine for what it could mean. Then they decide to go there and not even take one of us! I don't like being out of control, brother. I want to see her with my own eyes to make sure she's okay. I can't just walk away. I know I don't even know her but Gray, I know somewhere deep inside my dead soul that she belongs here. With me, with us, with the club.

"So today I thought a few shots would help. Then it turned into a bottle. I know I don't have my anger under control yet, so drinking on top of my anger didn't do me any good, and those damn fucking prospects wouldn't shut up about stupid shit and one made a comment about us being sucked in by some tight pussy and he wanted a turn and I just flipped out."

"Ry..." he says in a soft voice. I glance up and make eye contact with him. "It's not just your anger you don't have under control. It's your emotions and, well, everything honestly." He gives me a small smirk.

That asshole. I kick him with my foot, then move to stand up.

"Well, we can't all be nerdy, perfect Grayson Tanner, can we?"

He laughs and gets up, putting a hand on my shoulder. "Seriously, though, thank you for being honest. I won't get mushy on you, but I am proud of you. You told me your thoughts, and that's all I asked for. I won't push for more now."

He turns around and walks out of the room, I stand there frozen, my heart beating faster and a small, real smile on my face. Fuck. How does he do that to me? I groan, then flop onto my bed. I fucking hate when I have a panic attack like that. It always puts me on edge. I know one thing for sure: I'm definitely sober now. I feel like I could drink again, though, which won't help, so instead I head down to the gym in the basement and start in on the punching bag as shitty memories surface.

When I was five, my mom got pregnant again. My dad said she cheated on him, but that wasn't true since he wouldn't let her leave the house. My dad worked under Rage's dad, and I remember seeing Rage when I was younger. He was a newer member, but he was always nice to me and spent time with me. He was like a father/brother figure I never had but always wanted. When my mom found out that she was having a girl this time around, she was terrified to tell my dad.

When he finally found out, she was seven months pregnant. He beat her until she lost the baby and got away with it because back then, the club had dirty cops on their payroll and were able to make it go away.

After that, I tried standing up for my mom because she wouldn't do it for herself anymore. She slipped into a depression and never came out of it. When I tried to protect her, my father saw it as weak and turned his fire on me. He'd lie to me and keep things from me about my mom or my friends or anyone in my life.

I started having panic attacks when I was twelve. My father found out because I had no way to hide them and anyone in my life who I thought I could trust was lying to me and would report back to my dad.

Rage was going through his own things by then, so I never saw him. Noah and Cade had just had shit go down and had to deal with it, and Gray I only ever saw at school. So I was on my own. My dad saw me as weak and blamed my mother for it. So he came home one night, took me into their room, handed me a gun, and told me to shoot my mom because she made me weak and I needed to prove myself. I refused. I wouldn't do it. He said if I wouldn't, then he would make her death even worse.

My mom told me it was okay and to just close my eyes and remember she loved me and didn't blame me. I couldn't close my eyes as I watched him beat her, cut her, rape her, and completely destroy her body before very slowly cutting her throat open.

When he was done, he stood there with a beaming, sick smile on his face and said, "Boy, that's what happens when you are weak. Your no-good mother raised you to be a pussy, and we are going to have to change that now."

Before he could get another word out, a red haze filled my vision; it was like something else entirely took over my body. I couldn't even think about what I was doing as I picked up the gun from where I had dropped it earlier and shot my father. It only hit his knee, but he dropped down cursing. When the knife fell from his hands, everything turned completely red.

I don't remember any of it, and that's the scariest part. I killed someone. No. I didn't just kill someone; I brutally murdered my father, and I don't remember most of it.

Sometimes I'll have a dream with some small memory of that night. Stab here, stab there, blood flying, father yelling at me, father getting so weak he couldn't yell. But it's always in pieces and never fully comes together.

Rage has always told me it's my brain's way of protecting itself. But sometimes I still think it's just because I really am weak.

The club protected me after that. I was only twelve. They took care of the body, and Rage had been the president for one year when it happened. He helped and did everything he could for me. The club was still into some bad shit then, so it was easy to get covered up and written off.

Just after I thought it was all over, an aunt I didn't know existed came into the picture and took custody of me for two years since she was my legal guardian. I came back at fourteen and have been here since with Noah as my guardian.

I come out of my haze and realize my knuckles are bleeding from hitting the bag so hard with no protection on. I stop and clean them up, then head back upstairs to my room. After I shower, I land in bed, exhausted enough from the shitstorm today to just pass the fuck out.

CHAPTER ELEVEN

GRAYSON

The next morning I'm up early waiting to hopefully get this meeting over with as soon as possible. After leaving Ryker's room last night, I headed outside to walk around the grounds of the clubhouse.

They own about twenty acres out here. We are slightly on the edge of town and there isn't much around. It's peaceful. I know Rage wants to build out here, but I have no idea what. Still, I like to walk whenever I need to clear my mind or just think.

Ryker is really falling for Harley. I'm not too sure how I feel about that. I really hope this girl doesn't break his heart. Don't get me wrong, I really like her too, and she's gorgeous, but I barely know her. I just want to help her out of whatever bad situation she's in. No kid deserves what we've all been dealt in this shitty life. I hate keeping what Rage and I talked about to myself, but I guess I get it. All I know is he has to spill today or I will. I never want to be in a position like this again. Especially when I don't know what I believe with everything I found.

When I came back to my room last night, Nerds was waiting outside of it with his laptop ready to show me a few things he found. Putting some things into perspective for me and making me regret my decisions from how I handled things with Rage the other night. He told me it was going to be okay, but I'm not sure I believe him. I slept like crap all night, which is why I am up so early now.

I head downstairs to get something to eat and see a very tired-looking Nerds at the counter, downing coffee. "Are you okay, Nerds? You should probably get some sleep instead of drinking more caffeine."

He nods his head. "All good, brother. I was looking into some shit last night and had to monitor a run, but I gotta be up for this meeting. Rage wants me there. I'll just eat some nerds. They fuel me."

I shake my head at him. That guy has a serious addiction to nerds candy. "You are an addict, you know that?"

"What? You think they call me Nerds for shits and giggles? Get a grip, brother. We know this already. Leave me and my nerds alone," he grunts before draining his coffee and getting up to grab more.

Jeez, I forgot how sensitive the man could be over nerds candy.

I decided to make some breakfast for everyone since I don't think anyone should go into this meeting hungry on top of everything else going on. Plus, I enjoy cooking, so it might calm some of my nerves going into this.

The club has a surprisingly big kitchen. There are two entrances. One on the left that goes out to the hall where the stairs and main doors are, and one to the right, which goes straight out to the main room. When you come into the kitchen from the hall, there is a huge fridge, and on the other side of the fridge is a door to a walk-in pantry. The back wall holds counters that wrap around the room to the other entrance. There is a decent-sized island in the middle with a few bar stools that gives extra counter space.

I really enjoy cooking in here. There have been a few times that I have taken advantage of how much space there is, and the double ovens we have to bake a lot of sweets. It's a nice stress reliever. As I'm finishing up cooking, Ryker comes stumbling in still half asleep and makes a beeline for the coffee pot. Shortly after, Rage, Noah, Cade, and Sugar come in.

"Wow, smells good, brother. Did you make all this?" Noah asks, glancing at all the food laid out. I kind of went overboard and made eggs, bacon, sausage, pancakes, and french toast.

I shrug and give a tiny smile, gesturing for everyone to make themselves a plate.

After we eat in uncomfortable silence, with everyone just seeming to want to hurry up and get this over with. Rage clears his throat. "Everyone, my office, thirty minutes."

Everyone nods and heads off to do whatever they need to do before the meeting.

Since I made breakfast, the club girls will clean up everything, so I wave for Cade and Ryker to follow me.

We head into one of the random offices, and I shut the door behind us. "Ry, I figured we could fill Cade in now on what happened the other day at school when you asked Harley about her voice."

Cade leans against the desk that's in here while I sit in the desk chair, and Ry leans against the wall by the door. Cade crosses his arms over his chest and raises a brow at us.

"Right, so when we were standing at Harley's locker before her math class the other day, I asked her if she had never been able to talk or if she could at one point when she lost her voice and how. She freaked out and started panicking—"

Cade grunts, cutting off anything else Ry was going to say, and pulls out his phone to text us.

Cayden: The first day of school when she came into the office, she opened her mouth like she was going to talk but then shut it. I've always thought that she probably can talk and just is like me and doesn't for whatever reason, so her parents said she was mute.

Before I can say anything, Ry shakes his head. "No, brother. This was raw fear. She was terrified. It was almost as if she was terrified that we would find something out that would get her killed or some shit. Her face paled and she immediately started panicking and trying to get away from us, but Gray stopped her and helped her through the attack."

I nod. "She didn't even know what was happening. I explained a panic attack to her after, and she looked shocked but then like so many things made sense. She tried to take off after that, but I told her it was okay and she didn't have to tell us anything and then she calmed down. But guys, I think I messed up during math class."

"How?" Ry asks.

"I told her a tiny bit about me. How I had panic attacks after my brother died. How my parents treated me. I meant to just leave it at that, but it's like I couldn't let this girl keep thinking whatever negative thoughts were going through her head. Her misery was written all over her face. So I told her she didn't have to go through it alone. That there were people there to help her through the darkness and help her to take down her demons, that she just has to trust them to help. She said what if you trust them and they turn out to be bigger monsters, and I told her that I can't answer that but there are people who would ask how high if you asked them to jump. She asked me why, but we didn't get to talk much more.

"I feel like I pushed it. What if she thinks I am crazy now? I didn't mean to say so much, but it's like I couldn't stop my mouth. I just needed her to understand because it wasn't that long ago that I was hiding and didn't understand I had people, all I had to do was go to them. But just throwing it all at her at once probably terrified her even more and—" I get cut off by Ry squatting down in front of me with a soft smile on his face.

"Gray, breathe. You didn't do anything wrong. You did what we all probably should've done. It's okay. Hell, you were probably the best person to say something like that to her because you do understand. You are amazing at seeing what a person needs to hear and saying it without thought. So stop overthinking this."

Cade nods his agreement, and I take a breath. It helps when they support me.

"Should we bring this up to Rage?" I ask.

Cade nods, and Ry sighs, "I guess. Sometimes I hate taking things to them because I feel like they are going to shut us out any day now, and we won't know what their plans are, which I want to be involved in when it comes to Harley."

Wow, I swear every day he is showing more and more that he is falling in love with her. I want to be happy for him, but I am terrified he is going to get hurt or even worse... *No, don't go there, Gray.*

"I don't think they will cut us off, Ry, but it's important for them to know because her reaction to you asking could mean that things are worse than they seem at home for her." Ry sighs but nods. We all leave and head towards Rage's office since it's time to get this meeting going. When we get there, everyone else is also walking in, and we all stand around or take the few empty seats.

The silence is getting weird now. It's giving me the urge to speak, so I take a deep breath and remind myself I'm comfortable with everyone in this office.

I clear my throat. "Maybe we should backtrack and start with when I met with Rage, then work our way through everything in order?" Everyone nods. "Alright, well, I guess that means I'll start."

I pointedly look at Rage, and he nods, giving me the okay to dive into this.

"So Tuesday night after we all talked, I just felt like we were missing something and things felt off, so I decided to do more of a deep dive with Nerds, and we uncovered a lot. Basically, this operation they are running goes back at least twenty years, if not more. Luckily, they aren't working with any Mafia or gang groups that are around here. It seems they work alone and cater to the wealthy in surrounding areas. The thing is, there is no way they could've just randomly had the money to do all of this. Taking girls, keeping them somewhere, paying hush money, getting them ready, moving them... That all takes a lot of cash. So I dug deeper and found lots of offshore accounts connecting back to a lot of wealthy people; honestly, they made it easy.

"But here's the thing: Rage's dad was involved. Wait!" I say before they can all start going off and getting angry. "There is more. Let me finish and get this all out at once."

They all nod, so I continue.

"So Rage's dad has been a part of it and had a full group of people working with him. I haven't found out how Tammy and Richard got involved, but Nerds and I are still looking. The weird thing is, everyone we have found connected in some way from the group who ran things before Tammy and Richard took over are dead. We are still looking into it to see if it's a coincidence or not. What makes this worse is that there is an offshore account that is funding everything. The account sends money to Tammy and

Richard, and they use it to do everything they need to make their operation work."

I stop and prepare myself for what I say next. I know how I reacted, and it wasn't good. I assumed the worst and acted without thinking.

Apparently, I'm taking too long because Ryker looks pissed. "Who the fuck would do that? Who is behind the account? Can we take them out? Maybe that would put a roadblock to selling more people before we can find a way to take them down."

I nod. "Well, the name on the account is—"

Before I can finish the sentence, Rage speaks, "It's me. My name is on that account."

"I'm sorry, what?"

"What the fuck?"

"That can't be right!"

"Who the fuck would do that to you?"

Everything is shouted all at once, but I hear it all. I hear every single one of the brothers in this room back their president. Not assume he is involved in any way. I take a step back, then another, preparing to leave the room. I just need a minute. How could I have reacted the way I did and everyone else reacts this way? They are mad *for* their president, not at him.

Before I can even think of turning around and leaving, Nerds stands and yells out, "Shut up!"

Everyone goes silent and looks at Nerds, who is staring at me. I make eye contact with him, and I feel like he can read every single thought on my face.

"Grayson, no. You found it and reacted. You did nothing wrong. Don't."

Before he can say more, Ryker pipes in, "What the fuck are you talking about, Nerds?"

I look at Ryker then back at Rage and say, "Me. He's talking about me because I am the only person in this room who didn't even stop to think for one second that Rage couldn't be involved."

A pained look flashes across Ryker's face for a second before he retorts, "The fight that night?"

I nod, averting my gaze to the floor.

"We have a problem."

"We do." Rage nods, but before he can continue, I slam the door shut so the brothers out in the hall can't hear as much. In a deadly calm voice I didn't even know I could use, I say, "What the fuck is wrong with you? You're taking after your father? I thought you wanted to change the ways your father ran things. You know what Ryker, Cade, Noah, and I have all been through. I won't let my family be dragged into your mess. I can't let this go, Rage."

Rage narrows his eyes at me. "What the fuck do you think I've done, Grayson?"

"You're funding them!"

He laughs, but there is no real humor behind it as he turns a glare on me. "Are you insane? You think I'd get involved in this? I get how it looks, but no, Grayson, no."

I shake my head, not knowing what to believe right now. "I have to tell the others."

Rage steps around the desk coming towards me. I steel my spine, refusing to back down, even if it's the stupidest thing I've ever done. "You will not speak a word of this. Has anyone else seen this?" I shake my head, refusing to put Nerds on the line. "Good. Keep it that way. Grayson, I am deadly serious. Not a word. I need to figure this shit out first."

I sputter, "You've got to be kidding me. You can't expect me to keep this to myself!"

"You will. Or I will take out the punishment on your brothers. I don't like having to threaten you, Grayson, but you are forcing my hand. Keep. Your. God. Damn. Mouth. SHUT. Now, GET THE FUCK OUT!"

I turn around and storm out of the room, making sure to bang the door against the wall. Brothers are all around looking with wide eyes.

Ry comes up to me, concern etched into his features. "Gray?"

"No. Don't ask me anything. I won't tell you." I storm off to my room and slam the door.

That just made me believe that he really was behind all of this. I still feel unsure, but after Nerds came to me late last night, I realized I fucked up by not giving him a chance. Nerds looked into it more, and it used to be Rage's dad's account, but when he died, it went into Rage's name. Rage never knew, and the account has continued auto sending out money for years.

Cade rises to his feet and moves to stand in front of me. He puts a hand on my shoulder and looks me in the eyes. "It's okay, brother."

139

I relax a little. Cade rarely, if ever, speaks after some shit happened to him when he was younger, so him speaking to help calm me means more than he could ever know. I know I have huge trust issues, but I shouldn't have assumed he was involved. I should've known better. *I do* know better. But that didn't matter to me that night. All that mattered then was that I felt betrayed.

Rage clears his throat, and we all look at him. "Grayson, it's fine. That whole night was fucked up, and I didn't react well or reassure you. I was overwhelmed. My dad has been dead for five years, and I haven't thought of Tammy in years either. Everything threw me through a loop, and that night was just my final straw. You had every right to react that way. What I said and did wasn't okay, so let's just all move forward now. We are going to need to work as a team to get through this shit."

I nod and feel some tension leave me, but I still feel guilty.

"So what can we do? How do we approach this?" Sugar asks.

"Right now, nothing. I need to keep looking into this. We deal with Harley because her life could possibly be at risk right now. I will keep digging. We know that the account belonged to Rage's dad before it got changed to Rage," Nerds says.

"Right, my best guess is that my dad had it set up somehow so that everything was transferred to me if he died. I'm betting he assumed I would take over all of his 'activities' in the future. I doubt he expected to be murdered, or even to die when he did. But he was also so damn cocky that he probably couldn't believe that anyone would ever dare to try. So he never finished training me,"—he air quotes training—"because we kept fighting and he wanted to mold me to be his shadow, so he never shared everything he was into with me since he couldn't trust me. I'm guessing he thought he'd change my mind about it long before he died. But that obviously didn't happen."

Rage signs and runs a hand down his face. Now that I'm looking more closely, I can see how exhausted he appears from everything going on.

"This isn't the first thing that has come up that I've found out my dad was involved in. I will say, though, this is the worst. I want to prioritize getting it shut down and getting my name off this shit before we move on to deal with making other things legit like we had planned." He pointedly looks at Noah, Nerds, and Sugar.

They all nod, and Sugar says, "We need to have church ASAP. Bring this to everyone and have everything else go on the back burner besides things that are bringing us money. We also need to tell them about Harley. They are already wondering what's going on and speculating about it, which we don't need in the club. That shit leads to fights."

Rage nods. "Church Monday night. Make sure everyone is there."

I clear my throat. "Um, speaking of Harley..." I glance at Ry, hoping he will take over.

I need a break from talking so much and having so much attention being on me. Luckily, my best friend picks up on that right away and jumps in. Going on to explain what happened at school when we asked about her voice.

"Well, that is an odd reaction to have. There are plenty of reasons that could be. So we will keep an eye out and feel out Tammy and Richard about it. My best guess is if she is being abused, they did something to stop her from talking and she got scared when asked, not sure what to say or maybe thought you'd react the same way her abusers would," Rage ponders.

"We would never!" Ry protests loudly.

"Boy, we know that. But if this girl is bein' abused, her mind would go to all sorts of fucked-up places. You know that first-hand," Sugar retorts.

Ry sighs and drops his head in defeat.

We move on to talk out everything else, with Ryker and Noah getting their punishments for yesterday, and they tell us how it went at Harley's house. We are all mad, but all we can do now is keep looking into shit and wait until Monday. Hopefully Harley will be there, and we can pull her aside and make sure she knows she can come to us.

Rage warns us to keep the drama down. He has to be president first, and he doesn't want us to put him in the spot of having to kick us out or put us above the club. We get it. We want this life too, when we can have it, so we won't put him in that position. The guys and I decide to find Harley before school and pull her aside. Rage wants to see if she would trust us enough that we could bring her here and skip school to talk. Nerds can hack into the system and mark that we were all there if she'll come back with us.

We all leave the office to go about our day, with Cade, Ry, and I heading upstairs to get some homework done before we go back to school.

As we are walking upstairs, Ry says, "Why do I have a feeling shit's about to get way fucking worse?"

Cade grunts his agreement, and I can't help getting a cold shiver down my spine and thinking that he's right and things are going to get a lot worse before they can ever get better.

CHAPTER TWELVE

HARLEY

Today is Sunday. I've been left alone since Friday night. Although that's not saying much considering Friday was the worst day of the week.

I don't know what happened, but somehow, they decided Noah was the person I spilled whatever secrets I don't even know to. I don't even know a Noah. I've never met anyone with that name. I know I heard people upstairs at some point on Friday, but I couldn't hear any conversations. It all sounds muffled from down here. I just know they wanted to make sure I didn't make a sound, so Father came down before gagging me and cuffing my hands behind my back.

Shortly after I heard the voices stop talking upstairs, Mother came down with Father in tow. They proceeded to torture me in any way they could. I don't think things could've gotten any worse than they did. It was like they were carving my insides from the outside. Even just thinking about it makes me want to burst into tears. They didn't stop until I was barely moving. I faintly remember them leaving as I let the darkness take over.

When I woke up, I had no idea what day it was or the time. It had to have at least been a day. I could barely move—hell, I still can barely move. The cuts all over my body make every little movement send pain through me, and I am covered in bruises.

My voice is weak. It sounds more like a whisper now if I try to talk. I really hope there isn't permanent damage.

I feel like I am fighting a battle that is impossible for me to win. It's not like I could ever get out of here on my own. I don't know why this is happening, and it's the most frustrating part. I keep telling myself I can fight and hold on and I will find a way to get out of here, but the reality is, if she doesn't let me go back to school or leave the house again, I will have no way to escape. I've tried to get the ankle cuff off before, and I can't.

My body is too weak to run from here, and they would catch me in a heartbeat. I'm done for. There isn't anything else I can do. Part of me wonders why I am even trying; I should just be hoping they beat me until I die at this point.

Tabby comes down and uncuffs me. "Mommy wants you upstairs," she sneers, looking at me like I am trash.

I rasp out, "Do you really think what they are doing to me is okay?"

Tabby laughs, and just like her mother, it's an evil cackle. "You have no idea what I think. Nor will you ever. You are trash. I am not. I get a nice big stack of cash for helping Mommy and not saying anything." She turns and goes back upstairs.

Well, at least that answers that question. Although, I don't think I could be paid any amount of money to turn a blind eye to something like this. But then again, it's me down here. Not her.

I try to stand, but the pain is so excruciating as it shoots through my body that it has me wobbling on my feet. I grab the wall to steady myself, then limp towards the stairs and take as deep of a breath as I can. I very slowly work my way up. Everything hurts, and it feels like the pain gets worse with each step.

By the time I make it to the top, I am sweating and breathing hard. Tabby is waiting for me. "It's about damn time, you lazy bitch." She walks off towards the dining room, and I slowly follow her.

Mother, Father, and Tabby are all sitting at the table with a feast of food in front of them. My mouth waters and my stomach grumbles at the smell. I don't even know the last time I ate.

Mother points the spot along the wall she always wants me to stand at whenever she has me come in here. I slowly go over and lean against the wall, trying not to breathe through my nose. I don't want to smell all this food I know I won't get to eat.

They all start eating, and about halfway through their dinner, Mother looks at me. "I am sending you back to school tomorrow." Something flashes in her eyes, almost like she doesn't want to let me go back. But it passes so quickly that I am not even sure I saw it. "You will keep your goddamn mouth shut this time. Things can get a lot worse if you don't. Next time, you won't get off so easily. I will starve you for weeks."

She stands and walks towards me. I try to swallow over the lump in my throat.

"Make you stand in here for every meal as we eat, make you stand still while in pain from me breaking your ribs." She runs a hand across my stomach over my ribs, and I try not to flinch. "And if you move even one tiny bit, I'll tase you. It would be quite entertaining for me."

She smiles, a deranged, fucked-up smile. She raises her other hand and then quickly shoves me into the wall, pushing on my ribs.

I cry out involuntarily; the pain is too much for me to stay quiet. I fight the tears that try to come, but I don't win this time. They fall. Mother's smile spreads wider at the sight of my tears. Then she turns serious, pushing harder until it's hard to even suck in a breath. "Do we understand each other? If not, I can always give you another lesson until you get the message."

I nod my head and try to rasp out on a panted breath, "I un... under... stand."

She stares at me, the look in her eyes even more terrifying than what she can do with her hands to me. She nods and then lets go and walks back to the table. "You'll stand there until we are done, then clean up the mess. You will get a can tomorrow. I think until you learn to keep your mouth shut, we will go down to one can a day instead of my generous two cans."

They take their time eating, dragging it out for almost an hour. My stomach grumbles the entire time. I have felt hunger before, but having to watch them eat is a new level of torment.

When they are done, Mother and Tabby leave, but Father stays to watch me so I can't even try to eat some of their leftovers. I feel his eyes searing into me the entire time I move around the kitchen and dining room. He just sits back in his chair with arms folded over his chest and his eyes trained on me.

My body stays tense, which isn't helping the aches and pain I feel from being hurt. My mind keeps flashing back to the basement, when Father had come down and touched me. The way his hands felt like someone branding me with a hot iron at every sick caress... I never want to experience that again. I always thought he just watched me to watch, but now I feel like he is staring at my body. It makes me want to cower in a corner and cover myself.

My stomach grumbles at me again as I grab the last few dishes that still have food on them. A part of my brain is telling me to just stuff the food in my mouth. I may get beat, but they can't take away the food I would've eaten.

I shake myself of those thoughts. My body could not handle another beating right now, and with Father being the only one in the room, he would probably touch me, and that thought alone makes starving sound like a fantastic idea.

I clean the counters up and then head back downstairs. Father follows behind me to cuff me back up. He leaves a few medical bandages next to me, then turns around and walks back upstairs. He usually is more talkative or leering at me. Instead, this time he kept his head down, barely even looking at me. It was like this time he couldn't get away fast enough. Not that I mind.

I feel like I could be sick to my stomach after that. I slowly make my way to the bathroom and rinse my mouth with water from the sink, but it doesn't help. Next thing I know, I am on the floor, dry heaving into the toilet. There is nothing in my stomach for me to even hurl, but the need to vomit is making me heave over and over again as tears stream down my face.

The way that she acted makes me think that things can and will get so much worse. Who even is this Noah person? Is that who was here Friday? I fucking hate that I can't ever do good enough, that no matter what they find something to blame me for.

I have never seen the look in her eyes that I did upstairs. She has always looked at me with hatred, like I did something to her or ruined her life, but this was so much worse than that, this was like she was wishing she could kill me. She very well might one day... Would I even care? At first, probably not. But now? I want to get out of here. Find answers. Do something, anything.

The whole world isn't this bad. I know that. Mother is suspicious and has a lot of things going on that she obviously doesn't tell me about.

Let's just hope those things stop her from trying to kill me anytime soon.

I lay down for a few hours, trying to rest my aching body, and then decide to get up and clean myself up. I peel my shirt and leggings off. They were stuck to me because of the blood from all my cuts. I shower very slowly, and by the time I am done, tears are streaming down my face from the pain. I'm breathing hard and feel like I might pass out. I quickly pull on a new hoodie then lay down, refusing to put back on the dirty underwear and leggings I had on. I hate going without, but I can't put anything new on with the cuff.

I've been laying here, numb, for hours. I very slowly sit up and rest my back against the wall. It's like there are so many things running through my head that I can't process, so instead I am numb to it all.

I try to take some deep breaths, remembering what Grayson told me about panic attacks. He also told me I have people. But do I? I have no idea who I can and can't trust. I also missed some school, so I have no idea if he got my note or not. The only person I can truly depend on is myself. Which means I have to get myself out here, and luckily with school, I just might be able to.

It's a huge fucking risk. If I don't make it or get caught, I am risking worse punishments. But is that fear strong enough to stay stuck and probably never get out? I can't let it be.

Take it one step at a time, Harley.

So, since then, I've been deciding what I am going to do. My body needs to heal. That's the biggest thing. I need to find medicine to make sure I don't get sick. I also need to eat, so the first thing I will do is get some food when I get to school. Then it's planning a way to get the fuck out of this town.

I get up slowly, my body protesting against the movements. I grab the cash from the hole in the wall and stuff it into the bottom of my backpack, hiding it as best I can. I then fold my clothes up as small as I can get them so I can fit what I can in my backpack without making it look too big.

I don't want to pack up things too early in case they come down and look around. In the morning when someone comes to uncuff me, I'll claim I need to pee before going. I will probably get hit for it, but it's worth it so when they leave, I can toss more of my clothes, shampoo, and the throw blanket into my backpack.

It's a risk because they might not leave me alone. Or they might drag me upstairs anyways. But I can't risk packing other things early and someone noticing. I have the cash, and that's the most important thing. The other things would help me save a little money, but I can manage without them. I'll wear extra layers so I have as much clothes on as possible without it being noticeable.

I take a deep breath and remember that I am doing this for me. No one is coming to save me. There is no getting out of this unless I do it myself and become the badass bitch I know I can be. I watched my mom do everything she could to give me a good childhood. She was a boss. She worked two jobs and did everything for me still. She was always around and there for me if I needed her. She was the happiest person I ever knew and so strong. I want to be like her, and this is how I start.

The next morning, I try to keep my shaking under control as I get ready for the day. I slowly shower and wash everything and put on the last two bandages I have on the worst cuts on my stomach. I can't do anything about my back even though it's still bleeding a little.

Mother comes down and unlocks me. I tell her I have to pee and then I'll be up. As I suspected, she slaps me and says, "You lazy bitch. Hurry the fuck up."

As soon as I hear her hit the top step, I start shoving everything into my backpack and then run over and flush the toilet. I squish my backpack down as much as I can, making it seem more flat than it is. It takes me a while to work my way up the stairs, but when I do, Father is by the door to make sure I don't touch anything and leave.

"Be good today, Harley. I'd hate to have to have a repeat of last week," he says with a gleam in his eye telling me he wouldn't hate it at all.

I nod and head out the door to go wait for the bus.

Holy shit. This is really happening. One step at a time. One foot in front of the other. I can do this. My body is protesting so much movement, but I fight through it. I make sure to flip the hood up on my hoodie and tug it up my neck as much as I can. They didn't give me anything to cover the bruising up this time, which is odd.

When I get to school, I take off right away for the library. On the way, I pass a vending machine and stop and grab a few snacks. I have to get something in me before I pass out.

I don't want to run into Lex. We usually spend mornings together before class, and I don't want to explain things to her. In the library, I log in to a computer and look up where I'm heading.

I've been doing a lot of thinking this last week. My mom and I lived in Auburn, Massachusetts, so my first thought was to head there, but then I remembered a story my mom told me when I was little after I had come home from kids club crying because another girl pulled my hair.

"Baby girl, I'm going to tell you a story. Once a long time ago, there was a young girl who didn't want to stay around the people who were being mean to her and pulling her hair. She had this beautiful soul growing inside of her, and she didn't want it harmed, so she packed her bags and went and found a princess."

"What was the princess's name, Mama?" I ask, and she smiles.

"She was Princess Brielle of the Virginia Beach. The girl found a way to go to the princess and ask her for help. The princess held her and kept her safe and always promised to protect her and the beautiful soul she was growing. So, my sweet, sweet baby girl, you are also a princess. You are so strong, so incredible, and you don't need anyone to come save you from those mean girls at school because you are going to be strong and stand up to them and show them the kindness that they may need. Because you, my baby, are so much stronger than the girl in the story. You will be the princess who saves the day. So don't cry, my sweet girl, because everything will be okay."

I take a chance, *probably a stupid one.* It wasn't the only time she told me stories about Princess Brielle, so I Googled Virginia

Beach and see it's about halfway from here in Jacksonville, NC to Auburn. So I'm going to take a chance that Brielle is real and is my mom's friend. Let's only hope she will be willing to help me too.

I bring up directions and print them up to be safe. I also print local bus routes. I find an online service for cabs and order one to meet me outside the school by the main road and not come into the parking lot.

When I'm done, I take off to make sure I get out there before the cab comes. My heart is pounding. I can't believe I am doing this. Holy shit. I take off down the hall at a brisk walk holding my ribs, trying not to let the pain slow me down.

But then I hear someone call my name. I can't look back; I can't risk it. I need to do this. I am doing this for me. I need to get the hell out of here, no matter how terrified I am.

I soon make it out and duck into the trees at the end of the parking lot by the road so no one can see me. I make my way out towards the main road and wait when I see the cab pulling up. My heart is pounding, my hands are sweating, and I'm shaking nonstop. I make sure it's for me, then get in and ask him to take me to the nearest bus stop that is heading north. My voice is a whisper and very raspy, but he is able to understand me.

We get there in no time and I get out to wait for the bus. I can't believe this is happening. Fucking hell, I am getting out of here! Whether I find Brielle or not, I am getting out from under Tammy and Richard. Ha! It feels fantastic to call them by their names. I want to scream it from the rooftops.

The bus soon arrives, and I get on and start to relax some now that I am actually doing this. My heart is pounding so hard it actually hurts, and my body is ready to shut down and sleep for days, but that doesn't stop a small smile from crossing my lips.

That's when I see him. He looks almost... familiar? He's standing outside the bus where I'm sitting by the window. He has these eyes I swear I've stared into before, and his mouth curves in a way I recognize, but I don't know him.

Although, he is staring at me. Directly at me. Making eye contact.

I realize it and duck down, pulling my hoodie up more as the bus takes off. Shit! I need to get off this one and get a different one. I'll just wait until we are out of Jacksonville.

Doing just that, I hop off the bus and find a different bus stop to wait for that new one. It's going to be thirty minutes until it arrives, so I walk across the street to a gas station to get something to eat. I grab a few snacks and two bottles of water, staying as cheap as I can.

Once I'm on the next bus, I calm down and feel like I can relax since I'll be on here for a while. I take a deep breath and look out the window with a small smile. For the first time in who knows how long, I have some hope, even if I am absolutely terrified of getting caught and being all on my own with nothing but what's on my back.

Little did I know, this was only the start to a long and hard journey of finding answers, but the only answer I have for now is what step two is to becoming the devil: Learn to become your own motherfucking princess.

CHAPTER THIRTEEN

RYKER

"RYKER ANDERSON!" comes from the other end of the hall.

All three of us turn, confused as shit considering we just came in from outside.

When I see Lex come barreling towards us, my eyes widen. I know the girl hates us, but what the fuck is she doing? When she gets closer, I can see the pure rage coming from her eyes directed right at me. Cade must see it too because he slowly steps up closer to my side.

Me being me and not being able to stop myself, I say, "Problem, Lexington?"

She stops in front of us and glares at me. "Don't fucking call me that. I hate that goddamn name and yes, we have a fucking problem, Ryker," she sneers my name at me. "Harley wasn't waiting for me this morning, so I went looking for her and saw her coming flying out of the library and taking off down the hall out the doors on the westside, heading for the main road. She wouldn't stop to give me the time of day. So what the fuck have you fuckwits done to my best friend?"

My back goes stiff, and I glance at Cade and Gray to see them thinking the same thing I am. Being in my panicked state, I blurt out the first thing that comes to my mind as we all dash around Lex and take off for the west doors. "Sorry, Lexington, we can shoot the shit next time. Gotta go, places to be."

We bust out the doors as fast as possible while also dodging students coming in and stop and look around. That's when Cade growls and takes off for the trees leading to the main road. We sprint after him to follow, looking all over, but I don't see her.

That's when we see a taxi driving by through the woods, with a redheaded girl in the back seat. We break through the trees right as it drives past.

Cade looks ready to chase the car down, and I think he would too if he knew he could outrun it. "Fuck! Where the hell could she be going? Why would she come here just to take off again? This makes no fucking sense!" I yell while pulling at my hair.

I turn to look for Grayson, who hasn't said anything, only to find him a bit away from us talking on the phone. What the fuck?

I stomp over to him, hearing Cade right on my heels. "Grayson! What could be so important right now you have to be on the phone? Did you not just see that shit? She took off!"

Grayson gives me a glare that he doesn't usually direct towards me very often. I clamp my mouth shut, then take a deep breath, hoping to keep myself in check. I can't go off the rails right now. So instead, I bring my mask down. I shut it all down and become the carefree jokester.

Grayson gets off the phone and looks at Cade and I before sighing, "That was Noah. I called him as soon as I realized what she was doing. He just sent out everyone available to go search for her. But we are to stay here like everything is normal in case she comes back here. If she does, we'll pull her aside and force her to go with us if we have to." He grimaces as he says the last part. Grayson doesn't like violence, so he wouldn't do something like that lightly.

I smirk. "Don't worry, brother, I will be the knight in shining dickwad who tosses her over my shoulder and carries her away." I cackle as he scowls at me.

"Don't do that. Please don't shut down on me, Ry."

I nod and look at him with as much sympathy I can give right now. It's too little too late for that. The second she got in that car, I knew I wouldn't be able to keep it together without shutting down. Harley is a mystery among so many other things, and it's really pissing me off that we can't seem to get ahead of things with her.

Grayson exhales, running a hand through his hair, and we head back inside to go to first period, which we are now at least fifteen minutes late for.

Noah texts our group chat of him, Gray, Cade and I that they are out looking for her with who was available to help. And that they are having Church tonight to discuss everything at length because half the guys are clueless to what's happening, and they need to be in the know.

It's lunch time now and still no sign of Harley. Also, no word from Noah. My mind is reeling. Do they have her? Is she okay? What if she's hurt? What's going on? Why did she leave? Not having control of this situation is pissing me off, especially with Noah not answering.

Seriously... I'm going to kill him.

The last three classes go extremely slow. After sixth period, we race outside to stand by the bus Harley would take to see if by some chance she's here and coming to take it home. But nothing. Once the bus leaves, we head for the clubhouse.

I'm really trying to keep myself calm, but I can feel the anger building in me and breaking through my walls. This damn girl has gotten under my skin, and I barely know anything about her.

When we get to the club, no one is outside, which isn't the best sign. Usually, people are wandering around out here or smoking. We head inside, and Noah is at the bar with Rage, Sugar, the club's Road Capitan, Axe, and the Sergeant at Arms, Stone.

I head straight towards him with Gray and Cade at my back. He sees us coming and stands up with wide but calm eyes. "Ryker—"

160

"Where. The. Fuck. Is. SHE?" I roar, no longer able to control my anger while seeing them all just sitting around doing fuck all.

He sighs heavily, which has me tensing. "I don't know, brother. I... I lost her."

He doesn't get another word out before my fist is flying straight into his face. I watch as blood pours from his nose, and he stumbles back before his own anger takes over.

Then all hell breaks loose.

BLADE (NOAH)

6 Hours Earlier

I'm eating breakfast with some brothers, shooting the shit when my phone rings. I glance at it. Seeing who it is, a bad feeling hits me hard in the stomach. I answer it and quickly move away to hear better because the main room is pretty loud right now.

"Brother?"

"Yeah, Noah, we have a problem. We wanted to find Harley before school today, to hopefully get her to come back with us and bail on school, but as soon as we got here, a girl came running up telling us that Harley took off out towards the main road. We just got out here, and she's gone, brother. She got in a taxi and took off before we could stop it. Can you try to find her? We'll come back now to help. I'm worried. Something isn't right." He rushes it all out so fast that I don't think he is even breathing.

"Alright, okay, well shit. Take a breath, Gray. There are some of us here today. I'll get everyone to go split up and search and call me if they find her, but Gray, you guys need to stay there in case she comes back today. Alright?"

"No, Noah, we need to help. I don't even know if Ry can hold on without losing his temper on some poor kid here." I'm already shaking my head even though I know he can't see me. "Nope. I'm pulling the big brother card. Stay put. I mean it. If we need you to leave, I will tell you. Otherwise stay and tell me if she comes back. I'm off now, brother. Good luck."

I hang up and head back towards the main room and let out a loud whistle so everyone shuts up.

"Alright, listen up! We've got a problem. This was going to be brought to Church tonight, but now shit's happening, so I need all hands that have nothing of importance to do to get the fuck ready and get outside to their bikes, NOW!"

I take off outside, not waiting to see who is doing what. I know they will follow my orders. One, I am the enforcer, and you'd be stupid to cross me and two, Rage is like a father to me, so I get a little more leeway with things.

About two minutes later, at least ten brothers come out and three prospects. As they get ready to take off, I yell out, "We are looking for Harley, short redhead, about 5'3ish and has a scar on her face on the right side. I know that's not much, but it's what we have to work with. Split up in groups of two to three. Head out to the Wilson's house, snoop around quietly, some go by the school, the rest of you split off to heavy taxi areas, bus stops, I don't fucking know where else. We just need to find her. When you do, keep a distance. Do not lose her and call me immediately. Sorry, that's all you get, brothers. Be safe, let's ride."

After about two hours of nothing, we finally get something. A prospect, Connor, called me and said he saw a girl who looked like her at a bus stop farther into town.

I speed that way with another prospect, Daniel, riding next to me. We get there, and I tell them to hold back as I head up to the stop. When I reach the bench, she's not there. But that's when I see her sitting on a bus by the window.

She has the most beautiful large, round, hazel eyes that I want to examine up close because she's too far away. I feel like I'm stuck in a trance just staring at her eyes. *No wonder my brothers are so taken with her.* I know this is her from the way the guys described her hair. It's long and copper with beautiful flowing waves. I can see her scar on her cheek and something in me burns with anger at someone hurting her. Which is outrageous because who knows what it's from.

She has bruises on her face, and her left eye is a little swollen. I can just barely make out the top of a bruise on her neck where her hoodie isn't covering it. I clench my fists because this girl should not be getting hurt.

She has been staring right at me with an awed but confused expression on her face until something close to panic comes over her and she quickly turns away and ducks down.

Then I realize I've spent all my time stuck staring at her and not getting on the bus. I turn and take off towards the front of the bus but as soon as I get to it, it speeds away.

"FUCK!" I yell, startling people who had been walking around me.

I quickly memorize everything I can about the bus and what the route says on the back screen part before turning around and booking it back to my bike. I parked around the corner to keep from scaring her, which I really regret right now. I get on my bike and take off after the bus with both prospects' bikes sounding behind me. We get stuck at a red light sitting in heavy traffic since we are in the middle of the town now and it's always busy.

Fucking shit, I can't lose her. Not now. Not ever. Fuck, what am I thinking? I'm so distracted by my thoughts when the light turns green that I don't see the truck coming at me from my right until it's too late. I hear a sickening crunch as I get thrown from my bike. It wouldn't be the first time I have crashed, but I have never flown through the air before.

It feels like time slows, and I squeeze my eyes shut knowing I am going to hit the road or even another car hard. I try to tuck into myself as much as possible as I hit the pavement and slide. Son of a fucking bitch, that hurts like a motherfucker. My head is throbbing, and my body hurts, but I can't focus enough to tell where I am hurt the worst. Before I can even think to move or get up, my vision is blurring. I can faintly hear muffled shouts and cars braking before everything goes out of focus and I pass out.

Beep.

Beep.

Beep.

That sound is annoying as hell. My head hurts like a bitch; it feels like my brain is pounding in my skull, giving me the world's worst headache. I slowly crack my eyes open to realize I am not at the clubhouse. *What the fuck?*

My mind goes into overdrive thinking about where I was. Goddamn it, the crash. Why the hell would the prospects bring me here? They know better. We rarely ever come to the hospital. And if we do it's because Doc is forcing us to. I'd much rather get patched up and lay in my own bed doped up on pain meds or even just dealing with the pain than be in the hospital.

It's not that any of us have anything against hospitals. Well, Axe, one of my brothers, struggles because of past issues, but the rest of us just don't want to deal with it. And shit is expensive as fuck.

I finally get my eyes to work with me and open them all the way. Blinking at the harsh hospital fluorescent lights. You'd think they'd at least be nice enough to keep the lights off or down low. Or hell, get a lamp in here. Why make people wake up from an accident or a surgery to bright ass fucking lights?

As I look around the room, I notice that I am alone. Where the hell are those fucking prospects? I am going to beat their asses when I get out of here.

I slowly sit up and notice that I am at least still in my clothes. They just took my boots and jacket off, but they are laying close by on an extra chair in the corner of the room.

I swing my legs over the side of the stiff bed and groan. Fuck, that hurts. I don't see any bad road burns. It looks like my palms have some scrapes, but I can't see anything else right now. I am just extremely sore from being thrown off my bike. I get up and make my way around the bed, where there seems to be a door to a bathroom.

"Fuck." I groan when I see myself in the mirror. There are scrapes on the left side of my face and a small gash on the side of my head they stitched. I try to wash the dirt off my scraped-up hands as gently as I can and then go back out and pull my boots and jacket on. I am moving much fucking slower than I'd like. But whatever, as long as I can get out of here soon.

As soon as I go to open the door, it opens from the outside and a petite blonde girl is standing in front of me. I am by no means tall. I mean, my younger brother is about three inches taller than me at 6'3, but this girl is fucking tiny. Probably barely five feet.

She glowers up at me with her bright shimmering blue eyes. "You should not be out of bed," she says with much more authority and balls than I expected from such a tiny thing facing off with me.

I smirk down at her. "Yeah? Well, since I am already up and seem to be moving just fine, I think I am good to go."

She crosses her arms over her chest. "You need to be checked over again now that you are awake, and you just got stitches in your head. You need to stay overnight so that they can make sure there are no other injuries you might have sustained."

I shake my head. "Well, you can check me out as I walk out the door. Don't forget to check my ass out too. It's pretty nice, if I do say so myself." I gently push past her and start heading down the hall. I swear I hear her growl as I walk away.

The elevator at the end of the hall opens as I get closer, and Sugar steps out. He sees me and then glances past me and raises a brow, dragging his eyes back to me. I look over my shoulder and see that the girl is following me.

"Not gonna happen, pixie. Go help someone who actually needs it."

Sugar holds the elevator open, and I step in. He shakes his head and says, "Not worth it, darlin'. He won't crack."

She huffs and turns around, storming back down the hall, and I snicker, which is abruptly cut off as the elevator doors push shut and Sugar turns his hard eyes on me. "What the fuck happened? Why were you travelin' alone?" he demands.

My brows hit my hairline. "That is what I would like to know. We found Harley, but then when we tried to follow her a truck hit me, and I woke up here. I wasn't alone. Where the fuck are Daniel and Connor? They were with me." My voice raises as my temper spikes. What the fuck is going on?

"Connor is back at the clubhouse, said after y'all found the girl you sent him back, and no one has seen Daniel. Axe was actually callin' him when I got the call 'bout you. They called Rage first, but he didn't answer, so the hospital called me. You can wait 'til we get back to tell me everything so Doc can check you over before we rehash shit. Somethin' isn't sittin' right with me, Blade."

I grumble, "Yeah, I feel the same. We'll figure it out."

We head out to the parking lot to the truck Sugar drove over here and drive back to the clubhouse in silence. My mind is running with questions about what happened. Both prospects were behind me. I know they were.

After we get back, Doc checks me over and then I go and flop down on the couch in Rage's office, sprawling out dramatically knowing we need to talk but also needing to lay down. When Rage, Sugar, Nerds, Axe, and Stone come in, they all look at me and chuckle, besides Stone who just shakes his head.

"Fuck off, you assholes. I just got hit by a fucking truck! I could've died. Show me you love me."

Rage and Sugar both laugh while the others just shake their heads. I grin as they laugh; I hate it when shit is too tense. Gotta find ways to lighten the mood.

The mood turns serious, and I reluctantly sit up, my body aching. But we have shit to discuss. I walk them through everything that has happened so far today up until Sugar picked me up.

Rage looks at Axe. "Did you find Daniel?"

Axe nods. "Yeah, I did. Let me get him in here." I plug my ears, knowing what's coming next as Axe opens the door and yells, "PROSPECTS!"

Within two minutes, all four of them are there. Axe nods to Daniel and has him come in then shuts the doors on the other ones. I snicker because of course he'd scare them all like that. Any chance he gets, he will. I couldn't fully see their faces from where I am on the couch, but I am sure they all looked ready to shit their pants.

I glare at Daniel. He's one of our young ones. He graduated last year from high school and immediately wanted to prospect. He also thinks I don't know how he treats my brothers, but I'm the enforcer. I know all the shit happening in my club. He's a cocky shit, but so far, he's been doing just fine with all prospect duties.

"Prospect, walk me through today from your perspective. Don't leave a single detail out. Not even when you stopped to take a piss. I want everything," I say.

He gulps and then starts talking about helping to find Harley, following me out, staying with me, and then when the truck hit me. "I tried to signal to you that I saw it coming right through. But you didn't see me signal. The truck blew through, and I slid sideways to avoid hitting the truck and hit the ground instead. I hit my head and passed out. When I came to, some random guy was checking me over, and I noticed you were already gone. He said another ambo was on the way, but I didn't want it, so I jumped up planning to take my bike back here, but it was gone. I don't know what happened to it. The guy offered me a ride here.

When I got here, I got cleaned up then made my way back to look at the accident site before heading to get you. Axe called me on the way saying to get back here so I did, and I've been waiting since."

Before I can crush him for being stupid, Rage does. "Prospect, did you lose brain cells when you hit your head? What is one of the first rules as a prospect? Something, anything at all happens, what is the first fucking thing you do?"

He glares at Daniel, who says, "Call a member."

I study him as he answers, facing off with our president. There is a slight wariness in his voice, and the way he is acting, but he also doesn't seem worried. Which is odd.

As a prospect, it is very fucking easy to get booted out. I remember my year as one. I was constantly on edge, and if I got in trouble for anything, I was basically shaking in my boots or ready to shit myself. And I had an in already. I knew most of the guys already. But it was still scary.

"Correct," Rage grunts. "This is a first offense. We will let it slide, but Blade gets three hits. Tomorrow. Get the fuck out, prospect. You're on bathroom duty for the rest of the day."

He nods his head and turns to leave. Something about this whole thing is off, but I can't figure out what. I'm going to blame my headache for that.

Before he leaves, I call out, "Tell prospect Connor he has five seconds to get his ass in here." I watch as Daniel takes off to find him.

More than five seconds later, Connor comes strolling in like he owns the place. I can't bring myself to stand, and it's pissing me off. I can't do my part of enforcer right now, I know my body can't handle it.

Axe notices, giving me a nod and quickly taking over, "Did we say take your sweet ass time or to get your ass in here in five seconds?" He shoves him into the wall. "You aren't shit here, prospect. You have to earn respect. Right now? You aren't even close. Stop walking around like you're the shit and you own the place, or I'll put you in your place and you won't enjoy it."

Connor nods, his eyes wide with fear and what looks like respect. He knows he fucked up and is taking it like he should. Axe releases him, stepping away.

"Prospect, care to tell me why you drove off the opposite way when I came back to get my bike and follow the bus?" I ask in a deadly voice, glaring at him.

He gulps before shrugging. "I didn't know I was still needed, so I just came back here."

Rage sighs and mumbles, "Fucking dumbass prospects," before speaking to Connor, "You'll take three hits tomorrow from Blade. Next time, you don't do anything else until you are told to. He didn't say he didn't need you. You do not get to decide that. Obviously, you were still needed. Get the fuck out. You're on gate duty. Double shift starting now. Relieve the prospect there.

"Connor." He stops and turns back towards me. Surprisingly he makes eye contact with me even as his eyes give away his slight fear. "You ever leave a brother alone again without permission and I will beat you into a coma. We are family here; we take care of each other and communicate to keep each other safe. Got it?"

He gulps again before nodding and excusing himself quickly. I can't help but chuckle as I say, "Think one day I will get one to shit their pants?"

Rage sighs, "That shouldn't be a goal, Blade."

We all decide to stop there and wait for the boys to get back to fill them in, since they should be on their way now and I have no doubt they are pissed. But my phone is gone, so I have to get a new one from Nerds.

We all head out and sit at the bar that is in the main room, with everyone getting their usual drinks, which is mostly just beer, but I opt for a few shots to take the edge off and hopefully numb some of my pain.

When the door swings open and slams into the wall, I turn slowly, my body still aching to see the boys coming right for me. Ryker and Cade are pissed, and Grayson looks annoyed but calm. Shit, this isn't going to be good. *One more shot before this shit? Fuck yes.* I turn back towards the bar, grab the shot glass, take it quick, and slam the glass down before standing to face the boys.

RYKER

As soon as Noah stands back up straight, looking ready to kill me for hitting him, his eyes roll, and he passes out. I watch Rage fly out of his seat to catch him and lower him to the ground.

"What the fuck happened?" As soon as the words are out of my mouth, a fist hits me fucking hard on the cheek. When that hit doesn't knock me down, another comes in the same spot, then two hits in a row in the gut, which drops me on my ass. I look up to see Stone staring down at me. Shit, he's pissed. He's one scary motherfucker, so this isn't going to be good.

"Did I knock any sense into you boy, or do you need some more hits?"

I throw my hands up. "I'm good, I'm good. I swear."

He stares down at me longer before nodding and stepping back, looking at Rage.

Rage sighs and then looks at my brothers and I. "Sit, boys. I'll catch you up, then you can go dig your grave, Ryker, because once Blade is healed, I don't think you'll be breathing anymore. You're lucky you're not one of mine yet because boy, that was disrespectful as hell. You never hit another brother out of anger like that. You know we only do hits here, and it has to be okayed by a ranking officer.

"You have no idea what happened today, and you didn't even give him a chance to explain. So sit the fuck down, shut up, and listen to me, and don't you dare speak a word until I say you can, or I will make things hell for you." He glares at all three of us.

Cade helps me up, and we sit at the bar while Rage fills us in on everything from today. Shit. I fucked up. I sigh and run a hand through my hair, looking at the ground where Blade is still passed out.

Rage lets out a humorless laugh, "Regretting letting your anger get the best of you?"

I nod, then decide to be honest with him because I trust him not to use shit against me, like people in my past have. "I just freaked out this morning and then not hearing all day about what was going on, I was trying to mask it and push all my fears and anger down, but as soon as I saw you all sitting here, I couldn't contain it. I know I need to work on it, I just don't know how."

Rage nods in understanding. "I get it. Let us help you, Ryker. But you gotta be honest with yourself and us."

I nod and drop my head on the counter, knowing the next few weeks will be hell.

Blade wakes up a while later and says he's glad Rage filled us in. We help him up to his room and I check over his face making sure he doesn't need his nose set or anything cleaned up, but he's good. One thing about always wearing rings is that my hits tend to leave nasty marks on people. *Oops? I mean, not really. I guess I kind of feel bad right now, but he'll live.*

Blade stares me down. "Brother, you royally fucked up. I won't be able to beat your ass because I'm hurt, but you'll be spending the next two weeks doing all the shit I tell you to. I'm not your brother and guardian, Noah, the next two weeks. I'm Blade, the SOS's enforcer and you, Ryker Anderson, are my bitch."

Shit fuck shit. I really am not liking my decisions right now. A lot of the time I couldn't care less, but I know he isn't going to go easy on me.

Grayson clears his throat. "So, what are we going to do about Harley? Where is she even going?"

Seriously! Where the fuck would she be going? It makes no sense.

Before I can say anything, Cade speaks... *Shit, that's just getting weird to hear.* "Ran away?"

Noah nods. "Yeah, that's my guess, especially with how she reacted to me. She doesn't even know me and acted like I might take her or something. She definitely didn't want to be seen."

I feel myself getting angry with Harley when I know I shouldn't be. "Why run? We can help with whatever is happening! Why the fuck would she run?" I angrily spit out. Noah raises a brow at me like I am an idiot, so I sigh and take a breath. "Okay, I know that isn't something she knows, though. Sorry, I'm just angry and worried. What if something happens to her?"

Noah nods in understanding. "I get it, brother. We have church tonight, so we will discuss everything, but tomorrow I'll have Nerds excuse you guys and pair you up with a member to go search. If she did run away, though, something is happening at home, and we need to be careful we don't lead those people right back to her. Especially with finding out the kind of business the

Wilsons run, we have no idea how involved Harley is or if maybe... maybe they were planning to sell her. We have to tread carefully."

Shit. I didn't even think of that. That enrages me and makes my blood boil. I need to burn off this anger before I end up doing something stupid again.

"Gray, go work with Nerds. He's going to try and track her and keep an eye on Richard and Tammy. Cade, Axe is going to go try to plant some trackers on them. You can go with him; he's already expecting you. Ryker." He gets a smug look on his face. "I need to rest, so for tonight, go find Rage and stick with him. Do whatever he says. If he even has one complaint about you tomorrow, I'll add another week."

Fuck me. I think I'd much rather take a beating, honestly.

I nod, and then we all leave so Blade can rest. Cade smirks at me in the hall. "Fucking stupid." He shakes his head.

My jaw drops. It fucking drops. I can't believe this shit! He decides to talk again, and he automatically is coming for me? Grayson bursts out laughing at that, so I turn to him and glare.

"As if you two were better. You were just as pissed coming in here today. I just happened to throw a punch first. Impulse control, you know." I shrug. "You should be thanking me for taking this shit on for you guys."

They look at each other, and then Cade laughs. Full-blown fucking laughs. I haven't heard him laugh in fucking years. I'm trying not to show my shock, but it's really fucking hard.

Cade looks at my face, then laughs even harder and wheezes out, "Brother, you don't even know what impulse control means. It's something Gray and I have that you lack. We wouldn't have hit him, fucking dumbass. And stop looking at me like I just killed a puppy. I wouldn't do that. But I might kill you one day." He then puts his normal stoic face back on and walks away.

Gray snickers and walks away as well while I stand there frozen.

I don't know what's happening but shit, if shit keeps shocking me, they will have to lock me away with the other crazies. *Fuck, maybe they should anyways. They'd understand me more than these assholes.*

CHAPTER FOURTEEN

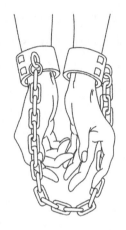

Harley

Day 1

I didn't realize that taking the bus would make this trip so much longer, but I guess with constant stops that makes sense. I'm guessing it's been about three hours. I really need to buy a cheap watch when I get there so I can keep track of the time. I think this will take most of the day to get there, so the first thing I need to do is find a motel. I'm worried that they won't let me get one because I'm a kid.

I take a couple of deep breaths. *One thing at a time, Harley.*

I am completely on my own, so there is no breaking down. I can't stop and grieve everything I'm feeling. I can't stop to think how absolutely fucking terrified I am right now. I have to stay on track and keep myself focused to keep myself safe.

I didn't run away from hell to end up dead or in another hell just because I can't keep my shit together.

The bus comes to a stop at a gas station to refuel, so I have a few minutes to run inside and see if they have a map I can buy. I find one easily, and I also happen to find a cheap watch for $5. I ask the clerk for the time so I can set it, then head out to the bus again. Looking over the map, I see we still have a ways to go. We are currently in Wilson, North Carolina, so not even in Virginia yet.

That makes me anxious. I just want to be out of North Carolina already.

A little while later, we are crossing the Chowan River on Edenhouse Bridge. We are getting close to the border of Virginia, and as much as I am terrified of what awaits me, I am so ready to be farther away from Tammy and Richard. I'm terrified they are going to come after me, but I just have to hope they don't find me and I don't get caught.

Laying low and just trying to find Brielle are my only goals right now. *If she's even real. Don't get your hopes up.*

I try to adjust in my seat to get more comfortable, but it's hard. My body aches and hurts everywhere. My ribs are killing me right now. I can't wait to be there so I can get off this bus and find somewhere to lay down. Hopefully in a motel.

I am worried someone is going to see all my bruises and get worried and call the cops. That would not be good. So since that guy from the bus stop I saw staring at me this morning, I've kept a hoodie on with the hood up even though I'm sweating and hot as shit on this bus.

The bus eventually pulls up to a bus stop that looks to be on a main street. There are businesses up and down both sides, and some people are out walking around. I get off the bus, my body protesting the movement after having sat still for so long.

As soon as I step off, I can smell it. The ocean. It smells crisp and almost salty. I know I can't be more than a block or two away from the water, even if I can't see it right now. There is a slight chill in the air with a misty breeze that feels amazing on my face. Part of me wants to go find the beach right now, but I need to wait and be smart about things. With the way I look, I can't be seen out much until my face heals.

I smile as I start walking and looking around. I can't believe I am out of there. I know part of me should be fucking terrified right now, but I feel almost giddy. I saved myself. I got out of there. I fucking did it.

I became my own motherfucking princess, Mom.

I check my watch as I keep walking; I left Tammy's at 7:15 a.m., and now it's 7:30 p.m. I need to go to a store and find something to put on the cuts on my body and maybe they'll have something to take the pain away, but I'd have to risk asking someone to help me.

I go into a store called Walgreens and there is a guy standing in the aisle with the medicine stuff. I take a breath. If anything, I'll just take off running and hide somewhere if he tries to take me or call the cops. I can do this. I shove my shaky hands in my hoodie pocket, hoping to keep them from shaking too badly. I walk up to him, and he glances at me. When his eyes land on my battered face, his eyes narrow and he sucks in a sharp breath as he clenches his fists.

"Hi." I try to give a sweet grin. "I was wondering if you could tell me what's the best medicine to get to take pain away?"

His narrowed angry eyes continue to stare at my face. I want to cover it, knowing it probably looks even worse now that it has been a day since I last got beat. I can feel the pain when I make any facial expression. The bruises and split lip making my face ache and giving me a wicked headache. After a few awkward seconds, he shuts his eyes and takes a deep breath before opening them again and attempting to give me a tiny smile; although, it looks more like a grimace.

"Of course, sweetie. Here, these will help take away pain. Take two every six hours as long as you need them. Also, you can use this. It'll help heal bruises faster." He hands me the pain medication and a tube of what looks like a lotion. I nod and smile. "Kiddo, do you need help? I know I'm just a stranger, but is someone hurting you?"

I keep the smile plastered on my face as I look up at the kind man. "Thank you, but I'm okay now."

I begin to walk away but he says, "Wait! Take this." I turn back around to find he's holding out a card. I take it from him and look at it.

Lincoln Tanner

Boxing Trainer

Self Defense Trainer

SWEAT FACTORY

On the back is an address and phone number. I glance up at him and furrow my brows. "If you need anything at all, come by there. Or call me. That's my name. I can promise to help in any way I can. Okay? Don't hesitate, kiddo."

I nod and turn around, walking away before I start crying. People can be better. Not everyone is bad, I remind myself. I check out and head down the street. I look for an old motel that might be willing to do cash only and no other verification.

Luckily, I find a place. It's run-down and doesn't look all that safe, but a room with a bed is better than the streets. I hope.

The guy barely even looked at me, just took my cash and gave me my room key. He had a look of it's not his business and he really doesn't fucking care, so I quickly walked out of the office and breathed a sigh of relief. That was exactly the kind of luck I needed right now.

I find my room, go in, lock the door, and make sure the window is locked and curtains are closed. Here goes nothing.

Day 2

I wake up feeling better than I have in a long time. I may have been constantly waking up to make sure I was still safe, but I was able to lay on a better bed and rest for hours. It's about noon now. I've been in bed since nine last night. Now I need to plan things out. I left one notebook from school in my backpack, so I pull it out and start making a list of what I can do. I look at the map I got yesterday and find where it looks like most places would be. I need to find a library to use, so that's today's goal. My body hurts, and I feel like I could sleep for days, but I need to keep busy and not let myself break down.

I shower in the tiny bathroom this room has and finally get a good look at my battered face. My lip is split in two places, and I have a black eye, as well as bruises on my cheek and jawbone. The worst part is my neck; you can see the bruising around it from the chain and Mother's hands. I reach my hand up to feel it and hiss when I touch my neck. It's tender and feels raw.

I will have to keep my hair down and my hoodie pulled up around my neck as much as possible. I apply the lotion stuff that the guy from the store gave me. It hurts rubbing it on, but hopefully it makes these marks disappear faster.

I take my pain meds and then before I leave to find a library, I count my cash. I started with $514 but after the taxi, the bus, two stops at gas stations, the medicine, and the motel I'm left with $333.20. I need to be super careful from here on out. If I get down to $200 before I find Brielle, then I'll have to start pickpocketing again. I guess the school was my practice round.

My body is most definitely objecting to having to move so much already, but I have to try to figure shit out, so that means pushing past the pain.

Maybe today is my lucky day? Not only do I find a library three blocks away from the motel, but they have free water and coffee. I've never had coffee, so I just grab some water and find a computer to start looking. My mom and I used to go to libraries all the time when I was little. It was the best place to get books since you don't have to pay. We'd pick out new fairy tales to read at home and mom would use a computer while I read and looked at other books. This library is much larger than some of the ones I have been to. It's two stories and is fairly busy.

But I found a computer in this little room on the back wall. It says private study room. You can be in here for two hours according to the sign on the door. Hopefully I can get one of these any time I come here to avoid people. The less I interact with people, the better. Especially considering the state of my face.

I've been trying to think about all the stories my mom used to tell me, and Brielle came up a lot, so I'm trying to piece things together. The one thing I remembered most is her living on the beach.

"Princess Brielle had a beautiful home. The back of the house looked out at the beach, and you could walk from her back deck down to the water. The girl loved to go down and sit, pushing her toes into the sand. It grounded her and was her favorite thing to do when she had sad thoughts like you are having, baby girl."

"Can we go to Princess Brielle and push our toes into the sand, Mama? Will it make me feel better?"

"Oh baby, I hope one day you will get to go to Princess Brielle and can do that, but not now, unfortunately."

I look at homes on the beach, then I look up Brielle in Virginia Beach, but there are too many things coming up. If I had her last name, this would be easier. So I go back to looking at houses on the beach. Any of the ones I can see on Google Maps that have a back deck that faces the water. There are six closest to me. Two are for sale, so that leaves four. I don't really know what to do with this information now. I map out other places around town so I can learn my way around and write down all the directions I need, then print some off for me to take home.

After that, I decide to stop for the day. It's been five hours, and I'm exhausted, so I head back to the motel and crash almost as soon as I hit my bed.

One Week Later

Nothing. Absolutely nothing. I have $203 left, and I've got nothing on Brielle. I'm starting to panic, and I'm really trying to hold it together. But I've been alone for a week now, and things are overwhelming. I'm starting to lose hope. Who knew that getting out of Moth—I mean Tammy's would be the easy part? That this would be the hard part. Staying strong because I am on my own. I have to depend on myself. I have no one else. Its fucking terrifying.

I ended up going to those four homes a few days ago but no luck. One of them, an older man, commented on my bruises and said he could call the cops for me. When I said no and went to leave, he tried yelling for me and I took off running. I found a place close by to hide, taking a breather. Running when your body is aching and banged up on top of very little moving over three years... it hurts.

None of the people from the homes on the beach even knew someone named Brielle. I don't know what to do next. Every day I've gone to the library to try and search for her. I've asked around at local shops, and I've just walked in about every direction trying to think of anything else I can do to find her but keep coming up with nothing.

I'm losing hope that she's even real, which means I'm going to need to start thinking about other options and what else I can do to survive since going back to Tammy is not an option.

I'll have to try and find a job. Maybe I can find someone who will pay me cash or under the table as I saw it was called when I Googled it. I am trying to stay positive and keep going. Every day I get up and move and leave the motel. But it's getting harder and harder. I feel like I am seconds away from a huge breakdown. But I didn't get this far to break and screw up and end up back with Tammy.

I have to fight. I am fighting for me, but I also need to fight to live a better life for my mom. *Just keep holding on. You didn't survive to give up now.* I feel tears burn the backs of my eyes, but I don't let them fall.

The only positive thing this week is that my bruises are healing. Slowly, but they are. I think a lot of the cuts on me are going to scar, and my ribs still ache, but they don't hurt as bad as the first few days. My face is still yellow and purple, but not as dark as it was. My neck is still pretty dark, but it hurts less every day. I can still barely make out the indent from the chain when she tried to choke me with it. I wish it would go away; I hate having a reminder there. I have enough scars to remind me of shit.

I decide I need to go out and try to pickpocket someone. That'll make me feel better, and I better start practicing doing it with adults and not just people at school. I really don't want to get under that $200 amount.

I get ready for the day and head out. Shortly after locking the door and walking down the stairs, there are guys standing around that are always there. They usually stare at me but have never said anything. Apparently, that isn't happening today because as I walk by, one steps in front of me.

"Look here, boys, the bitch's face is finally healing up. Maybe we can have some fun now and leave some new marks. Wouldn't want her to lose the color on her face that made her pretty."

The other guys all laugh, and I tense up. *Okay, breathe. Don't panic. Turn around and run back to the room. You can get in fast. It'll be okay.*

Before I can even try to turn around and run back upstairs, two of them step up behind me and block my way. One of them whispers in my ear, "Pretty scar you got there." He reaches forward and runs his finger down the scar on my face. "Maybe I should put another one on the other side to match." He cackles.

My whole body freezes up on me before I can even think of what to do.

Then the asshole in front of me pulls me to the side of the building and shoves me hard against the wall. I hit my head and feel my vision go in and out.

Don't pass out, don't pass out. Who knows what would happen if I did? I try to push him off, but he starts hitting my stomach hard, and I can't stop him. *Why is this happening to me? Why can I not catch a break? I don't understand. I just want to be left alone.*

When he goes to tear my pants down, I lose it.

This can't happen again. You are supposed to be stronger, Harley!

I scream as loud as my damaged voice allows, I scratch, hit, bite, kick, anything at all. I can feel my body protesting, but I refuse to be a victim. *Not again.* They all back off some when I don't stop. Asshole one says, "Shit, what the fuck is wrong with the bitch? She bit me. She's fucking feral. Let's leave her."

They move away some but then asshole two says, "I don't know, man, I like them a little crazy." He steps forward, and I kick him in the balls as hard as I can, then take off running.

I don't stop. I can't. Just keep running. Don't stop.

It hurts. I can't keep going, I'm just so tired. I need to stop. I can just lay down; I don't have to get back up.

No! I didn't make it this far for some assholes to stop me. I run and I run until... Oh. I don't know why I came here. I know I looked it up the other day to see how far it was, but I told myself I wouldn't do it. *He's a complete stranger, you idiot.*

I'm currenting staring up at the huge building that is the *SWEAT FACTORY.* I drop to the ground, my legs ready to give out. I don't even remember the run. My body was on autopilot to get away, and I couldn't stop or focus on anything around me.

But I need medical attention; I know I'm going to pass out soon.

Fuck! I pull the card out of my pocket, then slowly stand myself up, my legs shaking as I struggle to the door. As soon as I walk in limping, bloody, and bruised, all eyes turn to me. A huge guy comes running up to me, "Hey! Girl... what?" That's all I hear as everything fades to black.

When I wake, I don't recognize my surroundings and immediately start to freak out. When a hand lands on my shoulder, I scream.

Then the voice breaks through my panic, "Open your eyes, sweetie. It's okay, you're in the hospital, and I'm your nurse, Natasha. Open your eyes. Just do it slowly; it'll help the panic." Her voice helps bring me back, and I slowly blink my eyes open. She smiles at me. "Welcome back. You were out for about two hours. Do you remember what happened?"

I start to shake my head but then it all comes back to me. I gasp. Oh my god! Leaving the motel, the guys attacking me, running, the gym, then nothing...

Natasha looks at me with pity, and I fucking hate it. I don't want her pity. I need to get out of here. "Sweetie, there is a man here. He says he's a friend of yours, but we couldn't let him back since you were out and had no information or family here, but now it's your choice. His name is Lincoln."

I go to say I don't know him but the card, the guys at the store... I'm going to have to explain something to him. Maybe he can get me out of here.

I nod. "He can come back."

She smiles sweetly at me. "Okay, can you tell me your name so I can look you up?"

I freeze up. What do I do? Oh fuck, this is it. I fucked up and now I'll end up back with Tammy.

Natasha bends to look me in the eyes. "You need to breathe, sweetie, it's okay. Breathe for me. I'll get your friend and then maybe we can all talk."

I nod, hoping I can figure out what to do while she's gone. I try to practice the breathing Grayson showed me at school, but it isn't working. I close my eyes and picture his green ones and immediately I feel like I can breathe again. A few minutes later, the nurse comes back with Lincoln behind her; he seems worried but with no signs of pity, which calms my nerves a little. The nurse leaves us alone, saying she'll come back in a few minutes.

"I'm so glad you're awake. How are you? What hurts? Do you need the doctor?" His voice is calming but anxious.

I give him a small smile and say, "I think you need to sit, Lincoln. I'm okay, but I'm not sure you are." I didn't mean for that to be my reaction, and I worry he will get mad at me, but that worry instantly goes away when he chuckles, grabs a chair, and pulls it closer.

"I'm glad to see you awake and talking. I was so worried when they called me." I must be showing my confusion because he adds, "After you passed out, one of the guys I work with, Atlas, saw my card in your hand, so he called me, and I came straight here when he said he was going to bring you in."

I nod, not sure what else to say. I need to get out of here soon. They must not know I'm a minor yet, and I have no intentions of them finding out.

I look at Lincoln. "I think I'm fine. I should probably get going, though. You'll have to tell your friend, Atlas, thank you for me." I try to smile, but I know it's weak.

Lincoln narrows his eyes, and his lips pinch together.

Shit. I need to get out of here. I knew I shouldn't have showed up at the gym.

Before I can try to come up with something else to get him out of here so I can sneak out, he stands. "Actually, I have a friend who works here in the hospital. I want her to check you over and you can talk to her. Maybe she can help with whatever is going on. I'm really worried about you, kiddo."

I nod. "Okay that sounds great," I lie, hating it but knowing I have to get out of here.

He smiles and leaves the room and that's when I act. I jump up, holding in a whimper at the jolt of pain it sends through me. I find my clothes in a bag and throw them back on. I grimace when I realize there is dried blood on them.

Once I'm done, I quickly check the door. I don't see anyone right away, so I walk out slowly, then turn and look for a way to go. I see the exit sign and head towards it. Once I'm through the doors, I realize I have no idea where I am. I start walking through the parking lot when someone shouts to stop. I turn my head and see Lincoln looking panicked, running towards me.

Fuck! I have no idea what to do. So I freeze and just wait. This is going to be bad; he's going to hurt me for lying and running. *You should've known better.*

Once he catches up to me, I see a lady with dirty blonde long hair following a few feet behind him. She's the same height as me and in scrubs, so it must be his friend. She stops abruptly and gives me a confused glance over, her eyebrows scrunching as she examines me. Her bright sea-blue eyes are looking at me all over, specifically my hair and my face.

I don't like this. I want to run. What's the chance of me getting away if I just turn and run? Before I can even try, Lincoln steps closer, and I take a step back.

"Wait, I know something is going on, okay? Just let me help. If you don't want to be here, that's fine, but please let me help. It's just a gut feeling, okay? I can't just walk away this time. I knew I shouldn't have last time. Please don't run. I won't hurt you, and neither will Brielle." He points to his friend and continues talking, but I don't hear a single thing he says as I stare at her. She is staring back at me with a look of longing.

I cut off whatever Lincoln is saying, "Brielle?"

She nods, stepping towards me. "Yes, honey?"

I'm unable to get my brain to let out any words. There's no way... It's not the same person. I need to not get my hopes up. I don't know what to do. I feel like my tongue is stuck to the roof of my mouth. So I just blurt out, "Princess Brielle?"

Her face scrunches up. "I'm sorry, what?"

"Shit, oh fuck, shit. Sorry, I didn't mean to say that. Or cuss. Shit, this isn't going well." I take a deep breath, then blurt out, "You're Brielle? I don't think you're the actual person...There is no way my luck would turn around like that, but do you remember a Lilian Thomas? She's my mother and growing up she used to tell me stories of Princess Brielle, and I've been looking for her for a week now and haven't found her and she's literally my only hope for anything to get better in this shit storm of a life I've had so far.

"And I know it's stupid to hope or think some princess from childhood stories is real, but I had to try something to make my life better and now I'm spilling my guts to some random lady in a parking lot when not even two minutes ago I thought Lincoln was coming out here to fucking punish me for lying and taking off, but I forgot, or no scratch that, I didn't forget, I just really didn't know that not everyone is like that shitstain back home. Holy shit I'm losing it... And I just said all of that out loud. Fuck."

I'm about to try and figure out if I can outrun them or not when I hear a chuckle and look over to see Lincoln covering his mouth. Before I can question it, Brielle walks up to me and gently holds my shoulders. I flinch, and she immediately drops her hands.

"Honey, I know your momma. It's okay. Just breathe. I got you now."

Oh... This is happening. I can't believe this is real. I feel this huge weight come off my chest at the same time a huge wave of grief, pain, and sorrow comes over me and I feel like I haven't slept in years. I sag forward into her arms as the floodgates open and I cry. I cry for years of pain, for watching my mom die, for having no one to guide me through losing my best friend when I was only thirteen, for being alone at sixteen in a new state and trying to survive, for every single thing that has happened in the last three years.

I can't hold it all in anymore. I can't keep pretending that I'm strong and having fake courage. I shouldn't be taking comfort in a stranger who could possibly hurt me or be just as bad, if not worse than Tammy. But yet I can't bring myself to believe she is anything but the princess my mom said she was.

So instead of pulling it together, I wrap my arms around her and sob so hard I can hardly breathe. My chest is tight, and I feel everything going dark.

Before I let that darkness consume me, I whisper, "Please be real. Please be my princess. Mom said I didn't need anyone to save me, but I do. I really do."

Chapter Fifteen

Blade (Noah)

It's been a week since Harley took off. It doesn't look like she's been back at all, and from what the prospects we've had watching the Wilson's house have said, the Wilsons are searching for her.

The boys are angry. They wanted to protect her and help her. Normally those three don't give a shit about anyone but each other, me, and the club. So they must feel some kind of connection with her. I mean, I only saw a glimpse of her on the bus, and she's gorgeous, even covered in bruises. My fists clench thinking about how she looked that day.

I wish I wouldn't have been so distracted, otherwise I could've gotten to her. Who knows what's happening to her now? She could be dead for all we know. But we have Nerds searching for her, and we're keeping an eye on the Wilsons.

I'm at the bar waiting for it to hurry up and be 7 p.m. so we can have church. We filled everyone in last week on the situation, and they all agreed that we will extend our help to Harley if we find her. I haven't really been around to help with finding her. It's been a full week of working. The club owns all sorts of businesses, and we are still making them all legit after Rage's dad died and he took over.

I work mostly at our nightclub. I help keep watch over the dancers, and I am the main floor manager. I fill in for any job when needed, as well. When I'm not working there, I am the enforcer, so this week has been beat downs. Yep, I had to go hunt down some people who were trying to deal drugs at one of the diners we own. We no longer allow drugs to be sold on any club properties. It's been five years and you'd think they'd learn, but they don't. So I get called in to find them and teach them a lesson.

I like to switch it up a lot, so this week was some knife play... Let's just say they each have new bestie matching tattoos, honors of my trusty favorite knife. *Oh, and some broken ribs, but that wasn't the fun part.*

It's finally almost seven, so I head downstairs to the basement. When you get to the basement, you turn right into a wide hall. On the right are glass double doors that lead into a fairly large gym. Then as you keep going, on the left are three doors. The first a storage closet, then a full bathroom, and the third door is a locked safe room. At the end of the hall is another set of double doors. These are solid instead of glass.

A prospect stands outside the door to collect cell phones, as church is a no phone zone. We do it so there is no chance of someone recording or betraying us because everything the club does from money to businesses to illegal activities gets discussed inside this room. I hand my phone over to the prospect and head inside. The only electronic allowed in is Nerds's computer if he needs it.

Speaking of, almost everyone is in here except Nerds, which is unusual. He's always early. Rage comes in and looks around, seeing everyone here besides Nerds. He grunts and walks back out to the hall.

In church currently we have the ranking officers, Sugar, the Vice President, Axe, Road Capitan, Stone, Sergeant At Arms, me, the Enforcer and missing right now is Rage who is our President and Nerds, the Treasurer/Tech Guru. Then we have ten patched members as well. We also have three prospects right now, but they can't join church until they are patched in. They usually prospect for about a year depending on circumstances and either get patched in, which has to be a unanimous vote between members, or they get kicked out.

The room is a simple large rectangular room with not much to it. There is a long table in the center with enough seats for all of us. The club name is on the wall above the head of the table where Rage sits with Sugar to his right and Stone to his left. My spot is right next to Sugar. Axe sits next to Stone and Nerds sits at the other head of the table with a large TV screen behind him in case we need to look at anything. The rest of the table is full of the rest of our patched brothers.

All the ranking officers live here at the club. We have the second floor. I have extra rooms for Cade, Gray, and Ry since they are under my care. Prospects also live on the property since they are basically our bitches while prospecting. They have a small house out behind the club that they live in together. Some other members live in empty rooms or live close by somewhere.

Club sluts have shared rooms they can use if they choose to stay here full-time. They are here for the guys to use whenever and have to clean and help with upkeep if they want to live here and eat here. It's completely by choice.

No one has been forced here, not since Rage's dad died. He ran things differently. Let's just say that I wasn't going to prospect at eighteen if he hadn't died when he did.

Rage finally comes back in with an exhausted-looking Nerds in tow. Of course, he has his laptop in hand. He plops down in his spot, and Rage calls the meeting to begin.

We discuss the businesses and how they are doing financially. Everything has been on the up and up lately, so there have been no worries there. Rage asks if I got the drug dealers dealt with, and I smirk. "Of course, boss man. Who do you think I am? Stone? I get my shit done."

What can I say? I like stirring the pot. It keeps shit interesting.

Rage sighs, knowing I am pissing Stone off on purpose since it's so easy to do.

"Listen here, you little shit, I can take you on any day. I have eight years on you, kid. Don't fucking push me. I get my shit done."

I smile and go to mess him some more but before I can, Sugar who is sitting next to me slaps a hand over my mouth. "Don't.

Knock it off, Blade. I swear, one of these days I'm gonna cut your fuckin' tongue out. All you ever do is run your goddamn mouth."

I smirk behind his hand and then stick my tongue out, licking it.

He yanks his hand away and wipes it off. "What the fuck! You fuckin' shitstain! Why did you do that?" The room roars with laughter as they realize what I did.

I smile at Sugar and say, "What? You wanted to cut my tongue off. I was showing you why you shouldn't. I'm skilled with my tongue, Sugar. Just ask the ladies, they'll tell ya."

Axe yells out, "Why not just show him, Blade?"

Before anyone can say more, Rage slams his hand on the table. "Alright, enough! Focus! We have more to discuss." At that, everyone sobers up to continue on.

"Alright moving on from our normal club business, Nerds, anything new on Harley or the Wilsons?"

"Yeah, so far I got nothing on the girl. I can't find shit, and it's really pissing me off. She just doesn't exist before the last few years. Makes no goddamn sense. But I have her name tagged so if she does anything using her name, I'll be notified. Opening an account, getting a license, signing up for social media... Anything."

He sighs and then types on his computer again before speaking.

"As for the Wilsons, I've been making a list of all the high buyers they sell to. I have their names, addresses, bank information, who they bought, and for how much. I'm getting as much proof as I can. None of these people were very smart with this shit. The only thing proving to be hard is connecting Tammy and Richard to those sales. Also, your name on the offshore account that funds everything. I'm not sure how to approach that one. If we cut it off, then they are likely to either go underground or find a different way to fund things and we lose a big piece of our evidence," Nerds says.

"If we just want to take the Wilsons out ourselves, why does that matter? Remove his name, take them out, and then hand over all the buyers' information to the cops. Let them do the rest," Axe says with a shrug. It's not a bad idea, but I have a feeling Nerds has already thought that one through.

Nerds frowns. "Right, but we don't know what else is set up and where. Are there more accounts leading back to the club? Who else is involved? We know Rage's dad was one of the founders of this shit, but who else was? Who else is still involved? There's too many what ifs and questions I don't have the answers to yet. We can't have heat come back on us for this."

I look over at Rage. "What about Rob, Tammy and Richard's son? Where is he? Were you able to get a hold of him?"

Rage nods. "Yeah, Rob said he doesn't have much to do with his parents. He stays away as much as he can, and he also said he doesn't know Harley. That his mom most definitely didn't have another kid besides him and Tabby. So he doesn't know who she is and as bad as he feels for her, he wants nothing to do with them and is refusing to help us. I get it; he got away and is going to school to be a doctor. I'd want nothing of this life either.

"He did warn me that Tabby is a force to be reckoned with and can manipulate her way through anything. She's also a good liar and loves helping 'Mommy and Daddy,'" he says with air quotes. "So be cautious and if she's around, avoid her. Don't even try to get anything out of her. They'll most likely use her to go get any information they can on us."

"So basically, if you run into Tabby, run," Axe says.

Rage and everyone else nods their agreement. Well, this all kind of sucks.

"So where does that leave us? What's next? We can't have Tammy and Richard selling people under our noses in our town. Also, what about Harley? I have three teens out there waiting for me to come give them news over the girl they are obsessed with. I've managed to keep them tamed and in school all week, but that'll only last so long." I shudder dramatically, and the guys chuckle.

"As for the Wilsons, we keep doing what we are doing. Prospects on watch, Nerds keep digging, recruit anyone you want that has spare time to help you. I might be able to reach out to some other chapters that will have our backs and could lend a hand on how to handle this. As much as I just want to take them out, I know we can't. So we just keep playing it the way we have. Everyone in agreement?"

Most everyone nods. Some more hesitant to because none of us truly want to just sit and wait with this.

"Okay, good. As for Harley." Rage looks at me. "I don't really know what more we can do, brother. Maybe her taking off was a good thing. Maybe she found somewhere to hide from them if they were as bad as we are thinking they are. I still want answers. I want to know how this kid was under our noses and no one noticed. My father did a lot of sketchy shit, shit he never even brought to this table, which is a crime against the club. So he could have been involved with something with this girl. I mean, it is odd that she shows up two years after he dies. But then no one sees her for three years, until she randomly starts at the school. So yeah, I want answers, but we really can't do much with it right now. Just gotta keep our heads low so we don't draw attention to what we are looking into."

I sigh. "I get it, but it's frustrating. I saw her on that bus. Her face was all messed up, and she had bruises and marks on what I could see of her neck. I just wish I could've caught up to her and been able to talk to her or follow to make sure she was safe. Something about it all really bothers me."

"Speaking of that day, any new information on the crash?" Sugar asks.

Nerds pipes up before anyone else can, "I looked into that. All cameras around that area were cut. It's one of the reasons I lost Harley on the bus she took. They cut everything around that area so there would be no chance of seeing what happened or who could've been involved. There is nothing I can do about it. Also, the cops have not been looking into it at all. I've been keeping an eye on their system. The crash site was cleaned up and then nothing happened with it. I found the truck on a different street cam before the accident and got its plates. It was stolen, though, so that didn't get me anywhere."

Rage nods. "Alright, I know we've already been on the buddy system all week, but it needs to continue. I don't know what happened or how they knew Blade would be there at that time, so until we do, be careful, and make sure no club business goes beyond this room. Prospects are now on a need-to-know basis until we figure this out. I don't like not having answers, and right now, shit is a clusterfuck."

Holy shit. He thinks we have a mole. Before I can voice this, Stone does, which is shocking. He doesn't like to talk a lot unless you make him angry; then he goes off. "Mole?" he seethes.

Rage shrugs. "No idea, brother, but I'd rather be safe than sorry. So we deal with the buddy system for now. Blade, that extends to the boys. They are known around here as a part of the club, so I want them being careful as well."

I nod. As we wrap up church, I can't stop thinking about the accident. Well, maybe not accident. How the fuck would they have known I was going to be there? The only people that knew where I was going were all the club brothers who were out helping look for Harley. When Connor texted that he found her, he sent it to the club group chat so everyone knew they could stop looking.

But who would do that? And why? Seriously, if I don't find some answers soon, I am going to go on a rampage. This is such bullshit. I have three boys I have to protect and right now, like Rage said, shit is a clusterfuck.

After we make sure nothing else needs to be brought to the table, Rage dismisses everyone and I sigh, preparing myself to head upstairs where I am sure the boys are waiting for me.

Just like I thought...They are all right there waiting like eager little puppies.

Vicious puppies.

CAYDEN

My brothers and I are sitting around waiting for Noah to come out of church and fill us in. Gray and Ry are talking away like they always do, and I sit here quietly just listening. I hate talking. Talking is bullshit, and people waste too much time doing it. I love my brother Noah for getting that I don't want to talk. And my chosen brothers, Ry and Gray, understand too, which is nice. It makes it less lonely. But I still won't talk a lot.

Unless it comes to a certain redhead with hazel eyes. Fuck. She's perfect. I still remember the first time I saw her; I was in the office trying to get that bitch office TA to just get me the information I needed to take home for Noah to sign, but she kept batting those fake ass lashes at me and trying to get me to talk to her. I was tense and trying really hard not to lash out at her, but the bitch wouldn't take a hint. Until someone walked in behind me. I saw the TA's eyes go to the person behind me and narrow like she was annoyed and disgusted.

I had stepped to the side of the counter so I could see better because I do not like people coming up behind me that I don't know. When I looked back, the most gorgeous girl I had ever seen stood there. I was trapped staring at her, like my eyes could not move away from her. She was tiny, too tiny, and clearly needed to eat more. She had long, wavy red hair, high cheekbones, and bright, large hazel eyes that locked me in place the second she looked at me.

But she looked away when she realized she was staring into my eyes. Her lips were perfect and full and for the first time in my life, I wanted to willingly talk to someone, touch them, hold them, know everything about them.

I had to clench my fists to keep from touching her. I looked over the scar on her face; it didn't take away from her beauty whatsoever, but something inside of me wanted to know what happened, and if someone had hurt her, I wanted to hurt them.

My reaction to her had stunned me.

I had taken a few steps back to lean against the wall by the door and just watch. I felt like I was crazy for feeling so much so instantly for some chick. I couldn't stop watching her the whole time she was standing there. I could tell her clothes were old and didn't fit her properly and she looked skittish. Everything I noticed just made me want to know her even more. The only problem being, I found out later on how attached Ry was to her already, and Gray, even though he wouldn't admit it. So I knew

I had to keep my distance. I'd never mess up a chance at Ry or Gray being happy.

When I had come out of my daze of staring at her, I realized the TA had been a complete bitch to her, all because she couldn't talk. Such bullshit. I waited for the redhead to leave and before I followed her to stalk her around the school, I had stepped back up to the counter and let the TA bitch see my fury.

"Give me the fucking paper I need." She scrambled to grab it and when she brought it back to hand it to me, I latched onto her wrist. "You ever treat that girl like that again, I won't hesitate to kill you." I then snatched the paper from her and walked out, a small smile coming over my face as I heard her gasp and then cry behind me. Perfect. Then I went on to find my redheaded goddess to watch.

I come out of my thoughts from that day when we hear loud footsteps and voices coming up the stairs down the hall as all the guys come up and head out into the main room. We all look up, waiting for Noah to come out and talk to us. He walks out, sees us, and immediately sighs. I tense, knowing that's not a good thing.

He nods his head towards the hall with the offices, and we all follow him down to the office he uses often. We sit and wait. I can feel the tension coming off of Ry and Gray, just like it is me, as we wait for him to spit it out. I hate waiting; he better hurry the fuck up.

"Nothing new, boys. We just have to keep at what we are doing. I know that isn't what you want to hear, but it's all we got. Maybe talk to Lex at school and see if she knows anything. But other than that, I need you guys to keep laying low and showing up at school. I know it's frustrating, but we need to keep a low profile while we get information on the Wilsons and what they are doing. We don't have everything we need yet, and that's also slow going. I know you guys are going to be pissed, but I need you to understand where I'm coming from."

Gray nods and then speaks up before Ry can blow, "We do understand." He glares at Ry. "Is there really nothing we can do? We want to find Harley. There's got to be something else we can try that is still staying low."

Before Noah can say anything, Rage comes through the door and speaks up, "You're right. I know you boys won't let this go. So, Gray, you can work with Nerds whenever you aren't in school. Ry, I want you to stay close to Stone since he can tame you the best. You can help him outside of school and maybe you guys can travel to other towns and ask around at clubs to keep an eye out for her. But we have no pictures of her, so that'll be hard. Cade, you can work with Blade. Hopefully that'll keep you guys busy and still trying to find her without having you guys lose your shit on me and ruin any plans we may have."

We all nod, but Ry is clenching his fists. He's not happy about this. "I don't like this one bit. I want to go hunt her down and drag her back here. But I guess I get it and for now I'll behave."

I see the glint in his eyes; he is thinking of doing something stupid. I look over at Gray and see that he notices it too. Shit. Ry is up to something, and that is never good. Gray and I will have to corner him to get him to spill so we can help him, otherwise he'll do whatever his insane plan is alone. Fucking hell.

I need a release, so I whistle for Bear, my great Dane, and we take off outside to run the perimeter of the property. I've had Bear since I was twelve. He was my mom's dog. Bear was her best friend, and I can tell that Bear misses her every day, so I do everything I can to make him happy for mom. She may be a bitch for leaving us, but she's still my mom, and I get it.

I'd have run from dad if I could have too, but then again, I probably would've taken those most important to me with me.

I let those thoughts go because I am not out here running to go down memory lane. That would be a waste of time. I focus on running and letting the burn in my muscles give me a sense of calm, and the quiet air brings me solace. With Bear at my side, I feel like I could run for years.

CHAPTER SIXTEEN

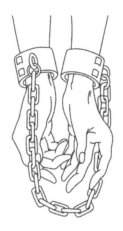

HARLEY

When I wake up, everything is foggy. I'm trying to remember everything that happened, and when it comes rushing back, I jolt up on... on the bed I'm on? Oh. I glance at the window, seeing it's definitely daytime based on the light beaming through the curtains.

I look around the room, finding it's simple. White walls, a big window to the left of the bed with a window seat that has blankets and pillows on it. There's a black bookcase with books on each side of the window, a black bedroom set that has a big bed frame with a headboard, two nightstands, and a long dresser directly across from the bed. The bed has light baby blue sheets and a light gray comforter, which I'm currently tucked under. The door is on the right of the bed with a closet along the same wall.

I don't know where I am, but it's a nice room. Before I have a chance to move or do anything, the door opens slowly, and I tense up before I see it's just Brielle coming in.

"Oh good, hun, you're up." She smiles kindly at me and sits at the foot of the bed.

I scoot up towards the headboard, leaving as much space between us as I can, not sure how this is going to go. I mentally prepare myself for a beating or hateful words thrown at me.

"I never got your name at the hospital. What is it?"

Part of me wants to lie and give a fake name, but I know that wouldn't do any good in the future, so I tell her, "Harley."

Her lips tilt up a fraction and she nods. "How are you feeling?"

Wait, what? "I'm... I think I'm okay... Um... Where are we?" I ask hesitantly.

She looks at me with such kindness that it sends a jolt through me. "We are at my home. Lincoln thought it was best to just bring you here because we don't fully know what's going on yet, and he thought the hospital was making you uncomfortable."

The first thing that registers is we are in her home. Princess Brielle's home. *I really need to stop calling her that.* Wait... I fly out of the bed, my body disapproving of the fast movement, and go to the window, but I don't see any water. I sigh in defeat.

Brielle must understand because she says, "The best view is at the back of the house. Would you like to come downstairs and see and maybe we can talk?"

I nod frantically, following her out the door and almost forgetting that I don't truly know her and need to be careful. She laughs lightly at my eagerness to follow her.

We head downstairs through the beautiful house we are in. It looks to be two stories from what I can see. Everything is open and bright. There are large windows on almost every wall. It's all white with oak and feels extremely peaceful. We don't walk through the whole house. Instead, we take a huge staircase down, and as I look over the banister, I can see her large open living room with a big fireplace to the right and straight ahead are floor-to-ceiling windows. They go from the ground floor all the way up the wall to the second floor.

It's beautiful. I can see the ocean before we are even downstairs. When we reach the living room, she walks up to the huge windows and starts pushing them open so they open up like giant doors and make the living room have full access to the outside.

My eyes widen at what I see: the beach. I can't believe I'm seeing it for the first time ever. Without thinking about what I'm doing, I take off running out the doors onto the large deck that appears to wrap around her entire home. I head down the stairs at the end of the deck and immediately hit the sand. It's chilly with the sea breeze, but I love it. I keep walking straight out towards the water. When I get close, I plop down on my butt and push my toes into the sand.

I allow a few tears to fall and breathe deeply, letting a small smile grace my lips. *I'm here, Mom. I really hope you were right about Brielle being a princess.* I never thought this day would come.

I feel the sand on my feet and running between my toes. It's peaceful. It brings me a sense of comfort I haven't felt in a long time. But it doesn't last.

The heartache that I'm experiencing this without my mom is so strong that I feel like my heart is being shattered into a billion pieces, and it makes it hard for me to breathe.

Brielle sits down next to me and drapes a blanket over my shoulders. I wrap it around myself tightly and silently cry. She doesn't say anything; she just sits with me until the tears subside.

She blows out a breath like she knows what I'm going to say when she asks her next question, "Hun, where is your mom?"

I blink, once, twice, three times. Then I turn my head and look at her. "She's dead," I say in a monotone voice. Having never been able to speak the words out loud to another person, I find it almost painful to do so now.

Brielle blinks away some tears and sniffles. "I'm so sorry, honey. I can't imagine what you're going through. But I need to know what happened. Why are you here?"

I want to lash out at her, I want to scream at her with all these emotions swarming inside me, but I stop myself knowing that none of this is on her, and she seems to genuinely care about my mom and maybe even me. "Mom died three years ago. I've been living my own personal hell since then. I have finally escaped and now, well, I am so lost and confused. I don't really understand anything." Unable to hold back anymore, I stand and walk back inside and follow the same path back up the bedroom.

Expecting some kind of punishment for how I just acted but not seeming to care enough to do anything about it, I get in the bed, curl up, and bawl my eyes out until I fall into a fitful sleep.

When I wake up later, it's dark outside, but there is a lamp on in here and I see Brielle sitting in the window seat staring outside, an open book resting across her legs.

I slowly sit up, rubbing the sleep from my eyes. "Brielle?" I say groggily. My throat is still tender from the abuse it's taken, so it burns slightly, especially from not having drank any water recently.

She looks over at me and gives me a soft look: content yet sad. I can see her eyes are red as if she's been crying.

"Hey, hun, was your nap okay?" I nod, uncertain why she keeps being so nice when I have done multiple things that normally would get me beat. "Good, I know things are hard right now," she says as she gets up and comes over to the bed and takes a seat. "But I need to know some things, okay?"

I nod again, not sure what to say, trying not to tense up while I wait for whatever backlash is going to come now.

"Okay, I did some math in my head and when I saw your mama last she was pregnant with you. Hun, you're only sixteen or seventeen. I need to know what happened so I know who to call."

Immediate panic builds up in me, and before I can think of the consequences, I shout, "NO! No, no," I say each one calmer than the last, trying to force myself to calm down. "I... I don't want to explain everything right now, but who I was put with after my mom died... it's been bad. I can't go back there. If you try to make me, I'll run. I came here because my mom used to tell me stories about you, and I just thought maybe you could help me. But I can go; you don't have to worry, I can be on my way," I rush out to say, realizing I might have made a huge mistake.

I move to stand, but she grabs my hand. I flinch hard and bite the inside of my cheek to keep the yelp from coming out. She lets go right away and pulls her hands up, showing she won't harm me.

"No, hun, wait. I don't mean that you have to go, and you are always welcome here. Let's just take a breath, okay? No calling anyone, but I will need you to talk to me soon. I'll give you a few days so you can see that you can trust me. I helped your mama out of some bad things. I will always be here for you too." She sniffles and quickly wipes under her eyes. "Sorry, I'll let you rest. The house is open to you. You are welcome anywhere and can help yourself to anything in the kitchen. The bathroom is right across the hall. Where were you staying before here?"

I tell her the motel name, and her eyes go wide with shock.

"Oh my. Well, give me the key and I'll ask Lincoln to go over and get your things and return the key."

I nod and hand it over, not really wanting to let someone else go get my things, but I've done and said enough. I don't want to push it and risk her getting mad. She leaves the room and tells me to rest as much as I'd like and let her know if I need anything.

She wants me to tell her everything, and I don't think I can do that. I head to the bathroom and take a really long, hot shower.

I feel like my mind is closing off. Like walls are building so high that I can't see over them. It's like every emotion I've hid or buried over the last few years wants to come out. I can't handle that, so up the walls go. I go back to my room. I should go eat since it's been a while, but the thought of food right now makes me want to puke.

So instead, I curl up on the bed and stare out the window until the sun rises the next day.

Then, I don't move. I stay curled up staring at the window. I don't know how long I stay. I eventually get up to go pee, and Brielle tries to get me to go downstairs and eat, but I tell her I'm not hungry and go get back in bed. It's just so comfy; who would want to leave it?

I saw Lincoln once. He came in and sat with me, but his pitying looks were too much, and I lashed out at him. I didn't mean to, but when I looked at him and saw his sad, sympathetic eyes, I started screaming at him that I didn't need his pity. I don't make eye contact with anyone now. I don't want to see the looks of sorrow and understanding from anyone. They will never get it.

Brielle comes in and checks on me a lot. She brings me food and tries to get me to eat, or come out, or just talk. She comes in and talks about her life sometimes. Working as a nurse, what she likes to do, her friendship with Lincoln, who goes by Linc, and her friendship with two other guys, Atlas and Ryan.

I listen to it all but don't move or respond. I get up and go to the bathroom to pee. When I'm done, I turn around and dry heave into the toilet.

I feel hands pull my hair back. "Honey, you need to eat something. Please, just crackers at least, okay? Please, I need you to try." I can hear her voice breaking, and I know she has tears in her eyes.

I nod just so she'll stop and leave me alone. She exhales and then gets up and leaves. I go climb back in bed and a few minutes later, she comes in with water and crackers. I drink and eat, but it feels like sandpaper in my throat as it goes down. She smiles weakly at me, and I quickly look away.

"Maybe a shower? That might make you feel better. It's been three days now that you've been in here. Maybe we should go walk the beach?"

I finally look into her eyes and rasp, "I don't want to go to the beach. I don't want to go to a place my mom loved that now she can't love. I don't want to do anything. I've fought for three years and now that I don't need to, I'm wondering why I ever did to begin with. I should've given up a long time ago. It would've been easier on everyone. I don't know what to do now. Nor do I want to do a damn thing." I spit out the last word.

I know I'm hurting her; I can see it on her face. She doesn't know what to do or how to help. *Guess what? Me fucking either.*

She stands. "I'll give you some space. Come down when you're ready." She smiles sadly and leaves.

I curl back up on the bed and stare out the window. I feel hollow; I have no tears. Nothing to let out. I'm just an empty shell wondering why I fought so hard to get away in the first place.

BRIELLE

I walk out of her room and slowly pull her door closed. I lean against the wall next to her door and let silent tears fall down my face. How do I help her? I've never felt so helpless. *I'm so sorry, Lil, I'm failing you.* I can't help but let the thought in. I'm failing her. Lilian would never let her daughter end up like this. It's been days and she hasn't left the bed unless it's to use the bathroom.

Linc comes up the stairs and sees me. He looks at me like he can read every feeling and thought I'm having, and he probably can by now. He's been my friend for ten years. He comes over, scoops me up bridal style, and carries me downstairs. I'd usually protest being manhandled, but right now, I need his comfort.

We get downstairs, and he sets me on the couch and plops down next to me. I look over at him. "What do I do, Linc? That girl is... she's broken, and I don't say that lightly. Lilian thought she was broken, but she wasn't. But Harley? She's shattered. There is no life in her eyes, Linc. I can't even imagine what she has been through. I want to know. But I can't force her to talk, and I can't get her help when we don't know if she's in danger."

Linc sighs, "I know, Bri, I get it. I think we should give her some more time. I just... I think whatever happened to her, she's kept it all bottled up and has been alone for who knows how long. It seems that you may be the first person that brought her any form of safety, allowing her to let those walls down. You've told me about Lilian, and I think she'd be proud of you and so glad that her little girl found you. Based on just what Harley said about her mom telling her stories, you were important to her."

I feel tears trickling down my face. "I can't believe she's gone, I always thought when she had to leave here that everything would get better. I did everything I could to help her. She was so scared, Linc, but she never ever thought to do anything but fight for the little one she was growing. I just don't know how to get Harley to see she has the same fight. She just doesn't know it."

"She was fighting for the baby, Bri. She had something she knew she had to protect, and she was willing to do anything for Harley. Harley gave Lilian a reason to fight." He sighs, "Harley needs to find it in her to want to get better. To know that life isn't always this hard. She needs you to hold her hand and not give up on her, because I think she is waiting for the other shoe to drop or you to turn your back on her. Someone has done a number on that girl, but she is not shattered, Bri, she is broken and needs to put her pieces back together. I will keep coming by too and show her she has more than one person here. Hopefully sometime soon she'll trust us enough to open up so we can help, and she can truly see she is not alone now."

He looks at me like he knows I'll hate what he says next. "Well, if we really need to, we can always let Atlas come talk to her." My eyes go wide, and he laughs. "I'm kidding... For now. He may be a scary son of a bitch, but he means well. You know he'd help in a heartbeat. But I won't push it... Yet."

I roll my eyes. Atlas is terrifying. He can be brutal and mean, but he does mean well. He helped me through a rough time about five years ago. He was not nice, to put it lightly, but he helped me look at things with a new perspective. I'll be forever grateful to him. I hope we don't need his help with Harley, and she'll come out of this and let Linc and I help. Unfortunately, things don't always go the easy way.

Two weeks later

I'm exhausted. Between trying to work a few days a week and worrying about Harley, I feel like I'm barely holding it together. I'm getting more worried.

One, because I need to know what happened. What if someone comes looking for her? She's a minor, and me not reporting that I have her is illegal. And two, it's been eighteen days total since she stepped foot out the door to run down the beach. I'm at a loss for what to do.

Linc comes over and tries to help, but we can't get through to her. She eats maybe once a day when I refuse to leave the room until she eats, and I know she's only eating something so I'll leave.

The girl was already skin and bones when she got here, and now it's not getting any better. I'm debating stealing an IV kit from work to get some fluids in her before things get even worse.

Lost in thought, the front door slamming makes me jump and almost spill my coffee. A few seconds later, Linc and Atlas come into the room.

Atlas whistles. "Damn, Bri, you look like shit."

Linc slaps him on the back of the head and shakes his head at him. "Don't say that shit, dude." He looks at me. "You look fine. But I'm assuming nothing is better?" His expression darkens when I shake my head.

Atlas runs a hand through his hair. "Alright, let me talk to her. She needs to move and eat. And you,"—he points a finger at me—"need to see a change so you can sleep and not be so worried. This is wearing on you, and it's not okay."

I shake my head. "Atlas, this isn't her fault. It's whoever did this to her and—"

"You're right. It's whoever did this to her. They are a piece of shit who doesn't deserve to breathe. But, Bri, she is letting them win. She's letting what happened to her, what they did, keep her in a bad place. She is showing them that they won, and she could be destroyed, and from what you've told us about Lilian, that girl is not weak. If she is even half like her mother, then there is fight in her. So let me find it. Go with Linc. Go down to the beach so you're still close, but go, because this isn't going to be pretty, and you don't need to be here to listen or coddle her."

I sigh and glance up the stairs. *Lil, if you're here, if you're listening, please give your daughter strength. I'm trying to do right by you. Please don't hate me.* "Come on, sweet girl, let's go walk the beach," Linc says as he throws an arm around my shoulder and guides me outside.

We soon reach the sparkling blue water and Linc stops walking. He turns so he is standing in front of me and cups my cheeks, bending down so he is eye level with me.

"You need to breathe, Brielle." He inhales, and I follow, exhaling when he does. I feel tears form in my eyes. "There you go. I know this is hard, and it was sprung on you out of nowhere, but she wouldn't have shown up here if this wasn't something that you needed as much as she did. Lilian leaving has always bothered you. This is your chance to mend that part of your heart and gain Harley as a permanent part of your life."

I let my tears fall silently, and Linc wipes them away with his thumbs.

"I'm scared, Linc." I whisper. He opens his mouth to speak, but I shake my head, stopping him. "I know I'll be okay and can do this because I have you, Atlas, and Ryan. But Harley... I think you're right that everything has been bottled up. That scares me. What happens when these walls she's built do come down? What if I'm not enough to help her through this? I'm terrified that she'll be so angry that she does stupid things or... or worse." My voice cracks.

I can't even say it. I've seen people come into the ER and have to put on a watch. It's scary, and my heart breaks for them. I have no idea what Harley has been through and what is going to happen, and that alone is petrifying.

Chapter Seventeen

Atlas

I steel myself for whatever I am going to be walking into. I know from experience that sometimes hurt people will lash out at you before things get better, so I prepare myself for it. Bri has filled me in on as much as she knows. I sympathize with Harley, but unfortunately, enough is enough.

I tap on her door lightly, then push it open slowly. She is curled up in the middle of her bed, facing the window.

"If you're coming to give me more pitying looks then just go away," she mutters, her voice muffled by the blanket pulled partially over her face.

I clear my throat, and her head whips towards me. I walk in and lean against the dresser facing the bed, crossing my arms over my chest. "If you don't want looks of pity then stop being pathetic enough to get them. From my perspective, you want the pity. Otherwise, you wouldn't be doing this shit." I gesture towards where she lays on the bed.

The look she gives me, it's pure fire, like a lit match behind her eyes, and it's burning hot now. Ah, there she is. Now to keep that fire. I smirk at her.

HARLEY

Who the hell does he think he is? He doesn't know me. I've heard Brielle and Linc talk about him and how close the three of them are, but that doesn't give him the right to speak to me like that.

I clear my throat, it being scratchy from the burning it has gone through and from not talking much the last two weeks. "Atlas, right? Why the fuck are you here? And who gave you the right to say that shit to me?"

The smirk on his face grows, and I feel like I could growl at him. He's really pissing me off.

Pathetic? I am not pathetic! I have been through hell. He has no idea the torment my own mind has put me through these last few weeks.

His smirk grows into a full-blown smile. "There she is; let it out. That anger you're feeling right now? Let it out. Release it. You won't hurt my feelings, Harley. But if you don't let it all out and find a way to live, then you *will* hurt Brielle."

I stare at him. This guy cannot be serious. He what? Wants me to yell at him? I'm not going to do that! He doesn't get that I can't risk him or anyone else turning on me and hurting me again. I wouldn't survive it again.

I feel myself shutting down again but before I fully can, Atlas stands to his full height and looks down at me. "Don't. Don't shut down again. You are letting those who have hurt you win. You are not living life anymore. What's the plan, Harley? Just stay in this bed forever? Let yourself slowly wither away? Bri has told me about your mom. How strong she was, how hard she fought to not let anyone else take anything from her. She fought for you, Harley. She battled for you. Don't disappoint her by refusing to do the same."

Before he can get another word out, I fly out of the bed, my body aching from the movement, but I don't care. I let the pain fuel me.

"Don't you dare!" I scream at him. I start pacing the room, "You have no idea what it's been like. What I've had to see and go through." I point at him. "You. Don't. Know," I seethe.

"You're right, I don't, so why don't you tell me? Why don't you tell any of us so we can help you? Why don't you stop pitying yourself and do something instead of letting those that have hurt you win?" he snaps at me.

Oh my god, who does this guy think he is? I'll admit, I've lost my way. But he has no right to say shit. He doesn't even know me! And right now, all I want to do is hit him. I want to hurt him because he is hurting me by making these walls come down. I don't want to hurt. I can't hurt like that again. I can't live through it alone. If I let my walls down, I don't know what will come out. I can't put Bri through the pain of my story. I can't even relive it myself. If I truly let my walls down, my emotions and raw heartbreak will kill me.

The next thing I know, he is kneeling on the floor in front of me. *When did I end up on the floor?*

"I know, Harley. If you really want to, you can hit me. I'll take it. Let me have it." *Oh, I said all that out loud.* "Let the pain, the grief, and everything you feel out on me. I can handle it. What I can't handle is you hurting yourself and in turn hurting Bri. She is my family, which makes you my family. Let us help. You aren't doing this alone anymore. We may not know what happened to you, and maybe you can't believe that people would be on your side, but you didn't get here for it turn out to be nothing. You fought your way here because deep down, you knew that you could trust Bri."

I'm already shaking my head before he even finishes talking. "No. I don't. I can't... this isn't... just no. You don't get it. You can't help me. They broke me!" I sob. God, why am I crying? I don't want to cry anymore. I don't want any of this. Why can't he just let me stay in the comfort of my bed where I don't have to feel these things?

"Harley, they couldn't have broken you if you got away. You got out. You left. You left as a goddamn child and survived on your own. Those are not things a broken girl does. But right now? Right now, you are letting them break you, and they aren't even

227

here. You need to fuel all your emotions into something. Find something that'll make you feel better. Fuel it all there. But at the same time, you have to talk about it." He stands up. "I'm going to go downstairs now. Come down when you decide to pull your head out of your ass. There isn't much more I can do now. I can help, but you have to get your ass down those stairs and tell me you want it."

He walks out, slamming the door behind him, and I scream. I scream as loud as my scratchy throat allows me.

His words replay in my brain.

"Stop being pathetic to get their pity."

"From my perspective, you want the pity."

"You will hurt Brielle."

"Don't disappoint her by refusing to do the same."

"Stop pitying yourself."

"You are letting them break you, and they aren't even here."

"Find something that'll make you feel better."

Oh, I know just the thing that'll make me feel better, I think as I get up and storm to the door, flinging it open so hard it hits the wall before I go storming down the stairs in search of the one thing that'll make me feel oh so much better. I have always told myself that I would never resort to violence like Tammy did, but right now I feel like I can't control this rage burning in me. *Maybe I'm no better than her.*

I find Brielle in the kitchen stirring something in a pot. She looks up when she hears me stomping through, and her eyes go wide with shock before she smiles. "Honey—"

"Where is he?" I grit out, trying not to aim my anger at her. She doesn't deserve it.

She looks confused for a minute before worry comes over her face. "Harley, I just want you to be okay. I'm sorry if he overstepped, I just—"

I shake my head. "Stop. It's not your fault. Just tell me where he is so I can talk to him."

Before she can answer, a deep voice speaks from behind me. "Right here, Harley. Glad to see you came down. Are you ready to talk?"

I turn around and look at him. He's standing at the entrance to the kitchen from the living room, and Linc is a few feet behind him.

I walk towards him, letting him see the anger in my eyes. "Oh, I'm ready for something," I sneer. When I get up to him, I slap him as hard as my weak muscles can manage. His head barely turns from the impact. I hear a gasp behind me, but all my focus is on the asshole in front of me. "You know, I should feel bad for hitting someone, especially after everything I've been through, but I really can't feel bad after all the shit you said. You don't know me. You had no right. NONE!"

He smirks at me. Fucking smirks. "I'll make you a deal. Start eating and getting healthier, and when Brielle says it's okay, you can come to the gym, and I'll teach you to spar." I'm ready to hit him again or hell, maybe kick him in the balls. That should knock him down a peg or two.

But before I can, Linc strolls up and steps in front of me. "Alright, little fighter, let's calm down now. Why don't you come sit and we'll eat and talk, okay?"

I feel my emotions start to calm down under Linc's soft gaze. But when I glance over his shoulder towards Atlas and see him still smirking right at me, my anger pulses. Turning sharply, I stomp towards the table as hard as my weakened legs allow. I take a deep breath to try and calm myself down. I drop my head, realizing what a complete ass I've been and that they might kick me out or punish me.

What the hell have I been thinking? I feel like I am going crazy with how up and down my emotions seem to be lately.

We sit down and a few minutes later, Brielle and Atlas follow suit. I know I need to apologize to them, so I take a breath and decide to get it over with now.

"Brielle, I'm so sorry. I can't explain to you how sorry I am for all this trouble. But I'm beyond grateful to you for letting me fall apart in your home and not giving up on me. I know you don't have any answers, but you were still there for me, and it meant a lot even when it didn't seem like it. I didn't mean to fall apart like that, but it was like I found you and finally, after three long years, I had a break and could let myself feel. But at the same time, the feelings were too much, so I built my walls so high I couldn't see over them to do anything." I blurt everything out, hoping that the truth will lessen whatever comes next.

"It's okay, honey, it really is. I just want you to be safe and okay. If you need to break down, this will always be a safe space for you.

I know this isn't easy, and I'm sorry to bring it up, but we have to start talking about things. I need to know what happened." She sighs and looks pained before she adds, "Honey, the only thing I can find on your mom's death is that it was an electrical fire. Can you... Could you tell me what happened?"

I slowly nod, not having expected her to just move past everything that I've done wrong. But I need to try and learn that they may not be bad.

I can try. I guess that means starting with the worst day of my life.

Taking a few deep breaths, I allow myself to go back to that day. Back to the day my mom was brutally taken from me, and I open myself up to Brielle. It's like I know somewhere deep inside me that I can trust her, which is the only reason the words come out of my mouth while I let the tears fall for my mom, who I never got to grieve for.

3 years ago - August 18th, 2015

Mom and I spent the long weekend going school clothes shopping before school starts in two weeks. I can't believe I'm going into 7th grade. I'm a middle schooler now. I've been homeschooled for many years, but Mom is letting me go to school now this year.

I get up this morning and run to my mom's room to wake her up like I normally do, but she isn't in her bed. Weird. She didn't even make her bed, and she always makes it. I run out towards the kitchen and see Mom staring at her phone. She's frozen where she stands, looking like a statue with wide, scared eyes.

"Mom, what's wrong? You're up before me, and you never are." My mom works late at night, so she usually doesn't go to bed until two or three in the morning, which is why she has me—her personal alarm clock, as she calls me—to wake her up.

She looks up at me, blinking before pasting on a fake smile and saying, "Oh, baby girl, good morning. Nothing is wrong. Mom was just her own alarm clock today. Come sit, let me do those curly locks of yours before they weigh down your head."

I laugh and follow her to the bathroom where she brushes and Dutch braids my hair. My favorite way to have it done!

When we are done, Mom says, "So baby, what do you think of a road trip? We can go anywhere you can dream of, but we have to leave today. How does that sound?" She says it excitedly, but I can tell something is off.

"But mom, what about school?" I say with a pout. We can't just leave. Why is she acting this way?

"Oh baby, for now we will have to keep homeschooling. But I promise someday soon you can go to a real school. Let's go pack our bags now so we can get on the road."

I cross my arms and give her an angry look. "But I don't want to. I want to stay here and go to school and meet friends like you promised!"

"I know, baby, but we can't, okay? We have to go on a trip. Please just pack a bag and we'll talk in the car."

She looks like she is going to cry but is trying not to. It makes me even more mad. She promised!

"No!" I shout as I storm off and hide somewhere she won't be able to find me. We moved here about two years ago and I found a small crawl space in the back of my closet. I never told mom about it. It was my little hiding spot. I like to take snacks in here and have alone time. Sometimes I dream about my dad when I'm here too. Mom doesn't like talking about him, so this is my spot to think about him. I just know he'd be a strong knight if I ever got to see him.

A few hours later, I come out hoping Mom doesn't want to leave anymore. Maybe she was just upset. She always tells me we have to calm down before discussing things because when you're scared or angry you might say things you don't mean. That must have been what happened. She didn't calm down before talking to me.

But when I come out and find mom pacing the living room, I realize something is wrong. She's still in sweats and a large t-shirt. Her hair is in a messy bun. Usually, my mom looks beautiful. Well, she still does, but she usually curls her hair. It's long and red just like mine. She always wears makeup, although she won't let me wear any yet.

Mom likes to have things super clean, and when she's sad, she cleans even more. But right now, everything is messy like she tore apart the living room and kitchen. She looks more frantic than she did before. Muttering to herself, chewing on her nails, which she always yells at me for, and her eyes are all red and puffy like she's been crying.

"Mom?" I whisper, feeling bad for hiding for so long now. Mom needed me.

She turns around and looks at me, her eyes wide with fear. "Oh, finally. Where were you hiding? It's time to go. I packed for you already. You can't have hiding spots I can't find anymore. We have to go now. You can yell at me in the car."

She puts her hands on my shoulders and turns me around, but before we can even take a step, there are three loud bangs on our front door. Mom jumps, grabs my arm, and pulls me towards the back door. Not even grabbing our bags. I go to say something, but as soon as she opens the slider, someone is pushing her back and coming in the door. I scream as my mom gets thrown to the floor.

Before I can get close to her, someone else grabs my arms and holds me against their chest, whispering in my ear, "Be a good girl now, sweet Harleyyyy." He sings my name, and I freeze, not daring to move.

Three more men are in my house, making it four total. One holds me, and the other three grab my mom. She fights, but they easily overpower her, tying her down to a kitchen chair.

The guy holding me whispers in my ear, "Be my sweet Harley and watch and nothing bad will happen to you. You'll come back to where you belong." I look down at the arm wrapped around me and see a tattoo. It's a weird devil of sorts, but my eyes aren't making it out clearly with the tears streaming down my face.

My mom screams, and tears begin streaming down my face. "Mom?" I sob, and she looks at me.

"Harley, be strong. Be brave. You can do this. Remember what I've always told you."

I think back to what she has told me every week since as long as I can remember, "If anything ever happens, you find an opening, and you run. You run, Harley. You leave me and run." She used to make me repeat it back to her all the time.

I nod at her, and she closes her eyes and exhales.

I try to fight the man's hold, but he is stronger than I am. I cry out for my mom and claw at his arm. What is happening? Who are these people?

"What do you bastards want? The old fucker couldn't come deal with me himself? How did you even find me?"

"Oh, don't worry, the old fucker is here to deal with you himself," says a voice from the front of the house.

A huge man comes into the room. I can see tattoos sticking out around his neck from the jacket he has on, and his lips are twisted into a cruel smirk. He walks up to my mom and starts hitting her everywhere.

I scream and cry and beg, but the guy behind me just holds on tighter, leaving bruises on me. I'm forced to watch as they tie my mom up on the table and hurt her. She screams. I don't know what he's doing, but it looks painful, and she's bleeding in between her legs. The other guys cut and hit her until she passes out. Then they throw cold water on her, and she comes to.

The huge man that mom called the old fucker says, "No passing out now. Before we finish up with you, I'm going to ruin you. You'll watch your precious baby get raped and beat and her throat slit, then I'll take you home with me and watch you die slowly... Or maybe I'll kill you and then take your little girl home and keep her for myself. You did run away from me."

I feel my mind closing off. Refusing to listen or see more. I squeeze my eyes shut. Tears running down my face. I can feel my entire body shaking.

"You would've killed my baby! I had to leave. You left me no choice, you bastard!"

The man laughs, "Ahh, someone grew a backbone while in hiding for thirteen years. It's really a shame I can't take you home with me. It would be so fun to break that backbone."

Mom starts screaming and trying to fight. I don't know what to do. I have a feeling they are going to do what they did to mom to me. I need to run like mom always told me.

The guy behind me grabs a knife and holds it against my throat, causing Mom to freeze and stare with wide eyes. She looks at me. "It's okay, baby. It's okay. You can do this. It's. Okay," she says slowly.

It takes me a minute to understand that she means it's okay to leave her. Tears fall down my face as I keep my promise to my mom and do what I can to get out of here.

I know she is talking about running, so I take a deep breath. Reminding myself of all the times Mom said I was strong. That I can be my own princess. My own warrior.

I throw my head back as hard as I can trying to throw the guy off balance, then I ram my foot down on top of his and kick back as hard as I can. When I stumble forward as his tight grip loosens, his knife flies at my face and slices it. I feel horrible pain searing down my face, but before I can cry about it, Mom is screaming to run, so I do. I take off and run and run.

My surroundings blur around me as I become exhausted. Finding myself stumbling more and more. I have to keep going.

I don't stop until I pass out. After that, everything is gone.

I stop and take a breath, preparing myself to tell Brielle and the guys the rest. "I apparently had passed out on the side of the road. Luckily a cop had been driving by and saw me collapse while I was running. I don't remember anything after that. I guess I was unconscious for about two weeks in the hospital. The doctor said it was because my brain was letting my body heal from the mental and physical trauma of it all. The cut on my face obviously left a scar." I point at it, as if they can't see it. "They had to put stitches in it because it was really deep. I never got aftercare, so the scarring is worse than it was supposed to be. My right arm was fractured where the man had been gripping it so hard, but I never got proper treatment for it after the hospital, so it isn't fully healed and still aches sometimes."

I take a shaky breath, feeling the tears still streaming down my face. I've been staring at the table this whole time, but I finally look up. Linc's eyes are misted over, and his breathing is ragged as he seems to try and get a control on his emotions. Atlas looks ready to hunt anyone who has ever hurt me down and kill them. His eyes are narrowed as he glares a hole in the table. His fists are clenched, and his entire body is tense.

Brielle is crying with a hand over her mouth. She nods her head at me, moves her hand, and says, "It's okay."

I exhale and then continue. Better to get it over with now. "My mom's sister Tammy, who was there when I woke up, told me my mom died in a fire. That's all I know, and I don't know if anything has happened with it since that day. I've had no way of finding out. Besides what you just said about it being an electrical fire."

"So when you woke up, did anyone besides Tammy talk to you? Cops or doctors or anything?" Lincoln asks.

"A doctor came in once, but he directed everything towards Tammy. Like I wasn't even in the room. Then they stepped out into the hall to finish talking and a nurse came in. She told me that there had been a fire and my home was gone, along with my mom. Before I could say more, because I was going to tell her what actually happened, Tammy came back in, and the nurse left."

"What did Tammy say about it all?"

I look over at Atlas. "Nothing. Anytime I brought stuff up, she'd say now isn't the time. I only stayed one more night after I woke up before they let me leave. I don't think I was supposed to leave, but it seemed like they all listened to Tammy. No cops ever came in and talked to me. And once we left the hospital, I had planned on trying to make Tammy talk to me, but..."

I clear my throat, memories threaten to surface, but I force them back down in a box. Now is not the time to dump all my shit on them.

"But she never brought it up again and wouldn't talk about it," I say in a detached voice.

When I look over at Brielle, she looks like she has questions, but after a quick glance at Atlas, who shakes his head, she stands and comes over to me with tears running down her cheeks, and she holds her arms open hesitantly. I go to shake my head and tell her no but then I remember, this is Brielle. Someone my mom loved and cared deeply for. Someone who could have hurt me in any way over the last few weeks and has done nothing but shown me kindness instead.

So instead, I take a deep breath, stand, and hug her and we both cry. *Holy shit, I didn't realize how much I've missed and needed a good hug. I never want to let go.*

After we pull ourselves together, we sit back down at the table and Linc brings in some food and water. He kisses my head and whispers, "I'm so incredibly proud of you. You are beyond strong, Harley."

There are so many emotions swarming in my head that I want to shut down. Before I can, Atlas starts talking, "Don't close us out, Harley. You just did something amazing. Now is when the real fight begins. You need to control the feelings. As soon as Brielle gives the okay, I want you to come to the gym. I can help with the rage, but remember you need to focus on something that'll help. Let everything you're feeling fuel you to be better."

I nod and let the tears fall. Thinking over everything in my head, I excuse myself and head upstairs and take a really long shower. I hear them whispering as I leave, but I don't even bother trying to listen. I need a break.

Thinking about this shit is not easy. Especially when, in the end, there are more questions than answers. I know Tammy is up to some shady shit. I have a feeling she is more involved with my mom's death than I thought and that she had something to do with how it ended.

When I get out of the shower, I wipe the mirror off so I can see through the steam and stare at myself. I stare at my scar, at how exhausted and horrible I look. My eyes are red and puffy with huge bags underneath them. I'm also thinner than before. My body doesn't feel any stronger even though it hasn't been a punching bag for someone in weeks. I feel... pathetic.

That's when I decide. Looking at this sad, pathetic person I've become, that's when I decide how to take back control of my life. It's simple really, it's the next step. Find answers.

And more than that, get revenge.

CHAPTER EIGHTEEN

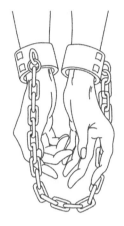

HARLEY

I t's now been almost a week since I told Brielle, Linc, and Atlas about my mom's death. I surprisingly feel a little lighter after being able to talk about it and cry over it. That night, Brielle and I sat down and watched one of my mom's favorite movies, The Notebook. We cried and then laughed about us crying. It was... incredible. I felt like I had a piece of me given back that day.

There is still so much pain, sadness, and anger inside me, but I also just feel like I can breathe a little easier.

I've been trying to eat more, but it's slow going because of the fact that I've spent three years not eating a lot. Brielle said my stomach has shrunk and it will take time to work it back up to be able to eat enough food for a day. She did ask me about what has happened over the last three years, but I shut down, not being able to talk about it. She said she would give me more time. But I don't know if I'll ever be ready to talk about it.

After I had told them everything about my mom's death and found out that it was said it was an electrical fire, I couldn't help myself and looked it up. The article I had found was short. It just said that there was an electrical fire due to old wiring and my mom was home alone. She was unable to get out of the house in time and unfortunately died.

It mentioned nothing about me. As if I never existed. I can't help but wonder if Tammy had something to do with that. Especially since she always said she had connections. Were those connections law enforcement? How could she just make me disappear?

I'm currently sitting on a couch in the living room. No one is home right now. Brielle had to work today, and Linc is at the gym working. He said he'd be here as soon as he was done. They don't really like leaving me alone for long periods of time. I opened up the big sliding doors so I can hear and smell the ocean. I'm sitting here staring at it trying to tell myself I can go out there.

After that first day, I was so excited to feel sand, and then I immediately realized that it was heartbreaking for me, and not long after I shut down for over two weeks. I know that wasn't the main cause, it was just part of my breaking point.

But I'm terrified to go out again. Brielle told me to wait for her and she'll do it with me when I'm ready, but I feel like I need to just do this by myself.

But instead of stepping outside after I opened the doors, I sat down and have been listening to the light waves of the ocean. I can't keep letting things get to me, and this is an easy one to overcome. *It has to be.* This can be turned into a good memory, knowing my mom was out here sixteen years ago, looking at the same view, going through hard times. Fuck, I have to do this. My leg bounces, and my hands are shaking. It shouldn't feel this fucking scary. It's just sand. *Just sand? Right...*

I stand up and very slowly head out the doors onto the huge deck. From the deck are stairs going straight down to the sand, and I walk down them at a snail's pace. When I reach the bottom, I take a deep breath, look up to the sky, and say, "Mom, I really hope you're here with me."

I take the last step off and feel the sand on the bottom of my feet. Tears burn the backs of my eyes, and this time I let them fall. No more holding it all in. I can do this. I can learn to control them in a healthy way.

I take a few slow steps and then stop. God, this is ridiculous! It's sand. It's not a bomb that's going to go off. It's not any of my demons. It's something my mom loved; it's something my mom always told me stories about. I steel my spine and make myself keep walking, letting the tears fall as I let a memory surface.

"Hmm, want me to tell you another story, baby?"

I nod my head like a lunatic; I love my mom's stories. "Yes! But it has to be about the princess! She's my favorite."

Mom laughs. It's a sight I never want to forget, her head tossed back, a huge smile on her face, and her eyes shining with love as she looks at me. "Well, luckily, Princess Brielle is my favorite too. I could tell you stories about her every day. This time, I'm going to tell you about a time when the girl who Princess Brielle saved got really, really sad, so she went down the beach and sat in the sand.

"She was feeling really lost, but then the princess came down to where she was and asked her if she had ever built a sandcastle. The girl hadn't, so Princess Brielle said we must! The girl thought princesses can't get dirty, and they most certainly can't build their own castles! But Princess Brielle was so much more than a princess; she was a warrior too, and warriors can do absolutely anything they set their minds to! So the girl and the princess started building a sand castle.

"They made it so big that it was as tall as they were! They were so proud of it, but also so dirty! They went inside and cleaned up, and when they came back to see their sandcastle, there was a storm coming. Well, not even an hour later, the storm came and took the castle away. It got swept up into the water along with rain pelting down on it. The girl was sad. She said that's just her luck! Make something beautiful and the world ruins it. But you know what the princess said?"

I shake my head, eager to hear the rest.

"She said the most beautiful things are created in the midst of a storm. Do you know what that means?"

I shake my head again. "No, Mom, what does it mean?"

"Well, it means that the girl and the princess spent a lot of time and work building the castle and then it was torn down by the weather so that the earth could make something even more beautiful." She whispers the next part, "A rainbow."

I smile. "I love rainbows!"

"Me too, baby. Want to know what my rainbow is? What the earth brought me after the storm?"

I nod, bouncing up and down. "Yes! Tell me! I need to know!"

She laughs. "Well, silly girl, my rainbow was you. Harley Brielle St. James. You were the rainbow after my storm, and you shine for me every single day." She kisses my nose and whispers again, "The end."

Mom says it's time for bed and sits with me like she does every night until I fall asleep. Before I drift off, I ask, "Mom, can I be a warrior, too? What if I want to be a warrior and not a princess?"

Mom doesn't answer right away and as I drift off into dreamland, I hear, "Baby girl, you are a princess because you have a big heart and are kind. You are also a warrior because you are brave and strong. I hope there never comes a day where you have to fight, but if you do, I know deep in my soul that you will be okay, because you, my baby, are so much stronger than I could ever be."

I smile as I draw closer to the water, letting the tears fall as I finally grieve my mom. As I let myself feel the full force of what I went through. Of how I survived, of the guilt I feel for not staying with her. Everything. I decide while my mind stays on the grief that I need to also build my first sandcastle. I get to work building away with some buckets and things Brielle has on the deck.

I'm about halfway done when I hear someone say my name. I glance up at the deck and see Brielle, wide-eyed with tears running down her face. She comes down to me and just stares. I can see all the questions in her eyes, so I decide to answer a few.

"Do you want to know how I knew you even existed?" She looks at me confused but nods. "Well, my mom never actually told me about you. But ever since I was a baby, she told me stories before bed. A lot of them had to do with Princess Brielle of Virginia Beach. The stories all centered around a princess who was also a warrior who saved this girl who was lost and broken." I smile sadly at her. "I took a chance that they were all based on real stories. That the girl was my mom, and you were real."

I take a deep breath. Here goes nothing. I'm opening myself up.

"You saved her, you know? I know now that I kept her alive, I gave her something to fight for. But you? You saved her. I don't know why, but you did, and you're doing it again now, with me. You don't even know my story, and you've let me into your home. You've let me turn your world upside down and still have shown me more love and affection than I've seen in three years."

By now Brielle has picked up a bucket and is helping me finish the castle.

She murmurs, "I knew your mama when I was little. We went to school together, but then I moved here after my mom died. My dad remarried really fast, and he lost himself to his grief and drowned himself in alcohol. His new wife... she was, well, she was awful. I struggled for many years and was trapped in a bad situation. So when I got out, and your mom had just happened to find me, I knew I'd do anything for her, and for you. To keep you guys from going through even a fraction of what I went through. Little did I know that Lilian had been through even worse.

"When you showed up, I was shocked. I had no idea what was happening, but I saw the look in your eyes. I heard what Linc said about seeing you in the store, and I knew I'd do whatever it took to keep you safe. Not only for your mama, but for you too. She was my family, and so were you. I loved you like a niece before you were even born, and I have wished for sixteen years that I could've seen you grow up. I know the circumstances now are god awful, but I am glad to have you here. I love you just as much as I loved Lilian. I see so much of her in you. It breaks my heart and heals it all at the same time."

I stop building, letting the tears fall. I walk to Brielle and take the bucket from her hands, then take her hands in mine. Shocking us both since I've never initiated touch with anyone since I came here.

I look at her. "Bri." She grins at me finally using the nickname. "Would you like to know my full name? I never really truly understood why I was named what I am, and I still don't. But now, one part of my name makes so much sense, and I will yell it from the rooftops and carry it with pride."

Bri nods her head. "Your mom never got the chance to tell me your name, but she told me it was meaningful."

I smile, feeling great pride in getting to tell her this, knowing my mom up above is smiling down at this moment like it was meant to be. "Harley Brielle St. James."

Her eyes widen before she breaks out into huge sobs. I pull her to me and hug her, not letting go. Feeling my own tears fall down my cheeks as we both grieve the loss of a beautiful soul that was taken from us too soon.

After a few minutes, I feel another set of arms wrap around both of us and look up to see Linc with tears in his eyes. He must have heard. I can tell from the look on his face. He holds both of us as we cry, resting his head on top of ours.

A few days pass and it feels like my life might be kind of normal for once. I've started helping Bri around the house with things. She also tried to teach me how to cook, and to say I suck is an understatement. I'm pretty sure I should not be left alone in the kitchen, and by Bri's perplexed facial expression, she thinks the same thing but is too nice to tell me.

There have been a few times that she has brought up where I came from, who I was living with, and what happened, but I shut her down. I'm trying not to be rude, and it's not her fault, but I don't want to talk about it. I'm not ready. But if she doesn't stop pushing, I think I might blow, and I really don't want to lash out at Bri.

The cup I was drying hits the counter a little harder than I intended with these thoughts in my head, and it shatters and pieces go flying all over. "Fuck!"

I feel like my blood is boiling under my skin. I keep getting angry like this from even thinking about everything that has happened. I can't control it. It's just this intense rage; it feels all-consuming and like if I don't lash out, I'll explode. I should be aiming this at Tammy, not Bri. But it's not like I can just go show up there and scream at her no matter how badly I want to. I scoff at myself, *You wouldn't. You'd freeze and be weak and submit to her ways.* That thought pisses me off more than anything else does.

Bri comes into the kitchen and freezes, taking in the sight of me looking pissed with broken glass all over and grabbing the broom to come clean it up.

I take a few steps back, but before I can leave to try and calm myself down, she says, "Wait. I, uh, I want to talk to you about something. I've been putting it off because I think it's a bad idea. Okay, scratch that. I think it's a bad idea because it's not something I could ever do, but I think you need to." She runs a hand down her face and sighs. "You're getting healthier, and you have no more lingering injuries. Atlas has offered to take you to the gym and help with the anger and grief you feel and to learn self-defense. I don't fully agree, but I can't keep watching you suffer like this.

"You are doing so much better, but even I can see the anger at the surface ready to explode at any second. I know you're trying to contain it, and I appreciate that more than you know. I don't do well with anger, but I don't want that to ever stop you from coming to me if you need me." She exhales. "Okay, anyways, enough of my rambling. I think you're ready." She pauses, then grimaces. "I mean, if you want to. It's completely up to you. No one is forcing you to do anything."

"I think it's a great idea, and I really want to. Thank you, Bri."

She gives a hesitant smile and slowly nods. "Right, okay, good. I want Linc there, too. I hope that's okay. It's just that Atlas can be really intense." I give her a sharp look, and she lets out a humorless laugh. "Right, you know that. Anyways, as long as you continue eating and let me keep up my checks on you health wise, I think you are ready and will be fine to go."

I nod and smile. "Thank you, Bri, I know this is hard for you, but I really think I need it." She gives me a shaky nod and returns to cleaning up the broken glass.

I still sometimes get nervous or anxious with things. Or I feel like I am dreaming, and the beating is going to come at any moment for the way I've acted since I've been here, but the way Bri just put aside all her issues with fighting and me learning to defend myself shows me that she is not like anyone else.

It helps heal a broken part of me that I didn't realize needed healing. To have faith in people again, that not everyone is going to hurt you. But it also is a reminder that you can't just trust anyone and have to be wary because they could end up being a Tammy.

CHAPTER NINETEEN

RYKER

I t's been six weeks since Harley took off, and to say I am pissed is an understatement. I still don't know what it is about that girl, but she consumes my thoughts. I also have this intense need to wrap her up in a bubble and keep her safe in ways I couldn't keep my mom safe as a kid. So, I decide it's time to take things into my own hands. I've been playing by Noah and Rage's rules. I've stuck with Stone for weeks, but we've found nothing. Gray works with Nerds, who has been teaching him everything there is to know about tech shit. But they haven't come up with anything on Harley. They've just been building more information about Tammy and Richard.

They are trying to make sure the club will be safe when it's time to take them out. I am someone who prefers to have control in all aspects of my life. I trust Noah and Rage with everything in me, but I'm starting to feel out of control. I know there is a real chance that Harley will never come back if she's been through even half of what I think she has, and I don't blame her. But I need to know she is safe, and my patience has run out. Which is why I am currently in my room pretending to sleep waiting for the right moment to sneak off club property.

I'm not stupid. I know they are keeping a close eye on me because this wouldn't be the first time I've lost my shit. Besides when I went into a blind rage and killed my dad, I've lost it a few other times. I'm not proud to say I've hurt people. Not that they haven't deserved it, but it's the not being fully in control part that really worries me, which is why I try to stay in control of every aspect of my life that I can. It helps keep me a little more centered.

A year ago, Gray was really struggling to find himself, and a part of that was dressing differently. His hair actually used to go to right below his shoulders, but he got it cut a little shorter about six months ago.

Anyways, we were out after school one day with Noah and Cade. We had gone to a diner in town we go to often.

I was already on edge around that time. It was coming up on one year since I had last seen my aunt, which made me testy. I was also constantly getting into trouble at school for stupid shit and had been suspended. Basically, too many little things at once will set me off.

So when we were in the diner, some kids kept making snide comments towards Gray, calling him gay, fag, and lots of other nasty terms. These boys had been known around town to be causing trouble. They were all eighteen and older but were constantly going after younger kids. There were even rumors going around that they had sexually assaulted an underage girl, but no one had proof. The club was going to have Noah go and *talk* with them, but things had been busy.

So that day they wouldn't leave Gray alone and kept trying to pick a fight with him, which was pointless. Gray was insanely patient and wouldn't have ever given in to them.

But me? Well, I lost my shit. To be honest, I don't remember a lot of it. I can't tell you how it started or how bad it got; I just remember a red haze taking over and it felt like I was someone else altogether. Then I remember being pulled back by Cade and Noah, with Gray standing in front of me trying to get me to calm down.

Then next thing I know, half the club is there. Doc was patching up the boys that looked close to death. I had beaten all four kids by myself. Then marked them with the switchblade Rage had to tear out of my hands. I do not remember doing any of it, but hearing that I wrote the very words they called my brother all over their bodies while listening to them cry out for help was too much. I shut down for a week before I was able to put my facade in place and become the happy, carefree Ryker again.

So that leads me back to now, lying in bed waiting until 2:30 a.m. Usually things go quiet around here then, and I'll be able to sneak out. Luckily my brothers and I like to keep in good shape, so I'll be able to go out my window and down the drainpipe instead of having to go through the clubhouse. It's 2 a.m. now, so just thirty more minutes.

Waiting here is the hardest part. I hate being still for too long. But if I am pacing up here, someone is bound to hear me and to everyone else, including my brothers, I am sleeping right now.

I am so obsessed with Harley. I know it's not healthy, especially since I barely know the girl. But she is perfect and most importantly, she's perfect for me and my brothers. My worst fear is losing my brothers to women. Them going off and getting married or some shit and their wives not wanting me around because I can be a fucking handful.

But Harley? She's fucking perfection. She's caught all our attention. My brothers like her, I want her, and I want her for my brothers.

I don't think it's all that weird, especially since none of us are normal, so who gives a shit?

So I am going to head out and go over to Tammy's and break in. I want to look around, see if I can find Harley's room and any clue as to where she might be.

And it's time to move.

I get up and throw on some running shoes, then head to climb out the window. I get out and down the drainpipe with no problem. Now to get over the main fence.

To no surprise, the prospect is asleep in the gate house. They are most definitely not supposed to be. I snap a picture and then head towards the gate. Since he's asleep, I can just jump the gate instead of trying to find a place to climb the fence.

I get over it with no problem. I have to walk, which is lame, so instead I turn it into a nice workout and run. Not weird to see a guy running at in the middle of the night, right? *Oh well.*

We are about five miles from the school, and Tammy's house is another five in the other direction from the school, so it takes me about a little over an hour to get there. My legs burn, but I soak in the pain and burn of running so hard and so long. I love running. It puts me in complete control and lets my mind blank and just enjoy being outside. It's something both Cade and I love and sometimes do together.

When I finally reach the house, I know I don't have much time now that it's a little after 3:30 a.m. and they will probably start getting up in an hour or two. I head right to the front door and start picking the lock. People make this way too easy. I get in in under five minutes and head towards the stairs. Upstairs, I find Tabby's room, which she is sleeping in. The master, which Tammy and Richard are both asleep in. Next is another bedroom, one much more masculine and must be Rob's. Then a full bathroom.

Huh, there isn't another bedroom up here. I head back downstairs and start checking doors, finding a half-bath, laundry room, an office, and then a door to a basement.

The stairs are old and creak really badly, so I have to move carefully. It stinks down here too; it smells like something rotten. When I get to the bottom, I see that the basement isn't much bigger than probably 500 sq ft. The floors are concrete, and the walls are old and cracked. It's completely empty in here. There is a small hole in the middle of the floor where it looks like maybe a screw was or something, then off the corner there is a door, and inside is a small bathroom. It smells, but there is nothing in here either. I don't think they ever come down here.

As I am walking back to head upstairs, I see a small spot on the wall that doesn't look right. I walk over to it and push on it, but it doesn't budge. I stick my fingers in the crack between the wall and where it's not flush and pull as hard as I can; it opens with a creak, fuck. Hopefully that wasn't heard upstairs.

I have to pull really hard to get it fully open. Once I get it open enough for me to go in, I step through. It's pitch-black in here, so I pull out my phone and turn on the flashlight.

What. The. *Fuck.* There is a ratty old mattress leaning on its side against the wall with an old, stained pillow on the ground next to it. There is most definitely dried blood on the mattress and pillow. There's a chain that has a cuff on one end of it thrown in the other corner. I feel my anger rising, I have a feeling I know why this is in here. Pieces start to come together in my mind. *Holy fuck.*

Before I can do anything else, my phone starts buzzing. Thank god I remembered to turn the ringer off. Gray is calling me. Fuck, they know I left. This should be fun. I don't answer since it's not a good idea. A few seconds later, I get a text.

> **Caveman Cade:** Get out! We are outside. Lights are coming on upstairs from the right side of the house. Get the fuck out!

> **Gray:** We are partway up the driveway, off the left side in the trees. Hurry up! Get out of there. Meet us. We have Noah's truck.

Well shit. I leave the small room, making sure to close the door behind me. Before I can go to head up the stairs, I hear voices, "Yeah, I think it came from downstairs. I'll go check." It sounds like Richard talking.

A few seconds later, the door opens, and he is coming down the stairs.

I quickly dart into the bathroom, standing behind the door. Hopefully he doesn't come in here or shit's going to get a little hairy. I send a text back so the guys don't freak out, which how the fuck are they even here? Or even knew I was? *Questions for later, Ryker, focus.*

> **Me:** Hiding. I'll be out as soon as I can.

Richard walks around the space in a circle. He stops by the bathroom door. I hold my breath but prepare myself to knock his ass out before he sees me and get out of here. He steps into the bathroom, and I know I'm going to have to make my move quickly so he never sees my face and I can get out. He turns so he's facing the shower, giving me his back, so I jump, getting my arm wrapped around his neck and using my other arm to hold it tight. He starts thrashing trying to buck me off and pull at my arms. I try to keep him as still as possible, waiting for him to pass out but with minimal noise.

I hear Tammy call out to him, fuck. *Come on, you old bastard, pass out already.* He finally stops fighting, so I hold a little longer until I know he's out, then slowly lower him to the ground. He most definitely isn't that strong, but the bastard does have some sharp nails. He sliced my arm up pretty good.

Damn. *Okay, now to get out of here unseen.*

I leave the bathroom and slowly make my way up the stairs. I don't hear anything, so I sneak out to the hall and make my way towards the closest window to jump out of. I have a feeling Gray and Cade aren't the only ones who know about my little adventure. *Oops?*

GRAYSON

I am going to strangle him.

I prefer things calm. I leave all the violence, raging, and hate for Cade and Ry.

But right now? I could strangle Ryker Anderson. That boy is trying to kill me. He's always been a little crazy and on edge. I know we have to watch him in case he is going to lose his shit on someone, but he is taking all this stuff with Harley to a new level.

I like the girl; she's nice, and she's really pretty. But I don't know how I could ever truly be with someone when my heart belongs so fully and undeniably to someone who would never look at me as anything more than family.

But Ryker has it in his head that she is what we need. That this girl, who showed up out of nowhere, has probably been through just as much, if not more shit then we have, and who seems to be a ghost, is what we all need.

We've kept him calm and at bay for weeks. But both Cade and I knew it wouldn't last. Which is why we are currently tucked back into some trees watching the Wilson house while Ry is inside. He doesn't even know we are here yet. When a light comes on and we see movement, I am ready to run in there, but Cade puts his hand on my shoulder and shakes his head.

I try to call Ry, but he doesn't answer. Cade sends him a text. Then he texts me.

> **Cayden:** You dumbass. How is he supposed to answer a phone call right now?

Oh, oops. I didn't even think about that. This is what happens when I worry about Ryker. He invades my mind, and I don't think straight. We sit in the trees, waiting impatiently. My phone buzzes a few times with texts from Noah checking in, but I ignore them for now, knowing things are going to be bad when we get home.

A few minutes later, Ry comes running from the back of the house just as we hear a scream. We stand and wave Ry towards us. Once he's close, we all take off running down the side of the driveway, making sure to stay in the trees. We get back to Noah's truck and bolt.

I take a couple of calming breaths before looking into the back seat from where I sit in the passenger seat to Ry. He at least has it in him to look a little remorseful.

"Want to tell me what you were thinking? Which by the way, you are not as stealthy as you think. Well, maybe for other people you are, but for those that know you? Yeah, it was easy to tell you were up to something. Cade and I waited in the truck for you to leave and then tracked your phone."

"You made me run that whole way? You could've given me a ride!" Ryker whines.

I see Cade white-knuckle the steering wheel and sigh. "Ryker, that is not the point. You need to explain everything before we get back, because I have a feeling it's not just Noah waiting for us at the club."

He goes on to explain everything in detail. I have to take a couple of deep breaths to keep myself from losing it on him. I know he is already done for back at the club. And even though it's messed up, I do understand where his mind was at. It's just the way Ry is. He basically did the same thing to me. Forcing his way in when he decides you are going to be in his life forever.

While we drive, we all sit in silence. I'm assuming thinking about the same thing: what Ry found. I can only imagine what kind of hell Harley has had to live through. I wish we could've done something sooner, but we didn't know what was going on and then we had to trust Rage and the guys to know how to handle things.

Bile rises in my throat as I think over what has probably happened in the basement and I have to force myself to breathe through it as I tap my fingers on my thigh counting to calm myself.

As we get close to the compound, Cade speaks, "You need to keep yourself in check, Ryker. You fucked up tonight, and no one is going to be happy. Take whatever they throw at you. Don't get us kicked out before we are even in."

Ryker nods, knowing Cade talking means he is deadly serious. If Ry goes, we go. If they decide he can't prospect or become a member, we all walk.

When we get back, we all head into the main clubhouse together. Rage, Noah, Sugar, Stone, Axe, and a few other members are waiting at one of the tables.

Ryker freezes, and I see the moment he truly realizes he fucked up. I nudge him to move forward, and he walks towards the table. No one says a word; they all just keep their eyes glued on Ry.

I nudge him again. "Spill it," I whisper. He nods and sighs.

After he is done walking them through everything, including what he saw in the basement, everyone looks outraged. Noah wants retribution for her, and most everyone agrees.

That is, until Sugar reminds us, "She left. Whatever happened to her, she found a way to go. We can only hope that she got somewhere safe." He looks at his brothers. "We have rules and can only help when asked, and y'all know that."

Everyone nods, a few still looking angry and ready to storm over to the Wilson home and demand answers.

I scrunch my brows thinking about what Sugar just said. I am not sure what they are talking about. Club rules? Ry, Cade, and I don't know everything that club does since we aren't members yet, but we know a lot. Although, apparently not this.

Rage stands up, directing his attention to Ry. "Blade knew you were going to do something reckless. I had more hope that you wouldn't. But either way, Blade gave your punishment to me. You are forcing my hand here, Ryker. You can't be trusted. So until I talk with Nerds later and have him come up with a way to keep you locked down besides for school, you'll be coming with me."

Cade, Ry, and I all exchange looks, not sure what he is talking about. Noah still hasn't said anything. I glance at him and see all the disappointment he holds towards Ry right now.

Rage nods to Stone and Axe, and they get up and grab Ry by each arm. Rage leads the way, and the rest of us follow behind Ry, Stone, and Axe. Rage goes out back and towards one of the sheds we keep tools in, but he walks around to the back of it and lifts a huge door that goes down to some kind of underground bunker. I've never seen this before, but I am getting a feeling that this isn't going to be good.

When we get down to the bottom, there is a big open space, one made completely of concrete walls and floors. There is wall of tools, or should I say torture devices. And a metal chair in the middle of the room. On the back wall are six cells. Each big enough to stand in and stretch your arms out to your side. Oh fuck.

I see the moment Ry realizes where they are going. He starts struggling in Stone's and Axe's grips, but they yank him forward and shove him in.

"Noah! No. You can't let Rage do this!" Ry yells, his breathing turning rapid and his fists clenching as he glares at everyone.

I go to step forward, but a hand lands on my shoulder. I look back and see it's Cade, who shakes his head. Goddamn it. I can't just let him be in there. Ry hates being still too long.

"Sorry, Ryker, but you wouldn't listen to me. I don't know what else I was supposed to do, and this officially affects the club, so I left it to Rage. I hate this. A lot. But you fucked up. You put this entire club at risk," Noah says without even glancing at Ryker. I can clearly tell this is hurting him.

"You know I would never lay a hand on you like my father used to do to punish people. Do we exchange hits? Yes. But they are always fair, and you cannot do it out of anger. I am angry right now, Ryker, and I do not trust you. Until I decide what happens next, you are staying down here. I am sorry it came to this, but you need to learn that we need to be able to trust you around here."

"Alright, look, I get it, I fucked up. But this really isn't necessary." Ryker's eyes go wide as Stone locks the cell door.

I shake my head and step forward, shrugging off Cade when he tries to pull me back.

"Is this really what you're going to do, Rage? How is it going to help? This will just make him even more restless than he already is, and there is no saying what he will do when he gets out of it," I say, trying to plead with Rage.

"Gray, leave it alone. Rage knows what he's doing. Unless you want to end up in this punishment, too, then just leave it alone," Noah says quietly to me.

Before I can respond, Rage glares at me. "You want to join him? You can. If not, shut the hell up." He runs a hand through his hair and sighs, "Look, I love you boys as if you were my own, but one girl comes along and you all seem to have lost your heads. I have to protect my club. I need to know that Ryker isn't going to do something like this again, and right now I don't trust his word. So he stays until I figure out what happens next. It won't be for too long; I wouldn't do that to him. You and Cade can come down and bring him meals and stay to eat with him, otherwise he is left alone. Another word about this and you'll be joining him, got it?"

I go to open my mouth, but Ry speaks up, "Don't, Gray. It's fine. I can deal. Just leave it be. I deserve it."

I shake my head but take a step back and keep my mouth shut.

BLADE (NOAH)

I watch Cade and Gray leave to head back to the clubhouse when Rage kicks them out so we can talk with Ryker. I fucking hate this. But I don't know what I am supposed to do.

When we knew Ryker was up to something, I really hoped it wouldn't be anything big, but that wasn't the case. I don't even think Ryker understands the danger he put the club in. I look over at him, and he meets my eyes. I don't have any words to say to him. I am disappointed, so I just step back and let Rage handle it. Even as Ry scowls at me, I can see the hurt behind the anger in his eyes.

Fuck. I don't do emotions. I am the enforcer. I take care of people who are threats to my club, my family. But how the hell do I do that when this threat *is* my family and is damaged in his own ways and I can't fully blame him for how he acts?

"Ryker, you need to understand that what you did was beyond stupid. What if Richard had seen your face? It wouldn't take much for him to connect you to us and then what? They could use any information they have on us from Rage's father to take us down for things we didn't do. Or if you hadn't gotten out, they would have you and who knows what they would have done then? You risked way too much. I know you want answers on this girl. We are trying, but there isn't a lot we can do right now. You need to get that and find a different outlet and trust us to handle things.

"If you can't trust us then how will you ever be able to be a part of this club? We rely on trust. We have to trust each other to have each other's backs. Always," Axe says. Our road captain always coming in with the right thing to say.

I see Ryker begin to understand. The boy can hide his emotions very well, but right now, he isn't hiding anything. We can all see his pain, and everything he feels is on his shoulders. I didn't think I could say anything. I thought he needed time with knowing I am disappointed and me not giving him my words, which is something Ryker craves. He wants validation from those in his life because of the shit he's been through. I wanted him to sit here with not hearing a word from me, but I don't think I can do that now as I watch him hurt. *Fucking emotions.*

"Ryker." His head snaps in my direction as I step forward, "You did something stupid, but that doesn't mean we give up on you. But this is getting towards the end. Where you have to figure out your shit and learn to trust us fully or you won't be a part of this club when you turn eighteen. I need you to find a way to pull it together. If you are restless and feel like you have to have that control you need, come to someone you trust and let them help you find control another way. Don't run off. That can't happen again. You got lucky today, but you won't next time."

Ryker nods. "I get it. I fucked up, and I'm sorry." He drops his head and clears his throat. "I'll work on it. This club is my family, and I want to be a part of it when I can be. I don't want to fuck it up for my brothers, either. Can we move past this? Do I really have to stay in here still? I get it. I really do."

Rage shakes his head. "You're staying. Sorry, kid. I may feel for you, but I am not a pussy. I won't give in that easily. I'll figure shit out so you aren't here too long, but a little time will do you good. There's a bucket for a toilet. The boys will be down later with food."

Rage nods at the rest of us, and we all file out as Ryker tells us he fucking hates us all.

Sugar chuckles when we get back outside. "That kid... he'll learn and get better, I know it. But boy, sometimes I wonder if he has any brain cells left."

They all chuckle and walk away. It takes me an extra second to leave. This is my brother. Someone I promised to take care of and protect. Sometimes I feel like I am failing in doing that. We may be hardened from the outside, but inside these walls? We can let it all down and feel whatever we need to feel. It's what it's like having these guys as your family. You never have to go through anything alone, but no one would ever know that we are secretly softies.

CHAPTER TWENTY

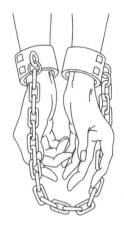

HARLEY

"**Y**ou're not trying hard enough, Harls! Push yourself! Come on, Linc can take a hit, so hit him!"

I slam my gloved hand into Linc's side as hard as I can. He barely stumbles back a half step. I feel like screaming; this is so frustrating. If Atlas doesn't shut up soon, I'm going to turn my punches on him.

"Harley! Get with it! Stop fucking around and fight him!"

That's it! I spin around and head towards the edge of the mats where Atlas is standing yelling out his fucking commands at me. "If you want me to fight so goddamn bad, get in yourself! Why stay out there, Atlas? Huh?"

He gives me a pointed look. He knows what I'm doing. Antagonizing him doesn't work. I've been trying for weeks now.

I sigh and try again, "You're pissing me off, so get in here with me. Give Linc a break."

"Hey! I'm doing just fine. I don't need a break, Harley! Don't make me seem weak!" Linc taunts.

I turn around and glower at him. "I don't know, Dad, you look pretty wiped out to me." I tease back. A week ago, we were in the store and someone made a comment about him being my dad and the poor man looked fucking horrified. I don't think I ever laughed as hard as I did that day.

"Not fucking funny," he grumbles and walks towards the benches on the far wall as other people in the gym laugh at him.

"Alright, enough fucking around. Back to the center, Harley. You want a fight? I'll give you one."

He wraps his hands and puts his own gloves on and meets me in the center of the mats. The big mats people can box/spar on are in the middle of the gym. At first, I could only do it if no one else was in the gym, but it's been three weeks now and I'm getting more confident being around other people. But I still don't like talking to anyone else.

Going in public at first really fucking sucked. I've had my scar for three years, almost four, but other people haven't seen it.

So while I forget it's there sometimes, they don't. Their stares bothered me at first, but I'm getting used to it, and Bri, Linc, and Atlas help me through it when it bugs me or I start to have a panic attack.

Some days are worse than others. Unfortunately, the worse days are coming more often than the good over the last week. I don't know what it is, but something is just bothering me. It's like constant bugs crawling under my skin.

My need to get revenge on not only Tammy and Richard, but also the people who hurt my mom, is getting more prominent in my mind. It's like now that my head is more clear, I am focusing all my energy on that. Well, I will be anyways. I just have to work around Bri because I have a feeling she won't be so on board with my need for revenge.

"Harley! Where the fuck is your head at, kid? You want to do this or not?"

God, I want to roll my eyes at him. Atlas is so broody, and he's always snapping. But I hold back from rolling my eyes because last time I did he made me run on the track outside behind the gym. I run every day now, but adding extra? Yeah, no. Fuck that. Running should be illegal. Seriously, who decided that's a way to exercise? I'd rather do anything than run.

The hit to my gut isn't as hard as it could be, but it definitely knocks me on my ass and grabs my attention. "What the fuck!" I yell.

Atlas is standing above me, glaring a hole through my face. "Get your ass up. I don't know where your head is, but this is the last chance. Get up and focus or call Bri and get the fuck out of my gym. I don't play games, kid, and you know that. Up!"

I jump to my feet and barrel right for him. Atlas pulls no punches with me. He goes hard and doesn't stop. It's what I need, it's what I crave now. The pain, the sweat, the body aches; it brings me some sort of twisted peace. It helps keep my fractured soul from shattering to pieces.

By the time we are done, another hour has gone by. Bri is here now waiting for me. She grimaces but tries to hide it. I don't know her full story, but I know she hates any kind of fighting or violence. She hates that I train so hard with Atlas, which is why even after three weeks she still wants Linc here with us the whole time. It makes me wonder if something is wrong with me because I seem to be thriving in this environment. Even though I was beaten and hurt for years.

Why would I want this? Shouldn't I also hate any kind of violence? I shake off the   thoughts. That's a problem for me to solve on a different day.

Today is for convincing Bri to let me look into things.

After I shower and grab my bag from Atlas's office and head out to meet Bri, we leave, and I fidget the whole way home. I know how she's going to react, but I need to do this shit for me. There are questions I want answers to, and some Bri might even be able to answer, so I have to talk to her first.

When we get home and head inside, Bri walks into the living room and sits down and stares at me. "Well? Something is on your mind. Atlas told me how distracted you were today, and you were silent during the entire the car ride home."

Well shit, she knows me, I'll give her that.

I sigh and move to sit across from her on the other couch. "Um, yeah. I, uh, wanted to talk to you about a few things... I just don't know how this is going to go, and I, uh, well... I don't know."

"Harley, it's okay. I won't be mad at anything you say. We will talk about it and go from there. I think I know what this is about, but I need to hear it from you, hun."

"Alright well, I want to look into my mom's murder. I want to know what happened, and I also want to..."

Shit, shit, shit, this is when the words are supposed to come out, Harley! Maybe just don't tell her about what else you want to do involving Richard and Tammy because she really just never needs to know what happened the last three years. Yep, perfect plan.

I swallow over the lump that has built in my throat. "Um, well, I just want to look into it. I also, um, I want to find out who my dad is. My mom never told me, and whenever I asked, she would look pained but then say that he was a good man but doesn't deserve us talking about him, which didn't really make sense to me, so yeah, anyways, I really just want to figure out who he is. I think I have a right to know, and I want to look into the details of my mom's death. There are things now that I can't seem to stop thinking about that don't make sense." I finally finish rambling, biting my lip.

Part of me still hopes that I can have my childhood fantasy of my perfect dad swooping in to save the day. Although I know logically, especially after everything I have been through, that probably isn't the case.

Bri has tears in her eyes that she quickly wipes away. "Okay, well." She clears her throat. "Lil didn't tell you anything about your dad?" I shake my head. "Honey, I really am sorry. I wish I didn't have to tell you this, but I don't think you should look into who your dad is."

That shocks me. "What? Why? He's my dad! I want to know who he is... Wait." Does she know who he is? Has she known this whole time and never said anything? Is that why she only asked about my mom and never asked me where my dad is? My fists clench in my lap, but I shut my eyes and take a few deep breaths trying not yell at her. Reminding myself I need to give her a chance to explain. I clear my throat, "Do you know who he is?" I say, keeping a blank mask on my face.

Bri looks down at her feet, her leg beginning to bounce uncomfortably. My skin is starting to get that crawling sensation, and I have a feeling I'm not going to like whatever she says next.

"No, hun, I don't know exactly who he is, but I have some ideas." Bri slowly raises her eyes, her own glossy and tears slipping. "Harley... your mom was raped. Whoever your dad is, he... he raped your mom. I am so, so sorry to have to—"

Before she can say anymore, I get up and run out the back door. I can faintly hear Bri yell for me, but I need to run.

I can't spar right now. I know none of them would let me. I just worked out for two hours, so the next best thing is running.

I run hard. I push myself. He raped her?

That means...

I came from rape.

My mom had to look at me every day knowing I came from something that possibly destroyed her.

How could she even look at me?

My knight in shining piece of shit sperm donor. How could I let myself fantasize about a man swooping in and being this wonderful dad that I have always dreamed of? I feel so stupid for ever holding onto hope that one day I would find him and it would be some great happy reunion.

I keep running. I can't stop. I feel like if I stop, I'll break, and I can't do that. I want to... I just really want to kill him. Yes, I want to destroy the people who hurt my mom. I want them to pay tenfold.

Fuck them for taking my mom from me. Fuck the man who thought he could take advantage of my mom. Fuck that man who lived in my dreams as a child or who I dreamed of as I was locked away. The man I thought would come save me. Who in reality ruined everything before I was even born.

I turn around and walk back towards the house. I need to calm my thoughts. I just... I am so angry, and I don't want any of that to come out on Bri. Bri is good; she is an angel, and I never want her to feel hurt. I feel like I need to protect her. I'm jaded, and yeah, she had things happen to her too, but she came out soft and loving. I don't think I will.

When I get back, Bri is pacing the back deck. "I'm so sorry, Bri. I didn't want you to feel any of my anger."

She smiles softly, but I can tell she's been crying. "It's okay, but I need to know you're safe. I got something the other day for you and haven't had a chance to give it to you."

Bri waves for me to follow her, and we head inside to her office.

She pulls out a phone. "Here, it's all set up. Please use it. I put myself, Atlas, and Linc in there. Also, it does track so I can know where you are. It's for your safety, so please don't fight me on it."

I nod; I understand where she is coming from. I mean, she still doesn't even know what has happened to me or how much danger I could be in. It makes me feel safer, too, knowing that they could track me.

"Thank you, Bri."

"Okay, so we do need to talk about what I told you." I grimace and nod as we walk back out to the living room and sit down. "Harley, I can only imagine how hard what I said is to hear, but I really don't think you should look into it."

"Okay, but why? What do you know, Bri? I need answers. I've had no answers for so long, and I need to start figuring shit out for myself."

She nods. "I understand that, but why this? Maybe Linc can talk to someone down at the station and see if we can find out anything on the case, but Harley, I really think you need to focus on moving on and not bringing this all up. I mean, honey, you haven't even told us what has happened to you for the last three years."

I look down. "I'm not ready," I mumble.

"I know, but we do have to talk about it someday."

This isn't the conversation I wanted to be having. I don't want to talk about me. I don't think I'll ever be ready to share my personal hell, and I'd never want Bri to have to hear it all. So I change the subject back to my mom.

"Okay, but I still want answers, Bri. I need them. It's going to help me heal." *And get revenge.* "So please, tell me what you know."

She sighs, "Alright, here's the deal, you have to tell one of us, me, Atlas, Linc, what you find out. Where your brain is at, everything. I am only giving into this because I see the fire in your eyes, and I don't want you doing this without us and getting hurt. Deal?"

Shit. I am about to lie to her. "Deal." *Shouldn't I feel guilty for that? Why do I not?* I guess I just didn't realize how revenge is an all-consuming thing and can and might literally destroy you.

Too bad it'll be too late before I really realize that.

Chapter Twenty-One

Brielle

"Alright, well, I met your mom when we were kids. I think it was first or second grade. We were best friends instantly. We were always together. I knew Tammy, who is your mom's sister. She was one year older than Lil. Tammy was mean; she always had it out for Lil and wanted to make her life hard, so she picked on her a lot and got others to, as well. Lil used to come over to my house all the time. I never knew why, but I did know that she didn't have it easy at home."

I take a breath. Talking about all of this isn't easy. But part of me is hoping that by telling Harley this, she'll open up to me about the last three years. I know the girl has been through hell. I can see it in her eyes. I have this odd feeling that whatever happened involved Tammy. I saw how she was when we were kids. I can't see her ever having gotten better.

"When I was fifteen, my mom died. Three months later, my dad packed us up and moved us here. I had an hour to say goodbye to Lil. It was really hard, and Lil was extremely upset.

I needed my best friend after losing my mom, but my dad was taking me away from there. We moved up here, and my dad moved us right in with his new wife. I didn't even know he had met someone and gotten married. When we moved in, he started drinking a lot more than I ever remember him drinking. I watched him slowly fade away in front of me.

"His wife was awful to me, and a lot of shitty things happened. As soon as I turned eighteen, I gave up on trying to help my dad get better and left. I was able to get this place with money my mom had left me for when I turned eighteen and more when I turned twenty-one. A month after moving in here, Lil showed up. Broken, scared, and extremely lost."

I start to think back to that time, and everything comes back to me like it just happened yesterday.

17 years ago

I have been in my own home now for a few weeks, and I couldn't be more grateful to be out of my dad's house. The future is finally looking up for me. I am curled up in my window seat in the office reading a book and listening to the sound of the waves from the ocean through the open window when someone knocks.

Before I can even get up to head to the door, someone is knocking again. What the heck? I fling the door, assuming it's my dad wanting something or his evil wife, but that's not who's here.

"Lilian? What on earth are you doing here? How did you find me? Oh my god! Lil what happened to you?" I open the door wider, letting her come in.

She limps inside holding onto her midsection like it hurts. Her face is bruised, and her neck has handprint bruises on it. She's thinner than I remember and looks like hell. She comes in, and I lead her to the living room.

I just moved in, so I just have an old thrift store couch. I help her sit and then go get my first aid kit. It's not much, but it'll have to do. When I return, Lil is in full sobs, her body shaking violently, and she's extremely pale. I drop down to my knees in front of her.

"Lil babe, breathe for me. I need you to breathe before you pass out. Please, please, breathe. Slowly, in and out."

After a few tense moments, she starts taking deep breaths with me.

She sniffles. "Bri, I tried my best. I made sure no one followed me. I got away. I don't know what I'm going to do. They know I'm pregnant. My baby can't live that life. Bri, please, please, keep me safe." She rushes it out so fast, barely taking a breath while gripping my arms tightly.

Pregnant? Oh my god.

"It's okay, I'm going to help you however I can, Lil, but I need you to tell me what happened. We are in this together. For now, I

want you to take these pain meds. I'll get you cleaned up, but then I want you to get some sleep. We can talk about this all tomorrow. The house will be locked up. No one can get in. You're safe here, Lil."

As much as I want to know everything now, I don't think she could even get through telling me she needs rest. It doesn't look like she's slept in days.

After I get Lilian cleaned up and to bed, I pace downstairs. What am I supposed to do? This is so bad. Something horrible obviously happened to her. She's only seventeen. The poor girl. I'm eighteen; I don't know how I'm supposed to help. I finally get away from my own crappy childhood and now this?

I don't even know if I want to know what she's been through. I need peace, I need quiet. But this is Lil, and I will help her through anything, even if it flips what I've always wanted upside down.

The next morning, I get up from a night of tossing and turning and basically no sleep. Lilian is still sleeping, which is good. If she's pregnant, then she needs the rest. I stress cook and make way more breakfast than we need.

By the time I'm done, Lil has come down. "Good morning, Lil. How did you sleep?"

She smiles. "Really good, actually. Thank you for last night. I needed comfort, and I was exhausted. It's been a long few weeks."

I nod. "Well, let's eat then we can go sit down on the beach and talk. It's pretty peaceful, especially in the mornings."

"You have a beautiful home. I couldn't believe it when I found you and figured out this was your house. You're doing so well, Bri. Your mama would be insanely proud of you."

I feel tears well in my eyes, but I don't let them fall. "Thanks, Lil. I think we've been through hell lately and could use this place to heal." She nods, and then we dive into the food, eating in comfortable silence.

After we finish eating, we head down towards the beach. Lil sighs when her bare feet hit the sand. She wiggles her toes and gives a tiny smile. We walk towards the water and find a spot to sit, gazing out over the sea.

I stay quiet, giving her time to open up. I know it can't be easy.

"Tam has been into some bad shit. She got pregnant at fifteen and had her son Robert. I've been helping take care of him for the last three years while Tam was off fucking around and getting into trouble and sleeping with multiple guys. Some knew about the others, and some didn't. There has been a lot of fights between her and other guys. You know how Tam and I have different moms?"

I nod. She told me that when we were younger. Her mom died when she was two and not even a week after, her dad was back with Tammy's mom.

"Well, Tam's mom hates me. She used to hurt me when I was little, but she stopped when my dad told her not to lay a hand on me anymore. I was around eleven. I thought he was doing it because he cared and loved me. But he just wanted me well enough for himself."

She shudders, and I can see her hands shaking as she clutches them together in front of her.

I look at her in shock, praying she's not saying what I think she is. "Lil?"

She nods, fresh tears running down her face. "He's been raping me since I was eleven. Tammy and her mom knew. They blamed me. So in turn, they treated me like shit. Tammy thought that I was perfect, and she hated me because all our dad's attention was on me. He is a part of an MC, and Tam wants to be someone's ole lady, so she thought if dad paid her as much attention, then it would make it easier for her. So she took out her anger on me.

"Anyways, after she had Rob, I made sure to take care of him since I only left the house for school anyways. This guy at my school, Gabriel, was always really nice to me. I had a crush on him for years. Tammy knew I liked him, so when he started being nice to me, she hated it. So she flirted with him and got him to give her all his attention and they dated for two years. Gabe didn't look at me as more than a younger sister, so he fell in love with Tammy. I think he is Rob's dad, but I'm not actually sure."

She rubs a hand over her face and then stares down at her feet. I don't say anything yet, staring out at the water focusing on the waves, letting them keep me calm. Silent tears run down my face as I grieve for my friend and what she has been through.

I can't imagine being raped by your own father. Tammy had a kid at fifteen? That's insane. I come out of my thoughts as she starts talking again.

"About four months ago, dad made me go to the clubhouse with him. Tammy had been kicked out apparently and wasn't allowed back, so he brought me as payment for Tam's screwup. I don't even know what she did. That day a few of the older members tested me out... raping me and beating me. Dad took me home after and told Tam to take care of me and not let me leave and he'd be back in a week. He had to go on a run for the club. I was so depressed I was ready to die. I didn't see a point in continuing on when this seemed to be my future. But Tam never left my side that week. Watching me like a hawk.

Since he came back from that run and took me back to the club, I've spent the last three and half months there, rarely ever leaving. I only ever saw the older members... They used me like their own personal toy. And then about a month ago, I was dragged into the main clubhouse and strapped down to a table naked."

She shudders and takes a few deep breaths. I wait patiently for her to be ready to keep going.

"The new guys who wanted to be prospects had to fight, and whoever won the fight got to have me as a prize. Most of the guys looked disgusted. Gabriel was there. He whispered to me that it would be okay. He promised he would win, and he'd find a way to get me out of it or be as gentle as possible. When he was dating Tam, he was always nice to me. I had that stupid crush on him, but he was in love with my sister. Never fully seeing the evil side of her."

I grab her hand when I see that she is pushing her nails into her palm, causing crescent moon-shaped marks to form, and hold it in my own.

She exhales. "He had no idea that I had already been brutalized. By his own father, by my father, by other older members. Shortly after the fights started, I was blindfolded. It didn't come off until I was home that night, so I have no idea who got me. I found out I was pregnant not long after. I know it was from the young one that was most recent because he didn't wrap up. All the old members did. Always. I knew when I saw that test turn positive that I needed to get away. I would do anything for my baby. So I started going through things at home and finding any cash or anything I might need to get away. They didn't make me go back to the club after that. Apparently, I had paid for Tam's mistakes."

She sighs heavily, all of this stuff weighing her down. She looks me in the eyes, and I can see all her pain. I have my own tears running down my face, but I don't say anything, letting her just get it all out, knowing sometimes it's easier to just spit it all out.

"He's not my dad."

I blink at her. "Sorry, what?"

She lets out a humorless laugh. "Yeah, that was my thought, too. I found my birth certificate. He isn't my dad. You have no idea how I felt a sick sort of relief knowing he wasn't my dad. It was a huge weight lifted off my shoulders. It doesn't change anything, but it's still good to know he isn't my dad."

"Holy crap. I can't believe he isn't your dad. I mean, I'm beyond thankful he isn't. Not that it makes things any better," *I say.*

"Yeah, it doesn't make it better. But it's nice to know the man who I thought was my father, David, who raised me and raped me for years isn't biologically related to me. It's a relief."

"So do you know who your actual dad is?" I ask.

"I tried to find him." She takes a shaky breath. "He's dead. There's one member of the Sons of Silence. His roadname is Sugar. I found out that we have the same dad. He's been a patched member since he was eighteen. He's twenty-five now. I wanted to talk to him, but I was too scared. His dad, or I guess our dad, was murdered about seventeen years ago. I couldn't find any more information on him, but the timing... well, it seems suspicious. I think my mom cheated and got pregnant with me and if I had to guess, David killed him." She lets out another humorless laugh. "Knowing him, he probably killed my real father in front of my mother as some sort of sick punishment."

She sighs and wipes the tears off her face.

"Anyways, while I was looking for my biological dad, I ran into Gabriel, who was prospecting. He looked sad and down. We both needed to get away, so he told me he'd take me away for a few days. I was too scared to ask if he was the one who, well, you know or not. But I just... I trusted him for some reason. So we left on the back of his Harley for a weekend of riding, laughing, and talking.

"It was the best weekend I had in my entire life... He admitted that it was him who won the fights. We both cried. He told me he was sorry and explained to me why it happened."

"Lil, he still raped you. Him being upset about it after doesn't change the fact that he made that choice. He hurt you."

She sighs, "It wasn't like that. There were other things going on. He didn't want to—"

"But he did! He raped you. Why are you making what he did okay? Does that mean it's okay what all the other men did to you?"

"No! Of course not. But... Ugh, can we just not talk about this right now? Let me finish getting everything out because I just want to get it over with."

I take a breath, trying to calm myself. I know I need to let her finish, but what she is saying is worrying me about where her head is at. "Sure, but Lil we aren't done talking about this. You're holding onto something with him that you need to let go of."

She nods, but I don't think she believes me. Which scares me.

"When we got back, things were bad. I watched as Gabe's dad beat him. Telling him what a pussy he was for catering to some whore." She sneers at the word.

"Then Gabe's dad, Killer, turned on me. He told me how the fights didn't go down. Gabe paid everyone off so he could have me and he's been telling others about my hot, tight snatch," she spits. "I was so angry. I couldn't believe I let my heart run away for a stupid childhood crush. He was in love with my sister. I should've known better. My dad, David, well the man who raised me, was so angry he started strangling me.

"I was terrified. Eventually Killer pulled him off before I passed out. I took off and ran home. I knew then was the time I had to get out of there. I was so glad I didn't tell Gabe I was pregnant. I didn't want anyone to know."

"Wait, if he really said and did that shit, why the hell are you protecting Gabe with me? He's a piece of garbage who deserves to go to hell!"

Lil glares at me. "Either shut up and let me finish or we can stop now. I'm sorry but don't talk about Gabe that way. You don't have the whole story."

I stare at her stunned by the change from the broken-down girl to this protective one. Wow, okay. Maybe she's sick and this is some kind of twisted Stockholm thing.

"Okay, continue," I sigh, crossing my arms.

"Tam was home when I got back to the house. She was talking to Richard and telling him how Killer was bringing Tam and Richard in to work with him. I heard her telling him about Gabe and I taking off but someone else had followed us and saw everything and recorded everything we talked about all weekend... including when he kissed me one of the days. What happened when we came back was a setup. Gabe didn't pay off anyone. He won fair and square and tried to be gentle with me without letting on to others that he was trying to protect me. He never lied to me over the weekend. Everything he said was true."

I watch as she wipes more tears from her eyes aggressively like she's tired of crying.

"They set it up because Tam still wanted Gabe and had plans to get him back even though she was banned from the club. She is also working with Killer; I don't know what they do, but it can't *be good. I know Gabe was in love with her in high school. She was his first love. But he said over that weekend how he'd never look at her the same again for whatever she had done.*

"I started getting all my stuff together to leave as fast as I could, but that's when Tam came in... She had the pregnancy test I took in her hand. She started screaming at me asking whose it was and calling me a whore. She said she was going to tell Dad—David—about it, so I panicked. I freaked out and hit her as hard as I could with my lamp and knocked her out.

I wanted to take Rob with me. He was only three, and he didn't deserve any of this, but Richard had him and I couldn't get caught, so I had to leave him behind. I ran and ran. I've been on the streets for three days, but I finally tracked you down and now I'm here."

She takes a shaky breath, new tears streaming down her face.

"I tried, Bri. I tried to do everything right, but I knew without a doubt that I had to leave to protect this beautiful soul growing in me. They don't deserve to have their soul shattered like mine."

She sobs hard, the weight of the world baring down on her.

I hold on to her while she sobs. "Wow, Lil, that was a lot. I still don't think Gabe is as good as you think he is, hun, but we'll talk about that later."

Lil scoots away from me with a glare. "I loved him. I know I can't be with him, and I can't tell him about his kid, but I will always love and care for him, and I hope he gets out from under his father someday."

I nod but say nothing. This is something she needs professional help for. I understand, after everything through her childhood how this could happen. The first time someone shows any kind of affection, you want to latch on and never let go of that feeling. But I just hope she doesn't ever think she can actually be with him.

Chapter Twenty-Two

Brielle

I look over at Harley, knowing I just threw a lot at her about her mom. She's crying, and I almost want to laugh as I watch her do the same thing her mom always did, pushing her nails into her palm, making crescent moon-shaped indents. She doesn't say anything. She's just staring off into the distance.

"Harley?" She finally looks over at me, blinking her eyes to focus on me again.

She clears her throat as best she can. I think her throat was damaged by something, but I haven't asked. Every time I do, she shuts down.

"That was a lot to take in, Bri. But thank you for telling me," she says in a detached voice.

"Are you okay? Don't bottle that all up, Harley. Please, let me help you process it."

She shakes her head, her brows furrowed. "I um, don't really know how to feel right now. But can we finish? There's more, right? Why did she have to leave here? Why did we end up in Auburn?"

I exhale a breath. "Sure, we can finish, just promise me you won't shut me out."

She nods, giving me a small tilt of her lips. "I promise, Bri."

"Okay, good... So after that day when she told me everything, she took time to heal from her injuries. She wanted answers about everything but didn't have it in her to find them. Her main goal was protecting you. She stayed with me for seven months. We didn't think to have her use a fake name for the doctors when she would get checked for you, so someone eventually found us.

"They taunted Lil, so after a week we knew she had to run again. I helped her sneak away and get out and told her she can't tell me where she is going. If for some reason they went after me, I didn't want to have any answers so I couldn't give them anything." Goosebumps rise on my arms remembering how scared I was back then.

"The men who showed up were from the Sons of Silence MC. They came storming in; there were four of them. They looked around but left me alone besides questioning me and said I was lucky they knew my father or I would've been screwed. I knew they meant they would have hurt me. I don't know how they knew my dad, but I didn't care. I just was glad they left and hoped your mom got away. After that, I got a letter three years later. A picture of you and a letter from your mom updating me. She told me we'd get to see each other again one day and that's when she would tell me your name. I never heard anything again until you showed up."

"Wow that's all, um, it's a lot. I'm not shutting down, Bri, I swear, but I think I need to spar. Can we call Atlas and see if he's busy?" She is fidgeting with her fingers and her eyes are glossed over, but she isn't fully crying now. Almost like an empty shell.

Did I just make a huge mistake?

"Honey, you already spent two hours at the gym today, and you ran for an hour when we got home. Can you wait until tomorrow?" I should've known this would be too much for her. I didn't want to overwhelm her, but there really aren't any easy ways to tell someone everything I just told her.

"I know, Bri, but I need to. It'll help. Then after we can talk, and I'll tell you how I feel. I appreciate you telling me everything." Her voice is so detached, it scares me.

I sigh. If I don't give in, I have a feeling she'll find another way to let out whatever it is she needs to let out. I can't tell what it is; she's hiding it well. Whether it's fear, anger, sadness... I have no idea.

I send a text to Atlas asking him to come over and then let Harley know he said he's on his way. Harley excuses herself to go get ready, and I go to the kitchen to cook and keep myself busy. About ten minutes later, Atlas shows up with Linc in tow. No surprise there.

Linc comes into the kitchen and hugs me. "What's going on?"

I fill them in and then feel tears streaming down my cheeks. "Did I mess up? I didn't want her to ever have to know, but I thought it would be better coming from me instead of her finding other ways to get the information she wanted." I sob into Linc's chest, taking comfort from my best friend.

"You didn't fuck up, babe. You did the right thing. Harley is stubborn. I'll take her back to the gym and see if I can get her to spill. We'll spar but not go hard. Ryan is there too, so he can help if needed. Linc will stay with you. Don't beat yourself up, Bri, you're doing the best you can," Atlas assures me.

Ryan is the other guy who runs the gym with Atlas and Linc. They've all been friends for years and brought me into their fold when I met Linc. I trust them with my life. So I trust them to take care of Harley with everything she is dealing with. I just really hope that I don't regret how I handled things later on.

There are so many unknowns with everything. We can't find answers on anything. Even though Harley won't tell us what happened during the last three years, we know it involves Tammy. The guys have tried to look into things, but Harley just doesn't exist besides when she went to be with Tammy. It makes no sense, and we have no way of getting answers.

I feel helpless and clueless and have no idea what to do besides try and be here for Harley.

Harley

Rage. Rage like I have never felt before is running through my veins. It feels like my blood is boiling. I've kept my face blank while Bri told me everything. I know that wasn't easy for her. But the thing is, I can't let this go. I know that I am going to hurt Bri by looking into everything and getting revenge. I know that. But I have to, and I really hope someday she sees that and doesn't hate me forever.

All I know is that right now, my brain is a fucking mess, and I need to spar. I feel my thoughts tumbling. I want revenge, I know that for sure. But how am I supposed to do that if I can't keep my mind together? So instead of dealing with it, I am going to spar until my muscles hurt so bad all I can think about is the pain.

I get out of the shower, get dressed, and head downstairs. Atlas is waiting at the bottom, and there is no sign of Bri. "Where is Bri?"

"She's with Linc calming down. She's worried about you, kid. I'm only doing this because I have a feeling you are like me and need to spar in order to break down your walls. Let's go." He walks to the front door and out to his truck, leaving me to quickly gather what I need and run after him. Asshole.

We soon reach the gym, and Atlas throws hand wraps at me. I quickly wrap my hands and watch as Ryan, the other owner, comes out, and Atlas says something to him too quiet for me to hear. Ryan nods and walks off to the benches against the wall, then sits down.

I scowl at him but don't say anything. We don't need a fucking babysitter.

Atlas moves to grab the boxing gloves, but before he can, I say, "No."

"No?" He quirks a brow.

I shake my head. "Hand to hand. Please. I need it."

Atlas sighs and glances at Ryan.

I grit my teeth. "Hey! Don't do that. Don't go looking at Ryan and having silent conversations without me. If you don't want to help me, I'll find a different gym to go to!" I yell, not meaning to, but I can't seem to control my feelings right now.

Atlas stalks towards me, towering over me. "Listen here, kid, you will NOT go to another gym. We will do this here. My way. You are not the boss. I am. You want hand to hand? Fucking fine. But I will not be pulling any stops for you. So you better bring your all and stay fucking focused or you'll be going home with bruises that you'll have to explain to Brielle."

I nod and walk to the center. "Fine, let's go."

We get ready, and Ryan tells us when to start. At first, it's fine, and we go back and forth.

I'm getting in the groove. That is, until Atlas gets a hard jab at my ribs. Something about it sets me off. It's like it triggers me. I freeze for a second before I throw a hit back as hard as I can. My mind is racing with everything Brielle told me today. Part of me wants to lock it down so tightly that I never think of it. But the bigger part of me is enraged and can't let any of it go.

How could I think of my dad as some knight in shining armor? Someone who I was hoping would want me and protect me? I am only alive because of a vile thing he did. Why did mom not tell me? Or at least tell me he was a bad man? I don't understand.

Before my thoughts can keep spiraling out of control, Atlas clocks me on the head and sends me to the ground.

"Get up! Get your shit together, Harley, you wanted this! So fucking do it! Stop getting distracted!" he snaps at me.

I stand but wobble a little, shaking myself out of it and readying myself to keep going.

"What? Have you had enough? Come on, Harley! What the fuck is the problem?" He throws his arms out wide.

I narrow my eyes at him, keeping my fists up, ready to strike. I know what he's doing and unfortunately, it's working. My hands drop. I break.

"I can't do it anymore!" I scream. "I can't do what I need to do if I'm constantly fighting my own mind!"

"Then stop being a prisoner to your own thoughts. Stop letting them keep you prisoner in your own mind, Harley! You got out. You did that. You broke free. Fight. Scream. Let it out. Don't let everything Brielle told you today eat at you. You can't change the past. You can only make your future better, but you have to truly want it to be better. No one can make you."

I scream. I scream so hard my throat aches and I know I won't be able to talk tomorrow. It's raspy sounding and broken. Just like me. My soul. Broken, destroyed. I don't want to be better in the ways he says. I want to be stronger and tougher.

I want revenge. On *him.* For my mom. For me.

I come from rape.

My dad is a rapist.

That thought makes me go straight for Atlas needing a release.

I swing.

He ducks.

He swings.

I don't move. I let his fist hit me. I let the pain fuel me.

I swing, I hit, I kick, I give it my all until I can't anymore and I collapse onto the mats, letting out a sob as tears track down my face. I pull at my hair. This isn't supposed to happen! I am supposed to be focusing on revenge and not break like a weak bitch.

He doesn't comfort me; he doesn't tell me it's all okay. He just gives me the moment to get myself together. When I stand up and look at him, he smiles at me. "I'm so fucking proud of you, Harley."

Before I can hit him again like I really fucking want to, Ryan steps in. "Cool down, kid. Fifteen-minute cool down. You need it. Your body is going to be aching tomorrow."

I stomp off, angrier than I was before. Proud? He's fucking proud? Of what? Me being weak? Because that's all I am. Weak. Pathetic. Worthless.

After I cool down, I meet Atlas and Ryan at the front. We head to Bri's house. Ryan follows us because we are all having dinner together. When we get back, I ignore Atlas calling for me and go upstairs to shower again.

I'm so pissed. Why does he always have to push like that? Why couldn't we just have sparred? I know that they all care, but I have to build walls and be tough inside and out to beat these demons I'm at war with.

This anger inside of me is constantly growing and almost becoming uncontrollable, even as I try to take deep breaths and calm myself down in the shower. I get out, throw on some sweats and a hoodie Bri gave me and go to walk downstairs. Before I even get halfway down, I stop at the mention of my name.

"What? Atlas, are you insane? You can't do that! That girl needs someone to help her, not push her to jump off a goddamn cliff!"

"Bri, that's not what his goal is. He's trying to help. Let's just take a breath, okay? We need to work on a plan to get her to open up and tell us about the last three years," Linc says.

I'm sick and tired of people thinking they know what's best for me. But this all just pisses me off and I've had enough. I know without a doubt I'm going to regret this, but I can't bring myself to care.

I storm down the rest of the stairs, causing them to go quiet. When I get into the living room, Bri, Ryan, Atlas, and Linc all look over at me. I square my shoulders and bring my mask down because I refuse to shed any tears over this anymore.

"You're so desperate to know what happened to me? You want all the nasty details? You want to know how when I left the hospital three years ago after my mom died I was slapped, had my hair pulled, then shoved into a trunk and then locked away in a basement for three years? Beaten all the time, chained up so I couldn't get out of the basement unless I was let out, forced to clean up after them, not allowed to think of my mom. Not allowed to speak unless spoken to. Constantly told how worthless I was. You want to know everything? I'll tell you. But you won't like it. I don't want to relive what they did to me. I don't want to think about it. I don't want to put you through the pain of having to listen to it." I look directly at Bri as I say that.

"You want to know how I tried to kill myself? You want to know how I tried to run away and when that failed, I thought that ending my life was my only choice left? You want to know? Huh?" I yell, my arms flailing in front of me. My voice is raspy and aches with each word I speak, a constant reminder of something they did.

Before I or anyone else can say more, a horrid memory assaults my mind, taking me back to a day when I was the weakest I'd ever been.

It's been a year. The only reason I know is because Mother came down to taunt me about it. My mom died a year ago yesterday. I've been trapped in this house, in this basement, for almost a year. All I do is clean when they tell me to and then stay in the basement as they come and beat me whenever they want.

Mother comes down holding a flogger. "It's a special day today, Harley. Lilian was murdered a year ago, so let's celebrate." She cackles as she whips the flogger through the air and it hits my skin.

I cry out, still unable to hold in the sounds of pain I make, which causes her to scream at me as she hits me harder.

"Stupid girl! I can't even come down to have fun without you ruining it! You ruin everything! Lilian knew it. She's dead because you ruin things. I have to beat you because you ruin EVERYTHING!" The lashes come faster, harder, all over my body. I try to hold in the screams, but it's too hard. I can't. I scream until my throat is raw.

Mother finally stops, and I hear her call Father downstairs. I don't move. I'm bleeding all over and my body is aching. With each breath I take, I can feel the slices on my skin move.

When Father comes down, he goes and fills the sink with water. Oh god. Oh no. Please no. He walks back and grabs me by the hair and drags me to the sink as I try to fight him. It's pointless; he's stronger and I am tiny and weak right now.

He immediately shoves my head in the water, allowing me no time to breathe. He holds it longer every time with only raising my head for seconds at a time in-between. I'm getting light-headed, but I do my best to hold on. He eventually stops and throws me to the ground. They stand over me as I cough, gag, and cry.

"You worthless piece of shit."

"This is all your fault!"

"You make us do this to you!"

"Lilian would be disappointed!"

I sob and curl myself up into the smallest ball I can until their words finally stop when they leave. I can't handle this anymore. I want to run away. I need to.

I wait until it's nighttime and I don't hear any noise in the house. I walk up the stairs to find the door unlocked... They really believed I wouldn't try to leave? I head towards the back door and unlock it.

As soon as I step outside, I am roughly yanked back inside by my hair and thrown to the floor. The hits come so fast that I can't even tell who is hitting me. They keep coming. Hit. Hit. Hit. Kick. Kick. Then I see the fist flying towards my face, but I'm too weak to move and everything goes black.

When I come to, I am in the basement again. I try to sit up and move and hear a clanking sound. I startle and sit up too fast. My head pounds, and my body aches, causing me to cry out.

Then I look down and see the cuff around my ankle... attached to a chain... attached to the center of the basement floor... No.

"You'll never leave again unless we allow it." I look up towards the voice and see Mother standing on the stairs staring down at me with hatred in her eyes. She turns around and stomps up the stairs, slamming the basement door and leaving me in the dark.

I cry out, my body wracked with sobs.

I can't handle this. I can't be chained up. Locked away. Never to be found. No. It can't happen. I need... I need my mom. That's the only thing that can save me.

I get up slowly and make my way to the bathroom. I stare at myself in the tiny mirror above the sink, finding my eyes are sunk in. I've lost weight. I can barely move, and now I can never run away because I was so, so stupid the first time.

That leaves one option... I look around but see nothing. Then the mirror. If I just hit it hard enough...

I clear my mind. Not allowing any pain or grief or doubt in. I focus on what this could bring me. Peace. Rest. No more voices in my head. No more nasty words spoken to me.

It'll end it all. It'll save you.

I pull back my fist and punch the mirror.

Once.

Twice.

Three times.

It shatters. My knuckles are bleeding, but I can't feel it.

Peace.

I pick up the sharpest piece of glass I find.

Rest.

I sit on the floor, leaning against the wall.

No more hatred.

I test it on my leg, slicing my thigh.

Seeing my mom.

I gasp as blood drips down from the sharp edge of the glass. It works.

I hold the glass over my wrist and slowly slice through the skin. I can feel it slicing, but I feel no pain. I feel bliss. I feel my broken soul finding its way to peace.

Before I can do the same to the other wrist, the glass is ripped from my hand and Mother is screaming in my face while holding a towel to my wrist.

I frown. Did I do it wrong? Am I in hell?

As I come out of the memory, I realize someone has their arms around me. I scream and start fighting them off, before the voices register in my head. This isn't there, I am not there anymore. I got out. *Breathe, Harley.*

My eyes focus again to register everyone staring at me. All of them look angry and all four of them have tears in their eyes. *Why?*

"Because, honey, you said all that out loud. Everything about running away and trying to... Oh, honey," Bri sobs and drops to her knees, letting out a broken sound as she cries.

I can't handle this...This isn't what I wanted. This just pisses me off even more.

"Are you happy?" I snap as I look around at everyone to see shocked and confused expressions. "Is this what you wanted?" I point to Bri. I'm being horrible, and I don't even care right now. "This is why I didn't want to talk about it. This is why I wanted to keep it from you guys."

"But Harley, now we can help you better. We can help you heal. We can go to the police and figure this all out," Linc says with what almost looks like hope in his eyes. I'm about to crush that.

"No. No, we will not go to the cops. I want revenge." Bri gasps from her spot on the floor. I steel my spine, ready to face off with them. "I am going to look into everything. I am going to dig and dig. I won't stop until I find everything I need to know. Then I will destroy every person who hurt me and hurt my mom. So you can either back me up or I do it alone even if it means leaving the only family I've had since my mom was alive."

I try to keep the worry from my voice that they may actually not want anything to do with me. But I have to take the risk. It's the only thing that's going to get me past everything, destroying every one of them.

Starting with the man who should have been my dad.

I can't be weak anymore.

I can't be pathetic.

I will prove my worth by getting revenge.

CHAPTER
TWENTY-THREE

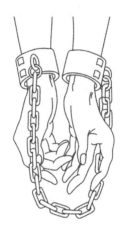

HARLEY

Two weeks later

It's been two weeks since I admitted I wanted revenge. Things have been tense. I still spar and workout with the guys twice every day. Ryan is teaching me how to shoot; he was in the military, so he has a lot of experience. Linc likes throwing knives, so he has been teaching me how to do that, as well. I pick up on things fast and don't stop practicing until I have it down.

Atlas trains me hard. I run at least two miles every day now. My body is building muscle, and I am getting stronger. I eat a lot more food now; I've come to love food again, so I eat all the time.

Bri has been distant. She hates all of this. She's still kind and is always telling me she wants me in her home and loves me. It helps reassure me because I'm still insecure. Very badly. It's stupid, but I don't know how to fix that. She told me that she wants me studying to get my GED while also looking into things and training. I gave in and have been studying. It's the only thing she's come down on, so I'll do it for her.

She's scared. She's worried someone is going to show up here, so she never lets me leave alone. She's also worried I'm going to get myself killed going down this path. I want to reassure her, but I can't when I don't know how this'll end.

I've been digging over the last two weeks but have hit a wall. My anger has gotten the best of me quite a few times. I use Bri's home office when she's at work because she works twelve-hour shifts at the hospital. I'm trying to dig into Sons of Silence again, which is what Brielle mentioned when she told me about my mom. I have been searching for them online, and today I have finally found something.

They hosted a charity event last year. *Charity event? What, to cover all the raping of women they do?* And there are pictures from a news article of some of them, so I have been able to search through the pictures and get some names. They shouldn't be allowed around kids! It's insane.

I'm able to get what is called their road names and what their job is from what it says on the vests they wear. The vests look familiar, but I can't think of why, so I push that thought aside.

Right now, I am going through pictures of the SOS MC from the charity event they did trying to make out faces and match them to the names on their vest things. I zoom in on one guy who looks kind of familiar. I can't make out his face or his name, but his cut says Enforcer. I go to the next picture.

Holy fucking shit. Enforcer is Blade; this is the guy from the bus stop! That's why I recognize their vests! He was watching me.

Ugh, this cannot be good. If they know who I am then who knows what they want with me? *Focus, Harley.* My main goal is to find out who my dad is. I want to kill him.

I've never killed anyone, and Bri and the guys don't know that I want to. They think once I find out who he is I'm going to get information on everyone at the club to take to the cops. But no. I want revenge firsthand. I want him to see me. I want to face this man and shoot him and watch him die. I know the chances of me making it out alive from this are slim to none, so I won't tell Bri. I'll leave her a letter when I'm ready to go find him and hope that she doesn't hate me.

I believe Bri when said she thinks my mom was misplacing love with Gabe when everything happened. She went through hell for most of her life, and it makes me question whether I might have done the same thing if I had stayed at Tammy's and was going to school... I'll admit I thought those guys were attractive and I felt good when they gave me attention, so I am glad that I got away from them when I did.

What if the same thing had happened to me? That I took any attention I could get and thought it was love? I shudder at that thought.

Gabe, my dad, does not deserve to breathe anymore. My mom doesn't get to. Why should he? It angers me so much. My mom always told me growing up that my dad wasn't a bad man and one day I would understand my name. She said she named me after something meaningful and important to her. I know what Brielle means, but what about Harley?

I think she still loved him up until she died. I hate him for that. He stopped her from ever getting to fall in love again because she was so messed up from him.

I need a way to find out these guys' real names. I wonder if any of them went to local schools. Or even the school I was at! I look up my school and see that luckily they have all school pictures for the last twenty years still up on here.

I start by looking for Tammy. If I can find her class, then I can look through them for a Gabe and then compare it to the pictures from the charity event to see if he's there. I find Tammy first, so I know it's the right class, and then I start going through the rest of the class until I find Gabriel.

I found him. Holy shit. His last name... This is my father. Holy fucking shit.

Why the fuck didn't I think to look up his first name with my last name? *Dumbass!* I Google his name, and then I find his information much easier. There are a few more pictures so now I can clearly tell he's a part of the club. I am just not sure what his roadname is yet.

I find out his father's name, Gabriel St. James. *Of course, he named his son after himself. Bastard.* He died five years ago. Murdered behind a bar owned by the MC. His road name was Killer. Based on what I've researched on how MCs work, his son, who is my father, Gabe, would have taken over. I just can't find any new pictures of him with his cut on to make sure and get his road name. But I know that's the name I need. Gabriel St. James.

I know I want to take down the SOS club, but I am not sure how I want to do that yet. I think starting with killing Gabe is my best bet, and if I survive that, I can make more plans. They ruined my mom, so I will ruin them.

I can't find shit on who killed my mom. Ugh! This is so hard. I know that the MC are probably the ones who killed my mom, but I have no proof. I wish I could remember if they were wearing vests or not and what they might have said.

I decide to call it a night and take a break. I can look into more tomorrow, and I am going to look into Tammy and her family tomorrow too. I am so glad that I'm not related to her in any way. I just wish I knew how she was able to get her hands on me after Mom died. Wouldn't there be proof that I was not related to her?

I gnaw on my bottom lip, debating looking into more now even though it's 10 p.m. *No, Harley, take a break. You've been in here almost all day,* I say to myself.

"Talking to yourself already, huh?"

I jump out of the chair and scream. "Holy fucking shit! Linc, what the hell? Don't do that to me!"

He laughs, "I wasn't even quiet there, kiddo. I slammed the doors and stomped around. I even called out your name. You were lost in la la land and apparently talking to yourself. Which, by the way, crazy you is right. Stop for the night and get out of this room. Bri should be home in an hour. Let's make something to eat."

I grumble and follow him out to the kitchen. "You know, I already know you can't cook after the stories Bri told me, and she's been trying to teach me. It's not going well. So what are you thinking we are gonna make?" I lift a brow at him and cross my arms over my chest.

He runs a hand over the back of his neck. "Uh, I didn't think that far ahead, but I'm hungry. Does she have anything easy?"

I shrug and go to look through the pantry.

"What about chili and cornbread? We can heat the canned chili on the stove, and I think cornbread is easy enough to make since it's from a box." I glance over my shoulder at Linc.

He nods, and I grab what we need. Then Linc starts prepping the cornbread while I cook the chili. While eating way more since being here and gaining a love for food that I didn't know I had, I have come to learn that I will eat anything, but I have a particular craving for Mexican food. Literally all of it. Anything. Bri orders from a restaurant that is close by, and I think I have tried literally everything on their menu. There hasn't been one thing that I haven't liked.

A little bit later, the cornbread is in the oven, and the chili is warm on the stove. It smells half decent in here. As we laugh and high five over our accomplishments, Bri comes in from the garage. She sees us and freezes.

"Is that... Do I smell food? Are you guys... cooking?" She looks so shocked that I can't hold back my laughter and burst out laughing at the same time Linc does.

"Jeez, Bri, you have so little faith in us?" I say.

She slowly nods. "Um, yeah... usually you just make a sandwich or heat up leftovers, and Linc doesn't step foot in the kitchen. Ever."

"Well, it's just canned chili and boxed cornbread. Easy enough." I shrug.

The oven beeps, so I take the cornbread out. We all get bowls of chili and some cornbread and sit down to eat. I take a bite and immediately spit it back into the bowl and start gagging. *Holy hell, how can that taste so bad?*

Bri chokes and chugs down water. Linc sighs dramatically and says, "I don't get it, I followed all the directions on the package. How did it not come out right? I didn't even burn it!"

"Lincoln, you seriously can't tell? It tastes like salt! Like salted bread. God, that's horrible! Why did you put salt in it?"

"I thought it would need it! I only added a little!"

"You only add what it says to, Lincoln Tanner!" Bri chides. Linc nods and mumbles a very not sincere apology.

"At least the chili tastes okay," I add with a shrug. Linc glares, and Bri holds back a laugh. We eat the chili, and then we all start cleaning up. Bri is loading the dishwasher when she stops and spins around. "Lincoln!" He freezes and turns towards her. I walk closer to see what she's holding up; it's a measuring cup... I think it's a quarter cup. "Is this what you used for salt?" Linc nods very slowly.

I burst out laughing. Holy hell. "Even I know that's a fuckton of salt, Linc! Holy crap, you can never come in the kitchen again."

Bri is nodding as I talk. "She's right. The kitchen ban now extends from your house to mine too."

Linc sighs and goes to the living room and dramatically falls back on the couch flinging his arms out. "I quit!" he says.

I start laughing again, but it's quickly cut off by the glare on Bri's face. I sober up quick. Uh oh.

She holds up the pan I made chili in. "Harls, how long did you leave the chili on the burner?"

I shrug. "Until the corn bread was done."

"Harley, you only have to heat it untill it's warm. You left it too long and didn't stir it enough. So what we ate on the top was fine, but the pan is trash now that you burnt the bottom of it up." She shows me the pan and the bottom is completely black.

I wince. Oops? "Am I banned from the kitchen too?"

She shakes her head. "No, I still have hope for you. But I need to be here with you."

"Well, dang, kinda hoped you'd just give up on trying to teach me." I sigh dramatically.

Bri rolls her eyes. "Children. All of you. Children. Lord, help me."

Linc and I snicker as she keeps going on mumbling to herself about stupid children.

The next morning, I get up and go to the gym with Atlas for training. By the time I get back, Bri is gone for work already. I lock up the house, shower, eat, and get back to work on researching.

I decide to take a break from looking at the MCs and look into Tammy and Richard. The first thing I do is look up Rob and Tabby on social media. Rob has nothing I can find. But Tabby has just about every social media platform there is. I don't even know what the point of some of these are... There is nothing I can use on here; it's all just her being stupid. She posts the most stupid shit every day.

I spend the next three hours looking into Tammy and Richard but unfortunately, I can't find anything. It's really starting to piss me off. I'm not tech savvy, so that makes it even harder because where the hell am I supposed to look? I know they are into bad shit. I've heard small things said over the years, and Brielle said something about my mom saying Tammy and Richard were going to work with Killer, who has been dead for five years, so who knows what they are up to now? As I get more frustrated, I decide to stop for the day.

I go through Bri's books; she is a huge bookworm and reads a lot, so she has quite the collection. I pick one out that I saw her reading not that long ago called Untamed Vixen by Luna Pierce.

A few hours later, I am a good chunk in and holy dirty, Bri has a naughty side. My face flames thinking of all things I just read. Reverse harem? This girl has more than one man. I mean, wow. The things I just read... I am fully innocent. I know nothing and have no experience, but shit my, well, I'm throbbing somewhere I've never throbbed before. I have this intense need to touch myself, and when I stick a hand in my pants and run a finger over my panties, I realize they are soaking wet...

Wow, that's kind of embarrassing. I lightly touch myself, and it feels like jolts of electricity go through me. I think about what I was just reading, and my mind automatically goes to the three hottest guys I've ever seen: Cayden, Ryker, and Grayson—

Oh shit! No, no, no. I rip my hand out of my pants and stand up and pace the room. What the fuck am I doing?

I sprint upstairs and take a cold shower and wash away all those thoughts. Holy shit, I can't believe that's where my mind went. Thank god I never have to see them again. That would be extremely embarrassing.

The next day, Atlas texts me to let me know we will train later in the day today because he has some other stuff to deal with this morning. So I get to work with my research. My biggest goal right now is to take down my dad, so I put Tammy and Richard aside and focus on him. I need to make 100% sure that he is involved in the club.

I go back to news articles and researching the name of the club and looking at every picture I can find. I search his name and try to find anything that way too. It takes a few hours, but I finally get it. Fuck. I finally know who he is. Fuck this, I need to just get it over with. I'm not that stupid; I know the chances of me living are slim, but it's not like I have much to live for anyways. Maybe I'll be lucky enough to run away. All I know is I need to take him out, and it needs to happen soon. Now comes the part where things get tricky.

I have the $200 that was left from pickpocketing when I came here that I never had to use. Bri didn't let me use it; she wanted me to save it. She also gives me cash all the time that I don't need, so I have an extra $200 from her. So I have $400 total. I don't know if I can come back here after I do it, *if I survive.* So I pack a bag. Bri has bought me a lot of clothes since I've been here, so I pack enough for a few days.

I don't want to carry too much on me. It feels like I get punched in the gut thinking about Bri and what this is going to do to her. I love her. She is like the aunt I never got to have, but I have to do this. I'll leave her a letter and hope she doesn't hate me.

After I am done packing my backpack, I stash it under my bed and get ready for the gym with Atlas. Here is the next part: Guess it's time to put my pickpocketing skills to the real test on a much bigger scale now.

Ryan has a small collection of guns at the gym where he helps people learn and get their carry permit. He was going to help me get mine when I turn eighteen, and this is probably ruining that now. Anyways, I know the code into the room because he had me go in there once to grab something. So I just have to get away from Atlas long enough to get in there and grab one and hope no one notices it's gone until it's too late.

A while later, Atlas shows up. He can tell something is off. I am doing a terrible job at hiding how nervous I am right now. Shit. I need to come up with something to tell him. So what do I do? I blurt out the first thing that comes to my mind.

"I read one of Bri's books today. It's one I saw her reading a while ago, and uh, it was uh... I don't even know, in a way like reading porn? But also with a good story that was interesting and, um, it had three dudes who all loved the same girl and they all ended up together. Anyways, I'm nervous for Bri to get home. I feel like I accidently found a side to her I didn't want to... Oh my god, I can't believe I just blurted all of that out." I put my hands over my face as my cheeks turn bright red. *Well, at least that worked as a distraction.*

Atlas doesn't say anything, but I feel him put the truck in park. I look up and see we are at the gym. When I glance over at him, he raises his eyebrows and smirks.

"Well, Harls, thanks for that interesting tidbit of information on Bri. But also, reading is something we do to escape our lives. It's a place to go when things suck or just when you want to pretend to be someone else. Don't worry about it. If you enjoyed the book, that's all that matters. So Bri likes a little erotica and multiple men? Who cares? I know I don't..." He chortles. "I doubt Bri will care. She'll probably be as embarrassed as you are, but it's really not a big deal. I'm glad you read today. Reading is good for the soul."

He gets a faraway look on his face that I can't quite understand. "Do you read?" I ask.

He looks pained before saying, "Use to. I mostly listen to audiobooks now. Let's get in there and get going, Harls." He jumps out of the truck before I can ask more.

We get started fast and before I know it, our workout is over, and I am exhausted. Atlas always goes hard on me and kicks my ass, and today was no different.

I tell him I need a shower and head towards the bathrooms. Before the bathrooms is a hall that leads to the offices and the storage room that is locked, and that's where the guns are. I look back and see him texting on his phone. I guess this is as good of a chance as I'll get.

I walk back to the storage room and enter the code. The door clicks when it unlocks, and I wince, hoping he didn't hear it. I go in and quickly find the gun I've used the most. A Glock 17. I make sure to grab extra bullets and then stuff the gun in the back of my leggings under my t-shirt, and the extra bullets go into the sports bra I have on. Luckily, the shirt is pretty baggy, so nothing really shows unless you look too closely. I head out and slowly shut the door.

As I am walking down the hall, a door flings open, and out steps Linc. He eyes me, and I make sure to lock down my fears and nerves as best I can and just look exhausted.

"Hey kid, what are you doing? Did you finish your workout with Atlas?"

"Yeah, I'm exhausted now and am going to shower before we head back to Bri's."

Before he can respond, Atlas comes down the hall. "Harls, what are you doing? Hurry it up. I don't want to wait all day. Linc, stop holding her up."

I mumble a sorry and duck my head taking off around them to go to the bathroom before they can say anything else. I lock myself in a stall with my gym bag and stuff the gun and bullets in the bottom of the bag to hide it. I take a deep breath, then quickly shower and try to forget about it so I don't break down in front of them. Shit, this is terrifying.

Luckily, we make it home with no problems. The guys drop me off because they have plans tonight since Bri doesn't get off until 2 a.m.

It feels like everything is falling into my lap way too easily, but I'm not going to think twice about it and take it as a win and do this. I head inside and get to writing my letter to Bri.

I cry as I finish, saying a silent prayer that everything goes well and that I can come back here and move on with my life when this is over and that Bri will still love me. I gather my stuff and call for a taxi. While I wait, I check over my research I wrote down.

Research

*My Father is: Gabe? - Gabriel St. James (Junior?)

*Sons of Silence MC, When mom was around them Killer was president. Can't find a picture of the SOS President, Killer also Known as Gabriel St. James was Killed 5 years ago. No longer President. Maybe his son is now?

*Vice President is "Sugar" real name Unknown. Mom's brother, same dad, he died 33 years ago.

*Road Capitan is "Axe"

*Sergeant At Arms is "Stone"

*Enforcer is "Blade"

*Another one with a vest says "Nerds" can't make out job title

*Hit List: Gabriel St. James - Road Name: Unknown

The taxi soon arrives, and I find out it'll cost me $150 to get to Jacksonville by taxi, so I do that instead of taking the bus again. I don't have time for that. The driver takes off, and I exhale.

Holy shit. I am doing this. I'm coming for you, you sick bastard. Today will be your last full day of breathing.

I smile out the window. *I'm doing this for you, mom.*

CHAPTER TWENTY-FOUR

RYKER

I strike out, hitting so hard that I hear the chain keeping the punching bag hanging rattle. I look down and see that my knuckles are split and bleeding. I grin. Fuck, I needed that. It's been a few weeks since I was forced into solitude. It's fucking bullshit. I have barely spoken to anyone since then. My mind can't comprehend what the point was. I know we live in a fucked-up world. Hell, I've lived my own fucked-up hell before I was even really around this club much. And then I turned around and lived through another hell with my fucking aunt.

I constantly find myself worrying about Harley. She consumes my mind. I wasn't fucking kidding when I said I was enraptured by her. She has this strength that I don't even think she can see for herself. I want to help her find it. I *need* to help her find it.

This girl can heal my brothers and I; I know she can without a doubt. And I know we can help her find that fire within her. I just have no idea how to go about things now. I feel stuck, and it's making my skin crawl. Rage made me stay down in that cell for three days. Grayson came down every day, three times a day, to bring me food and talk to me. He'd bring Cayden with him too, but he didn't say much. I think he is pissed at me.

On day three, Rage came down, bringing Nerds with him. Rage talked to me again about how I fucked up.

I get it, I really do get that I could have fucked shit up for the club in a huge way, but the other part of me just doesn't care. Harley is mine. *Ours.* And that's all that truly matters. Nerds put this weird looking black ankle bracelet on me that I can't take off myself. *Trust me, I've tried.*

"This is for your safety and for the peace of mind of everyone in the club. You have a lot of trust that you need to earn again. We aren't giving up on you. But this is a final warning. You fuck up like this again, you will not be joining the club. When you are eighteen, you will be asked to leave." There was no loving, kind Rage showing here.

I know he is serious, and I do happen to know when to keep my mouth shut, so I had nodded and didn't throw a bitch fit over the stupid fucking cuff that apparently tracks me anywhere I go and when I am in the compound. If I try to leave, it'll alert everyone unless someone turns it off for me.

After I had discovered the stuff at the Wilsons, they have been keeping a closer eye on them but still nothing. We all think Harley was being kept down in that basement. I wanted to go back again and look around and take pictures, but Rage said no. That they without a doubt would have fully gotten rid of the evidence I found.

Every day it's more clear that Harley ran away. Everyone is kind of coming to the same thought and wants to just leave it be rather than risk us leading Tammy or anyone else who could be wanting to hurt Harley straight to her.

But I just know there is more to this. I know it. But I can't prove it, so instead I am pounding as hard as I can on this bag, like I have been since the day I got out of the cell.

They want me to open up and talk to them and ask for help when it comes to my anger or when I feel I don't have enough control. But I can't do that when I want to punch every single one of them in the face for leaving me in a goddamn cell for three days.

The door slamming into the wall breaks me from my punching and thoughts. I turn towards the doors and see Cayden coming in looking furious, as per usual. I sigh, knowing he probably is going to piss me off.

"You know, I thought I was the one who didn't like to fucking talk around here. It only really worked because you don't know how to shut the fuck up a lot of the time."

I stare at him, shocked and slightly offended... even if it's true.

He scoffs, "Don't look at me like that. I can talk if I want to. I just chose not to. One thing that does is allow me to observe in a way other people can't. And you, Ryker, I have observed and come to a conclusion about."

I raise a brow and cross my arms. "What might that be, brother?" I snap at him.

"That you are being the biggest fucking idiot I have ever met. You may be slightly unhinged and probably need some kind of fucking help because of the shit you have gone through, but you aren't stupid. So why are you acting like it?"

I straighten my back, feeling my anger rising. "What the fuck are you talking about?"

He flashes a downright evil smile. "You. I am talking about you. After your punishment of being in the cell, you went quiet on everyone. I didn't like that they did that. I fucking hated every second you were down there. But do I get it? Yes. You fucked up. And you knew when you were planning and leaving here that you were about to fuck up. Man up and deal with the consequences that come with the decision you made.

"I heard them talking after they left you down there. They all hated it, but the only other option was for you to leave the club when you turned eighteen. And believe it or not, you do have a fucking family here. These people want to help you. They aren't your dad. They are not trying to manipulate you or lying to you at every turn. You have to trust them in order for them to ever trust you."

I just stare at him. Cade is my brother. Blood or not, I would die for him. We may have a weird dynamic around here, but one thing I have learned is that I can always, always trust Cayden and Grayson.

He hasn't said this much in years. Cade used to talk more. Still not even this much, though. I just stand here, staring. Processing everything he said.

He wouldn't take the time to actually talk and say those things to me if he didn't fully believe them himself.

Family.

Help... *me.*

I have to trust them...

Fuck, I get it. It feels like Cade just punched through a wall I have been building up and then when Harley came around, that wall built higher, but higher around my... my family. Because I know how I feel, and I didn't want them talking me out of it or using it against me like my dad would have. *They aren't your dad.*

I look at Cade in the eye. "How do I trust them? What do I do?"

He shakes his head. "I can't answer that. But maybe start with asking them to help when you feel out of control." He shrugs. "Come on, we need to go to school soon, and you fucking stink and need a shower."

I follow him out of the gym. "So does this mean you are going to start talking to me more?"

He snorts. "Fuck no."

I sigh. Back to short answers so soon. "We'll see about that," I say, giving him a huge smile when he glares back at me.

After I shower and get ready for school, I find Gray waiting in my room with a first aid kit.

I roll my eyes at him. "I'm fine, Gray."

He shakes his head and grabs my hand and starts cleaning and bandaging up my knuckles. I haven't been wrapping my hands because I just don't care to. I welcome the pain. Sometimes I feel like I need it to breathe.

"I don't know what Cade said to you, but you seem lighter. I'm glad," he says so quietly that I almost don't hear him. An emotion showing in his voice that I don't understand.

After he is done, we head downstairs, and I go to Rage's office so he can turn off my prison alarm. That's what I call the ankle monitor anyways. They make me wear it to school too because it can still track me but he can turn off the alarm part so I can leave without it triggering everyone's phones.

We go out to Noah's truck where Cade is waiting for us. We all know how to ride motorcycles, but only Cade has one right now, so we just take Noah's truck all together to school since Noah can use his bike during the day.

When we get to school, we pull up to our assigned parking spot and see Lexington waiting to the side, looking ready to kill. Cade grunts as he pulls in, and Gray and I sigh. Lex came up to us a few times before winter break asking where the hell Harley was, but we have mostly avoided her. No need to even try to play nice when Harley isn't here.

I get out first with Cade and Gray right on my ass, probably to make sure I keep my cool. "What the fuck do you want, Lexington?"

"I want to know why when I went to Harley's house over winter break, her mom told me that Harley had to leave because of your little gang. Because I swear to god, Ryker, if you so much as—"

I cut her off, "First off, it's a club, not a gang. Secondly, we had nothing to do with Harley leaving. We'd never hurt her. Third, you went over there? Tell me everything they said. Right the fuck now."

Lex smirks. "You can't demand for me to tell you shit. I believe Mrs. Wilson more than I'd ever believe you. Besides, I am going to go see her soon. Mrs. Wilson is letting me. So I'll get my answers on what you did." She glares at me and then looks behind me before sidestepping me to stand in front of Gray. "How are you, Gray?" She reaches up to run a hand down his chest, but I quickly grab her wrist and slide between them.

We know this game. She sucks at it. Steph, a bitch at our school, has been gunning for Cade and I for over a year. But she doesn't want Gray around us, so she has had Lexington trying to get with him. But she despises it so much that she can't pull it off without showing her hatred.

"You don't ever, and I mean ever, touch him. Got me?" I squeeze her wrist until I see the blood drain from her face, and she nods quickly. I release her with a shove and turn around to see the school's princesses coming over here. I groan, "Why today? Seriously? Let's just leave." Cade grunts, and Gray snickers quietly.

Steph steps up to Cade and me while her minions stay back. "Well hello, boys, looking nice," she purrs.

Gag. I look at Cade, and he just shrugs, then wraps his arm around her shoulders and leads her away. What the fuck?

We follow, unsure what is happening right now. Cade leads Steph right to an empty classroom and takes her inside, shutting us all out in the hall. We get a text a second later.

Caveman Cade: Might as well get my dick sucked.

What the fuck! Cade has only ever touched one other girl. It was a girl at the club a year ago, and he let her suck him off, but that was it. He has never fully been with a girl, so what the fuck is this now?

Gray just stares at his phone, his eyes wide like saucers.

I look back and see Lex and Steph's minions standing there. "What the fuck are you doing? Fuck off!"

The minions take off, but Lex stays for a second, watching us before storming past.

I am so fucking confused right now and it's only 7:15 a.m. Fuck.

Cade let Steph hang off him all day. She's insanely annoying, so I don't get it, but I can't ask him until we are away from the screeching fake bitch.

We are finally leaving for the day and as soon as we all get in the truck, I turn on Cade, "What the fuck was that shit?"

Cade shrugs and starts driving.

"Seriously, Cade. Say fucking something. Because I don't fucking get it."

He shrugs again then glances at me. "Free pussy."

I stare at him. I don't even know what to say to that. Gray speaks up before I can even think of what to say.

"Why though, Cade? You've never showed interest, and I thought you wanted nothing to do with Steph or her minions because of how they act and how they try to get me away from you guys. I don't get it. You don't care about free... girls."

If I wasn't so shocked by Cade, I'd probably laugh and tease Gray about not wanting to say pussy.

Cade white-knuckles the steering wheel, and when we stop at a stoplight, he grabs his phone and texts us. Apparently, he's done talking for the day.

Caveman Cade: It's just free pussy. I don't care about the dumb girl. Let it go. I am done talking about it.

I really don't want to let it go, but I know better than to push things with him, so I do. But there is something more to this, and Cade just isn't saying it.

When we get back to the club, there are way more bikes here than a normal day. Now what? I just want a break after the shit show of today. We get out and head inside, but Cade turns off and heads upstairs towards our rooms. I want to go up there and demand he tell me what the real problem is, but I'll give him time first. Instead, Gray and I head off towards the offices looking for Noah.

CAYDEN

I storm upstairs to my room, ripping the door open before slamming it shut. I change into workout clothes so I can go down to the gym. By the time I get down there, my irritation at today is just about maxed out. I'm not even angry with my brothers. I'm furious with myself.

I wrap my hands and step up to the punching bag, I know this isn't going to be enough to calm me down, but it will have to do for now. I start in, getting a good rhythm going as I let everything from today, the last few months honestly, out.

This girl, Harley. She won't get out of my head. I can't let her in there. The place is too dark for anyone to ever be. But more importantly, Harley is already Ryker's. He can get obsessive over things and people. He did when he met me. The shithead wouldn't leave me alone until I talked to him, which I still don't know if that was the best thing or the worst thing to ever happen because he hasn't gone away since the first time I spoke to him. All I said was, "Fuck off." And he started clapping and shouting, "He speaks!"

I feel things I have never felt before when it comes to Harley. But I can't act on them. If somehow or some way she does come back here, or Ryker finds a way to find her and get her in his life, I have to find a way to lose the feelings I have. I don't really believe we will ever see her again. I think she is long gone. But that doesn't stop her perfect face from popping up in my mind. All the goddamn time.

I slam my fist into the punching bag harder and harder. I hate myself for today. But I can't get her out of my head. I needed a distraction. Steph is always up our asses wanting to be around us. It's easy to just let her be my distraction...

There is just one big problem. The whole time I was in the classroom with her letting her go down on me, a certain redhead was on my mind. Fuck!

I push myself to my limits after I finish on the bag. I work out hard, to the point where my muscles will feel the burn for days after. I still feel disgusting for letting her even touch me today. But I can't keep letting Harley in my mind because either I'll end up like Ryker, obsessed and this need to hunt her down, or she'll come back, and I'll become a jealous, possessive asshole and destroy my relationship with my brothers when I know Ryker is in love with her.

I can't do that to my brothers. I won't. So I have to just keep doing anything and everything until I feel nothing for a tiny redhead that slammed her way into my mind without even knowing it.

I run back upstairs from the gym in the basement and whistle for Bear, my dog. He comes running out of the kitchen, of course. The dog never stops eating. We head outside and take off for a long run that will hopefully help clear my head more.

I just wish I knew my willpower was going to be put to the test much sooner than I thought.

RYKER

We find Noah in the office he usually uses, and he waves us in. "Gray, go ahead and head to Nerds's tech room. He thinks he got a lead on something and could use the help."

He looks at me, a question in his eyes, and I nod. "Go, I will fill him in." He nods in return and takes off.

"What's going on?" Noah asks.

I tell him what Lex said this morning. "Alright, let's go find Rage and then see if Nerds still has that mic I planted working. It should pick up on anything from the front door area."

"Alright, but before we go, I need to ask something."

Noah stops walking and turns toward me. "What's up?" he asks hesitantly, almost appearing shocked that I am talking more, but I guess after barely talking even to Noah for those weeks after being in the cell, that makes sense.

"Have you noticed anything different with Cade lately?"

Noah nods. "Yeah, but I just thought his weird behavior was because you weren't talking, and you know he gets worried about his brothers." He shrugs.

"Yeah, but he talked to me this morning. Like a lot. He helped me clear my head and said more than I think he ever has. And then when we got to school, you know that bitch Steph we've told you about?" He nods. "Well, Cade went off with her and let her get him off."

Noah looks taken back but then just shakes his head. "Maybe he's just ready to get out there more. The club sluts are off limits to you guys, so maybe he's trying at school. I wouldn't think too much about it. Let's go figure out this Wilson shit."

I nod and follow him. Noah knows us all well, but at the same time, he doesn't. So I don't know if he truly just thinks it's no big deal or if he's worried and trying to play it off so I don't freak out.

We find Rage and Sugar at the bar in the common room, and they follow us to Nerds's tech room. Nerds and Gray are already sucked into what they are doing. Nerds just nods and mumbles, "Ask Gray." The dude looks like a hot mess; he must have some lead to get this out of it.

Gray finds the audio files and starts going through them. Eventually he finds it and we listen to it. We've had someone always going through the audio to see what is going on, but it hasn't given us anything since we put it up besides normal conversations. They didn't even talk about Harley leaving which we found odd.

The doorbell rings. "I'll get it!" Richard says. "Can I help you?"

"Umm... yeah, I am a friend of Harley's. She has been gone for a while, and I just wanted to check in on her. Some boys from school knew her but won't tell me anything."

"And who are these boys?" a new voice says: Tammy.

"Um, some boys who belong to the gang on the other side of town," Lex replies.

"The MC?" Tammy asks.

"I think so, ma'am."

"Hmmm, well then, those boys are the reason she isn't here. She had to leave because of things they did. They are bad company."

"Oh yes, I know they are bad company. I even tried to warn Harley about that. But can I check on her? Or go see her?"

"Well dear, if we think we can trust you, then yes. But we need you to do a few things for us first. Why don't you come in?"

The door closes, and then you hear footsteps. "Come into the office, dear," Tammy says. You can hear movement, then nothing because they have moved too far away.

I frown. "So she didn't lie to us like we thought, but Tammy lied. Unless Tammy does know where she is and is keeping her somewhere else now."

The tension in the room rises as everyone spouts off different theories, but before we can dive into discussing it, Nerds turns around and jumps out of his chair. "Everyone, out! Everyone!

Gray, too. I need the room. Take this somewhere else! GET OUT!" he yells.

Wow. I don't think I've ever seen him so unraveled before. Rage looks just as stunned but moves everyone out of the room, and Nerds slams the door on us as soon as we are all out in the hall.

"What the fucking hell was that?" Rage demands. Ain't that the question of the year?

CHAPTER TWENTY-FIVE

NERDS

Thank god it's silent now. Don't get me wrong, I don't mind having them in here, and I love Gray's help and teaching him what I know, but right now I have something I need to focus on.

I have spent months looking into the Wilsons and all the shit they have done. It hasn't been an easy process, but I am slowly putting all the pieces together of just how deep this shit goes. Rage's dad, Killer, seems to have started all of this about thirty years ago with the other guys who started the club with him. They are considered the OG Members: Killer, the founder and then Hawk who was Sugar's dad, Chains, who was Axe's dad, and Buzz who was Tammy's dad; they are all dead except for Buzz, but he took off six years ago or so, so talking to any of them about everything is off the table.

It looks like they were a part of starting this thing up, and they ran it by themselves. They'd find girls through what looks like ads for different jobs that you'd more than likely see women take who are in desperate need of money. I found two warehouses where it looks like they are keeping them right now, more than likely to hold them until they get them trained and find a buyer. A shiver runs down my spine at that thought. I don't get how people could do this shit.

Then they create meeting spots for buyers to meet someone unimportant to do a drop once the money shows up in the account. It doesn't look like Tammy or Richard show their faces, which is smart on their end, so it doesn't appear from an outside perspective that they are involved.

But I have been able to hack into things from my side and see how everything operates. The only problem is, we already know Rage's name is on the main offshore account that funds the warehouse and everything they seem to need, but also Axe's dad, Chains, had everything transferred to Axe after he died. So now it also looks like Axe is involved. Along with Sugar. They all have their legal names on warehouses, vans, offshore accounts, and some of the job ads say they are for the club.

So we can't do shit to try and shut them down until I can clear everyone's name. But if I miss something, I screw us all over. So this isn't some easy process.

It's eating me alive to have to take my time doing this, which is why I've barely slept and feel like I want to rip everyone's head off. I don't want any more girls to suffer, but I can't do anything yet. It's killing me more than I am letting on.

I rub my temples; I could really use a joint right now. *No. No, don't go there.*

So with all of this shit piling up, I decided to set up a new program. It will keep an ongoing trace for anyone who searches any of the club members. Legal names and road names. Or if someone is looking into the club, it'll tag it so I can look into where they are searching from and find out who is searching if I need to.

It's something we should have done years ago. If we had, then some of this shit wouldn't be happening. *Shake off the guilt; it's not your fault.*

I shake out my arms and stretch before popping a handful of nerds in my mouth. The new system alerted me the other day to someone looking up the club, but nothing seemed suspicious. But now, the same place is still looking up information on the club and searching any names they seem to find. So I am tracking where it's coming from. They have a pretty solid firewall up, so it's taking some time, which is why I kicked everyone out.

I am already stressed out and trying to get past this firewall is frustrating my already tired brain, so I needed some peace and quiet. I know that whoever is searching is in Virginia Beach, Virginia, but that's all I have so far. I got the location down to a small area by the beach. When I searched that area, it looked like it had some beach houses, so I am not sure who would be living on the beach over there looking into us.

The firewall finally cracks, and I can get in to see their information. Brielle Ann West. I don't recognize the name, so I start looking into her. It looks like she's from here but left when she was fifteen after her mom died. She went to the same school as Tammy and Rage. That can't be a coincidence.

I dive into searching this more, discovering some old yearbook photos from their school, and it looks like Brielle was friends with

Tammy's younger sister, Lilian. I search for Lilian but can't seem to find anything on her.

My only thought is it would be Lilian searching for us maybe, although I couldn't tell you why.

This is pissing me off! It's been hours. Fucking hours! I can't seem to figure out why or even exactly who is looking into us, but they still are as I am looking! They are literally searching for everyone they can. I stand up and throw anything I can off my desk and into the wall. A few minutes go by before the door bursts open to Rage and Sugar.

They stare at me with wide eyes. "Don't look at me like that! I can't fucking crack shit! I am fucking failing at all of this! There are girls being hurt right under our noses, and we can't even fucking stop them!"

During my yelling, Stone also showed up. He pushes Rage and Sugar aside and tilts his head for me to follow him. I do, because I don't ever get like this, and if he thinks he can help, I'll fucking take it. I need to calm the fuck down.

We head downstairs to the gym. When we get there, he throws hand wraps at me. After I wrap my hands, we go to the mats, and he spars with me. Not taking it easy at all. I am not weak, I workout and have trained a lot, but I am no match for Stone, and I know that. The only sound in the gym is the music playing through the speakers, our fists hitting each other, and the sound of our breathing and grunts.

We don't talk, which I am grateful for. By the time we are done, it's been three hours. I am sweating, bleeding, and bruised, but I can relax my shoulders a bit.

Stone nods at me. "It's not all on you, brother. Take a breather when you need to. I know we all put a ton of pressure on you, but the rest of us know this isn't easy. Hell, almost none of us could do what you are doing. Don't overdo it. We are all doing the best we can. We can only truly save those girls if we are all at our best or else we risk them getting hurt even more or even getting ourselves into trouble. Got it?"

I wordlessly nod. Stone doesn't do a lot of talking to begin with, so I know I will take what he says to heart.

I decide to head upstairs to my room and shower and nap. A few hours later, I am feeling much better. It's getting late now, probably around eleven, so I head downstairs figuring nighttime will be my best time to get more work done peacefully.

When I reach the kitchen, I move to grab a new bowl of nerds. The prospects keep my stash stocked up for me. When I get in there, though, Daniel, one of our prospects, is standing in the kitchen eating nerds. I slam the door into the wall and glare at him. He smirks before masking it and dropping his hand to his side.

"Prospect, care to tell me what the fuck you think you are doing?"

He shakes his head. I look around and see Rage has now come into the room but is staying back, and another prospect, Connor, is standing with Daniel. He takes a step away from him. Smart boy.

"Prospect, has it ever been made okay to touch the nerds in here? Or fucking anywhere?"

The stupid kid tries to play dumb. I don't want to deal with this. I don't care if I have an unhealthy addiction. You don't touch my nerds and every fucking person knows that. Only Rage and Sugar know why. I grew up with addicts and because of that I also became one at too young of an age. It's how I came to meet Rage and join the club to begin with. They helped me get clean and along the way, nerds candy became a coping mechanism for me.

I mean, they taste fucking delicious. But they really help me stay clean every day. I don't go telling everyone this; it's none of their business. They all just think I have some weird addiction to the candy, which I guess I do, but you don't touch them. Ever. If you want some, go buy your own. You stay out of my stash.

Which Daniel damn well knows. So I decide it's time for a lesson to be taught to everyone here and it just so happens Daniel gets to help teach it.

I pull my gun out of the waistband of my jeans, and of course when I do a club slut walks in and freezes. Staring at everyone with wide eyes.

I glance over at Rage, and he has a smirk on his face leaning against the wall. He sees me looking and shrugs, telling me I can do whatever I want. He knows. He gets that nerds are my thing; they help me stay in control. I don't care if it's stupid. When recovering from an addiction like hard drugs, latching on to something like a candy is a good thing and most definitely allowed.

"Well, prospect, it's your lucky day." His grin turns smug. "You get to be the stupid one who everyone else can use as an example as to why you should never ever touch a man's nerds." Rage snorts and tries to cover his laugh.

I aim my gun at the prospect, and his smug look drops real fucking quick, but before he can react to anything, I shoot him in the thigh. He screams and drops to the ground, cursing at me like I did something wrong.

What the fuck did I do? You ate my nerds, bitch.

The club slut screams and flees from the room. *Well, damn, don't think she'll be wanting to suck me off anytime soon.*

Rage sighs, "Prospect!"

Connor jumps at the Rage's tone. Turning his head quickly. His panicked eyes connecting with Rage's.

"Get him cleaned up and make sure everyone knows why he was shot. Got it?"

Connor nods and gets to it. I sigh, feeling a little better, and go grab some nerds and head back to the tech room. Honestly? As much as that pissed me off, it honestly made me feel way better than sparring did.

I only grazed his thigh; it didn't even go through, so he'll live. I know I probably shouldn't have reacted like that, but I am finding it hard to really give a shit right now.

Rage follows me, with Sugar behind him. "Kids, huh? They never fuckin' learn," Sugar says with a small chuckle.

Rage laughs, "Prospects are like kids, huh? They surely act like it sometimes. They have no idea what kind of punishment they could've gotten from my dad if he had still been around. Didn't matter how small the rule, don't break it. Or you'd regret it."

They both laugh, but it sounds more like an evil cackle.

I stop dead in my tracks when what they said registers in my mind. Kids. A kid. Harley. Fuck!

"Uh, Nerds? You good, brother?" Rage asks.

I nod and get my feet moving, going into my tech room and slamming the door on Rage and Sugar. I hear them laugh and say, "Fucking Nerds."

I return to my searching and look for any birth certificates with Brielle's name on them but get none. So then I look for any with Lilian on them. Fucking hell!

Harley Brielle St. James. Mother is Lilian Fay Thomas and father is Gabriel Bennett St. James. It looks like Lilian was murdered three and half years ago. It was due to a house fire. There is no record of Harley after that. Like she just vanished. Although there isn't much on her before. The only thing set is I found a boys and girls kids club she went to. Looks like she went there when Lilian was working and they lived in Auburn, Massachusetts.

Shit! This is huge. This could be the same Harley. No, it has to be. Lilian died, and Tammy got custody of Harley. But the question is, why would Tammy try to erase Harley's past? And change her last name to Wilson? That makes no sense.

I jump up and run to the door. "Rage! Tech room right fucking now!" I yell.

Rage comes running in with Sugar in tow. "What's going on?"

"Sit." I point to the chairs next to my main desk. They do and glance at me with varying confused expressions. "Rage, what's your middle name?"

He raises a brow. "Bennett. Why?"

"Alright, well, I have some shit to tell you. It's not gonna be easy to hear."

I go on to tell him everything I learned and watch as his face goes from rage to utter confusion. "That's not possible. When Lilian ran away from here, they tracked her down months later and found her. They killed her and the baby."

Sugar puts his hand on Rage's shoulder. "Brother, it's not far-fetched to believe they lied to you. Maybe they couldn't find her and that was your father's way of tryin' to get you to get over it and not think of her anymore."

Before any more can be said, there is some banging and then shouting coming from the common room. We all jump up and run out, and the sight before me is not what I ever expected to see.

Holy fucking shit.

CHAPTER TWENTY-SIX

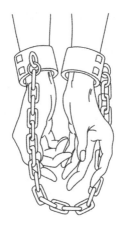

HARLEY

It's 8:30 p.m. by the time I reach Jacksonville. I have my taxi driver drop me off at the local mall. It's open for another thirty minutes, and on the way here, I decided I can spend a little money on myself.

I brought all the cash I have, and I have a few changes of clothes in my backpack, but I am looking for something different.

I walk through different shops, not finding anything. The only thing I seem to be getting is weird looks from the few people still wandering around here. The few times I did go out with Bri, it took me a while to adjust to people staring at my scar. But being out alone is different and kind of terrifying when you constantly have people looking at you like you are disgusting, or they stare at you with pity. I fucking hate it, but I push through it anyways.

I go into another store and decide to try something on this time instead of just looking. Maybe I'll have better luck. Being in a mall is so weird to me now. Luckily, with it being so late, there are barely any people around, but it still just feels odd. I have learned that I don't mind going places over the last few months. But I definitely prefer to be in a safe space at home, not that I have a home right now. I didn't really go out a lot at Bri's, not that she didn't try and offer all the time, but I never really wanted to leave.

I finally felt fairly safe after three years of always being on edge. I just wanted to soak in that feeling and breathe easy before taking on other things... Okay, well, or deciding I need to hunt down my birth dad. That got me out of the house.

As I browse the store getting ready to give up, I find a pretty pink top that makes me smile and decide to try it on. There is nothing wrong with it. It fits perfectly and is flowy, but I hate it. Ugh. I remember shopping for clothes with my mom when I was younger, and it was always so easy.

I know that I'll know the perfect thing when I find it. I head into one of the last stores there is, feeling a little deflated until I see it. The perfect outfit. I grab everything in my size and check out, not even bothering to try it all on. I know this is it. I then race to the bathroom to change. After I get dressed, I make sure the gun is loaded, safety is on, and tuck into the waistband of my jeans. I shove the knives I was given from Linc in my jean pockets and keep one in the pocket of my jacket. I come out of the stall and finger brush my hair and tie it up into a high ponytail then look myself over in the mirror, feeling a huge smile come over my face. Fuck yes.

I was wearing a black tank and sports bra under my hoodie, so I left those on, taking off the hoodie and put on my new leather jacket, with new black skinny jeans that have holes in each leg around the knee, paired with my new boots, black chunky lace up ankle boots.

Might as well feel good walking into what could be the worst decision of my life. Scratch that, this is most definitely the worst decision I've ever made.

I shove everything I didn't put on in my backpack, then head outside, taking out my phone to call a taxi.

The adrenaline is starting to kick in. I am terrified of the outcome, but I have to do this. I don't care how reckless it is. My life has been hell the last few years. So if I somehow do this and make it out alive, then I will take it as my sign to keep going and take down every other person who has hurt my mom and I. If I don't make it out of this alive, I hopefully will at least get to take my piece of shit sperm donor down with me.

I already miss Bri and it's only been a few hours since I left. I have come to love her like a real aunt I never got to have. I've gotten closer to Linc, Atlas, and Ryan too. They have helped me tremendously, and I don't ever think I could repay any of them for the kindness they have shown me. When I went to Virginia, I was not expecting to find a family. To find people who would help me.

Even when Atlas came storming into my life pissing me off, I didn't realize at the time that he was going to be the one to truly help me find my inner strength and remind me it's there every time I think it's not.

Linc is the calm in a storm. He will hold my hand and guide me through whatever inner turmoil I need to navigate. Atlas is the catalyst in a storm. He will demand for me to get up, be better, and do better. He's a force and sometimes can be too much, but in the end, he helped me to become stronger, tougher, and more resilient to the shit that life throws my way. Ryan is quiet but no less a storm than Atlas and Linc. He is kind and patient but can command a room with his presence. He wasn't around as much as Atlas and Linc were, but when he started teaching me how to shoot, he taught me to be patient but never give up.

And Bri, my sweet, loving Princess Brielle, who I grew up hearing stories about, that saved my mom. She has been my rock, a safe place to land. A place for me to go when things feel like they are too much.

A few weeks ago, I had been having a rough week; I wanted to try and get my license and learn how to drive, and I have been studying for the GED, so I wanted to look into a test to take for it, but then I was reminded of my haunting reality, and when I broke down, Bri was right there to guide me through it.

I go out and sit on the back deck hoping for some time alone. Linc, Bri, and I just talked, and I was reminded that I can't go getting my license yet or take my GED test because I am underage and they would need Tammy there since on paper, she is my legal guardian.

Ryan, who is tech smart, had looked into it a little and found out that she did have a fake birth certificate made. We talked about how we could go to the cops because Ryan has the proof that it's fake, but we have no idea how far her reach is so that just isn't an option because the thought of her getting her hands on me again sends me spiraling.

I thought this was supposed to get better, but I find myself panicking all the time. I fucking hate it. So now I am sitting outside on the deck, soaking in the scent of the ocean, letting the breeze and slight mist calm my mind.

Bri comes out and sits next to me but doesn't say anything. I feel tears fall down my cheeks, and I angrily wipe them away.

"Don't do that. Don't try to hide it or shove it all so far down you feel nothing," Bri chides, her voice holding more venom than I think I've ever heard from her.

"I am so sick and tired of panicking and crying. I want to move on and not let her get to me. I feel like she wins every time I let her in. The things she used to say... Bri, I really started to believe her. I have no idea why she put me in school, but I am glad she did, because it reopened my eyes to how people should treat others. I met some people at that school in the short time I was there. They reminded me I was worth more than what I was getting, and they didn't even know what was going on and it was the smallest things. Three boys, one girl.

"They showed me in just a few weeks how I deserve respect and peace of mind. It's what helped me get the strength to even think about getting out there and have the guts to just go and hopefully make it out alive because I had no idea whether or not you were real. It was beyond terrifying. But I did it because I couldn't let her win, yet here I am, months later, letting her win anyways. It's like her voice is engraved in my mind and will never leave."

Bri says nothing. We sit in silence for a while, and I really believe she is quiet because she knows I am right. Tammy will always win.

"You could not be more wrong." I startle, not having expected her to say anything, let alone that. "Yes, maybe you were able to pull yourself together enough to get out based on those kids at the school. But you still did it. You had to do it yourself. They couldn't do it for you. That shows tremendous strength, Harley. You were running away from your own personal hell having no idea if you were going to walk into another one or not. I could not have done that, and I mean that." She looks me in the eyes, "I mean it. I couldn't. I barely survived getting out from under my stepmom, and when I did get out on my own, I was struggling. Your mom saved me just as much as I saved her. I was drowning, and she gave me something to focus on."

She takes a deep breath and wipes away some stray tears.

"But Harley, things don't go away overnight. I still have nightmares. I still have moments where I am beyond terrified. It takes a lot of work to get to a spot where things don't bother you as much or you have less panic attacks. But they don't truly go *away. I wish I could tell you they did, but they don't. But I can tell you they get better. It hurts less, you notice less panic attacks, you notice their words dull in your mind. You just can't give up. If you give up, then they win. But every day that you get up, you fight, you train, you learn, you breathe, you smile, or you even cry, you are winning." She grabs my hand in hers. "You. Are. Winning."*

I take a deep breath, taking in her words. Letting the tears fall and knowing that Bri will hold me up as long as I need her to until I can do it on my own. Linc comes up behind us, wrapping us both up in a hug and making me chuckle. I swear it's his favorite thing to do.

He whispers to Bri, but I am close enough I hear, "You didn't tell us you still had nightmares."

She tenses, so I get up and walk down to the beach, giving them a moment alone and sitting in the sand so I can chat with my mom. I've come to love the moments I can come down here, run my toes through the sand, and talk to her.

I come out of my thoughts as the taxi pulls up, I take a deep breath then walk to it. I climb in and give him the address I found online for the club where I believe my dad lives. The taxi starts moving, and I wipe a lone tear off my cheek.

This is you taking back your power. This is you becoming the devil so no one else can ever be a devil in your story again. I text Bri. Even though I left her a letter, I just want her to know I really am sorry.

Me: I love you so much, Brielle. You are the aunt I wish I could have had. I hope you know how truly sorry I am.

I power off my phone, knowing she'll call the guys and everyone will be texting and calling once they read my letter. I have to stay focused.

When we arrive, there is a large gate with a small little gate house to the left. I see someone in it, but he appears to be sleeping, so I ask the driver to pull up farther past it and I jump out. Looking around at the fence, I notice that it's too tall for me to climb, but I know I could climb the gate. I just have to hope the guy in the gate house doesn't wake up.

I slowly make my way up to the gate, checking on the guy again, then I quickly climb it and jump off to the other side, landing on my feet. I start down the long road, staying to the side. I don't care if they know I am here, or if they know who I am, but I want to get in and make sure I don't screw myself and lose my chance to take him out.

As I walk down the road, I soon come to a warehouse-looking building. It's huge. At least three stories, four if they have a basement. There are large doors towards the left, which I am assuming are the main doors. I steel my spine, preparing myself for any outcome, and open the door slowly.

My heart is pounding in my chest. This is terrifying, but I have to do this. I have to win and take my power back. Bri may be okay to just live her own life and feel that that's winning, but I need payback. I need them to see me as the devil.

There are a bunch of bikers in here, and they are pretty loud. I get pissed at all these people looking happy and do something even more reckless: I slam the door into the wall, and it gets everyone's eyes on me.

I walk in and immediately there are catcalls and whistles. I ignore them, scanning the room. Someone yells for Blade, and a guy who looks familiar comes around the corner from the far side of the room. He sees me, and his eyes go wide. It takes me a minute, but I recognize him from the day I left when I got on the bus.

In the next ten seconds, three guys come barreling into the room from a hall straight across the room from me. I recognize one of them as Sugar from his picture online. The next guy I don't think I recognize, but the third guy, I do.

I quickly yank my gun out from the back of my pants and aim it right at *him*.

Gabriel St. James.

My dad.

The man in my fantasies who saves the day.

My mom's rapist.

The man who caused her so much pain.

The man who more than likely is responsible for her death.

I hear yelling around me, but all my focus is on *him*. He raises his hands and starts talking, "Harley, I need you to put the gun down. Let's talk, okay?"

I sneer at his calm voice. He goes to take one step towards me, and that's when I've had enough. I know without a doubt that as soon as I pull this trigger, I will die too. I have one shot. I have to get it right. I square my shoulders, making sure my stance is just how Ryan taught me. I black out everything else around me except for my target. I flick the safety off and put my finger on the trigger.

As soon as I start to pull, I hear a bang, then pain like I've never felt before explodes in my gut. My eyes go wide, and I drop my gun. It goes off as I hear someone yelling for others to get out of the way.

I drop to my knees, looking down as I touch my stomach. There is so much blood; I've never seen so much red before. Not even when I was being beaten within an inch of my life. The beatings hurt less than this does, but at the same time this pain is fading to a dull ache.

I feel my body going lax, and my eyes start to flutter as eyes I've seen before come into focus... green. So green and beautiful. They remind me of my favorite trees in Virginia. Green eyes is saying something, but I can't hear anything.

I let my eyes fully close as I fall.

There she is, standing in front of me in her favorite dress. It's white with yellow sunflowers on it. She always was so much more girly than I was. Her hair flows in soft waves down her back, the same hair I have. She smiles at me, and I smile back. She looks so happy, beautiful, and peaceful.

Before I can reach her to finally get that hug I've been aching for, she's glowing. Fire. She's on fire. She's burning alive. She smiles sadly at me. No!

"Mom!" I scream.

Then everything goes black.

To be continued...

TAMARA WILSON

'TAMMY'

17 Years Ago

I knew that faking my birth control was the best thing to do. Gabe always made sure I was taking my pill, but he didn't know they were all fake pills. He said he had too much to do and change before he could ever think about having kids. Which makes no sense to me because things are pretty perfect right now.

I am staring down at the pregnancy test with a smile on my face. This is perfect. I am not a huge fan of kids; they can be useful for my own gain, but other than that someone else can deal with them when they need something. I have a three-year-old right now, but my mom takes care of him most of the time or Lilian. Richard likes to help with him too and thinks he's a cute kid, but he's more of a pain in the ass.

My plan was to get into the club through Rob's dad, Cruz. But I broke it off with him when I got Gabe to fall in love with me. He thought we were soulmates or some shit.

But I couldn't have cared less. I wanted him and still want him so Lilian can't have him. I know she likes him, or used to at least, before we got together, and he is supposed to be the next club president, so what better place for me to be than the president's ol' lady?

I was meant to run shit and have everyone listen to me. But I can't only have one dick. I like to have multiple I can jump around to. So I have always kept Cruz on the back burner. But we got caught fucking at the clubhouse by Killer, who is Gabe's dad. Killer made a show of kicking me out of the club and later on, I found out that Cruz was just gone. They said he left the club, but I know better than that.

They killed him. My guess is either Killer or Gabe did it.

I was angry so I called the cops and left an anonymous tip that got them raided.

Daddy was not happy with me about that, but I was fine with it because it got me more attention from him. He stopped paying attention to Lilian for five seconds to yell at me, and I was happy about that.

I am not a jealous person, but I don't like it when people aren't paying attention to me. Especially my daddy. And Lilian is always ruining that shit for me.

I am getting ready to go to the club right now. It's been a few days since I got them raided, so they should all be calm now.

Daddy comes in while I finish putting on my makeup. "Where are you going?"

I bat my lashes at him. "To the clubhouse. I think Gabe has calmed down by now, and I can talk to him and we will get back together. Then I can be a part of the club in the future when he takes over as president. Wouldn't that be great, Daddy?"

He sighs heavily, "You are not going back to the club. Ever. Your little stunt got you kicked out. Permanently. Now I have to take Lilian over there for them as payment for your fuckup. You need to stop causing problems. The next one, I won't get you out of it."

I huff, "Daddy that's not—"

"Shut up. Stay home and take care of your child. Killer will probably come by at some point to talk to you."

He storms out, and I lose it. I scream and throw everything I can touch. That bitch! This is all Lilian's fault! Everything is always her fault. She probably asked to go to the club in place of me! She wants to be me. I know it.

Motherfucker! I throw the lamp at the door and scream, pulling at my hair. Why does she always have to get in the way?

I look at the door when I hear a knock and it opens slowly. Richard is standing there with Rob on his back. "Are you done throwing a tantrum? I need to talk to you about something before Killer shows up."

"It wasn't a fucking tantrum." I look around at the completely destroyed room and shrug. I'll make Lilian clean it up later. I follow Richard out to the living room, and he puts Rob down in his playpen. I roll my eyes. "You spoil that brat."

Richard shrugs. He drops to his knees in front of me where I am sitting on the couch. "You know I love you. I have loved you since we were kids on the playground. I want to be with you. But I know you want to be a part of the club. Well, maybe we can work together to get what we want and be together as a couple."

I scoff internally. He doesn't love me. He shouldn't anyways. I don't love him. "Explain," I snap.

"Killer is about to come over here to tell you that you are banned from the club and all club properties. But then he is going to offer you a job. Working with him in his side business that he and my father started with the other original club members. But the club doesn't know about it because they can funnel more money when it doesn't go through the club. My dad wants me to work for him and prove that I can take over for him someday. But he doesn't think I'll be able to prove I'm worth it. But you and me together could make a hell of a team.

"Which is why I asked Killer to offer you a job working with me. He always wants more people working with us, and we have no females, so you coming in would be helpful. So take it. Agree to whatever he says you have to do and take the job. You can work your way back into the club or we can destroy them all and take over their business for ourselves. We don't need the club for shit." He has a gleam in his eyes that I have never seen before, and it sparks something inside of me and I grin at him.

Killer does come by and offer me the job later that day. It's sex trafficking. He doesn't say what exactly I will be doing. He won't until I accept the job.

But if I do take it, then I have to forget about Gabe, never step foot on club property again, and do any jobs we are assigned to do. He said I have a few months to decide because right now things are slow for them.

This isn't what I wanted, but I can see myself working with Richard. I guess we could live together and have kids and be a couple. I could become powerful.

The club could be ours for the taking.

Four Months Later

Lilian has been mostly kept at the club for the last few months. I try not to let it get to me, but I fucking hate that. That slut gets to be there all the time. It's not fair. I have to give Killer my answer about the job by the end of this week, and I am thinking I am not going to take it, but I haven't told Richard that yet. The foolish man is happy thinking I am going to do it and be with him.

I have been having stupid fucking morning sickness, so I am currently huddled over the toilet, waiting to puke again. This is the other reason I won't take the job. This baby is my ticket back into the club and at Gabe's side.

I go to stand up, hoping that I am done being sick now and see something pink sticking out of the trash can. I pick it up and see that it's a pregnancy test. The only other person who uses this bathroom is Lilian. The bitch is fucking pregnant. I bet she did it on purpose.

I leave the bathroom and go to find my daddy. He knows about my pregnancy and isn't happy about it. He doesn't want more babies around here. Hopefully telling him about Lilian being pregnant will make him pissed with her more than he is with me. I keep hoping one of these days he will just kill her, but he doesn't.

My mom says he is obsessed with her, which is why my mom is out partying if she's not here helping with Rob. Daddy never pays attention to her anymore. All because of fucking Lilian.

"Daddy?" He is standing in the kitchen staring down at his phone with his brows furrowed and a frown on his face.

"Not now, Tammy. I have to go deal with this."

"I need to tell you something important." I toss the stick on the counter, and he raises his eyes from his phone to see what it is. He comes closer to look at it.

"I already know you're pregnant, Tam."

I shake my head. "That's not mine. It's Lilian's."

I watch Daddy's face go from pissed and annoyed to downright murderous. I bit my lip to hold back a smile, hoping this means he will finally want to be rid of her.

"I have to go deal with this. She took off for the weekend with fucking Gabriel. They have to be punished. We've had them followed so we know everything they are talking about."

She's with Gabe? Are you fucking kidding me? I bet the baby is his, too. That bitch. I will cut that baby out of her if I have to. She is NOT taking any more from me.

I need a plan. I have to do something. She will not take him from me. I call Richard, and he comes over and tells me what has been said between them. Gabe admitted to beating all the other prospects and trying to be gentle with her.

I scoff; she's a whore. He just apparently doesn't know she's been with lots of other men already. I form a plan and call Killer.

I tell him what he should do. I know he doesn't want this any more than I do. He wants Gabe focused on the club and is training him to replace him in all things. I tell him to make sure she knows he lied and come up with a whole story to go with it. Killer likes the idea and says he will check in later.

I have to take the job offer from Killer and work with Richard. I will find a way to destroy Lilian that way. And then someday Richard and I can run everything, and I'll find my way into the club. It's where I'm meant to be.

Richard left with Rob to take him for a walk while I was talking to Killer, so I just wait for him to get back so I can fill him in on what Killer is going to say.

Maybe keeping Richard around wouldn't be such a bad idea. I mean, then someone else can help with Rob and maybe even the new baby. He seems to like kids and wants to help with them even if they aren't his.

A while later, he comes back, and I fill him in on everything I told Killer and what is going down. He smiles at me. "You are beautiful and smart, Tammy." I preen under his praise. "This is why Killer wants you working for him with me. We will make so much money helping him with his side business." Before I can tell him I am going to take it, he looks past my shoulder and frowns. "Looks like we have an eavesdropper."

I spin around just in time to see Lilian duck into her room. I stomp to her room and swing the door open to see her shoving things in a bag. I take the pregnancy test out of my pocket and wave it at her.

"You stupid whore. Who did you let knock you up? I know you constantly throw yourself at everyone like the slut you are. I am going to call Daddy about this." Letting her think I haven't already called him so she can try to talk me out of it. I walk closer to her and scream at her, "WHOSE BABY IS IT?"

Her hands tremble as the clothing she had in her hands fall onto the bed. Before I can tell her there is no way in hell I am letting her leave, she moves faster than I have time to process and suddenly everything goes black.

Two Months Later

The day that bitch hit me, she left. There's no trace of her anywhere. We can't fucking find her.

Killer found out I was pregnant. Well, I told my daddy, and he told the club. So now I am sitting here with my boyfriend Richard. I had a plan to get Gabe back with this pregnancy so I would be a part of the club, but Gabe is obsessing over the bitch. Apparently, Daddy told them that she is pregnant, so Gabe wants to find her, which makes me think the whore slept with him. I knew she slept around but I can't believe she slept with my Gabe.

Killer is sitting across from us right now in our living room. Rob is playing on the floor. "I need you to find your sister. No one can seem to figure out where she is, so I am putting it on you," he says.

I scoff, "No. I don't want to find the bitch. Daddy will grow tired of looking and finally give me the attention I deserve. Why would I want to find her?"

"Because she is carrying my grandchild. That child belongs to me. So, if you don't find her, then your child, who I know isn't Richard's and is Gabe's, will be mine the day it is born."

I jump to my feet. "You can't do that! How am I even supposed to find her?" I yell, feeling my hatred for Lilian growing even stronger. She keeps stealing everything from me!

Richard just sits there calmly, not bothered by any of this.

Killer stands, towering over me. "I can do whatever the fuck I want, little girl," he sneers. "You will find her, or that child will be mine. A little boy is preferred. I need a real son to raise to take over for me, not the pussy my son is becoming. If it's a girl, that's okay too. She'll sell for a pretty penny."

"You can't! Gabe would never let you do that!"

"Gabriel won't know. You lost the baby during childbirth. It's easy enough to cover up. And if you open your mouth, I'll have you taken care of, and you'll never be found." He walks towards the door, his steps smooth and confident. "Two options, find Lilian before her baby is born, or I will take yours."

I throw everything in my sight at the door as he leaves screaming at him. The bastard! He can't do this. My daddy won't let him.

When Daddy gets home that night, I tell him everything. He looks at me, his face blank. "You did the things you did. You have to face the consequences. It's not my problem."

He walks away from me then, and I do something I haven't done since I was a baby: I cry. My mom taught me that crying is for the weak. That the Wilsons don't cry. Ever. But I do. Right now, I break down and sob.

Even with the bitch gone, Daddy still won't give me attention and show me he loves me like he did with her. She's still ruining my life!

I am tired of Daddy not taking my side with things. He should be protecting ME!

Day of Birth

I just had my baby. I didn't name it because I knew they'd take it from me. I never found Lilian. Killer said they hunted her down to somewhere in Virginia, but the prospects who were told to watch her until Killer and Daddy could get there fucked with her and taunted her like idiots, so she knew they were coming and ran. And now, no one can find her.

Those prospects are dead and because Gabe is obsessing over Lilian, they decided to tell the club that they found her and killed her and the baby. So only Richard, Killer, Daddy and I know she's alive somewhere. Hopefully not for long.

My baby starts crying as the nurse paid off to keep her mouth shut cleans it up. She passes the baby to Killer, and he walks out.

I never saw my baby again, and I vowed to myself to take down Lilian, Gabe, Killer, Daddy, all of them. None of them deserve to breathe. That was my baby to decide what to do with. Not theirs.

Also By Jessa

Beautiful Souls Series

Healing Souls — Book Two: Out now!
Intertwined Souls — Book Three: Coming 2024

Sons of Silence MC Series

Set in the same world as Beautiful Souls series.
Tormented in Silence Duet – Now a completed duet!

SCAN TO FIND ALL MY LINKS!

ACKNOWLEDGMENTS

Readers

Thank you so much for taking a chance on my debut novel! It means the world to me and I hope you stick around for more of Harley because her story is just getting started.

Sonia Lynn

Thank you for being by my side through all of this. If it wasn't for you I wouldn't have gone down this path and actually published. You are my platonic soulmate, best friend, therapist, roommate, co-worker, and everything in-between. Thank you for supporting me through all of my chaos. I love you!

Alpha Readers

Sofia Renna and Kloie Wiseman. Thank you for sticking with me through this whole process. I might not have had my shit together but you both kept me sane with your dedication to Harley's story. Thank you for taking a chance on a brand new author.

Beta Reader

Allison, thank you for sticking through the book and giving me feedback. I appreciate you!

ABOUT THE AUTHOR

Jessa James was born and raised in the lush greens of the Pacific Northwest. Her love of books began at a young age when thrilling adventures and magical cities sprang to life before her eyes in the form of words. Imagination, darkness, heroes, and villains filled page after page of her notebooks until one day a hobby became a passion. Reading transported her. Writing changed her. And now she hopes to spark the same joy and love of reading from her own words.

Made in the USA
Las Vegas, NV
10 March 2024